We Wandered in Scotland

Copyright

THE HAYTON COLLECTION

WE WANDERED IN SCOTLAND

Some journeys lead the heart to forever.

SHANNON STEEVES

To wintery landscapes that spark cozy dreams

December 22nd

London &
the Scottish Highlands

Chapter One

8:45 AM

The lift came to a stop on the third floor, and Cordelia stepped into the hallway at the Battersea apartment building. The scent of baked cinnamon mingled with pine cleaning products, a combination that made her stomach lurch. *Better than what they had before.* She balanced the white pastry box against her hip and knocked on the blue door marked 3B.

Thanks to Royce and the Countess, Jasper and Lucy were able to spend their days in comfort: dry, clean, and fed. They'd spent five years with a tent as their home, their comfort, using discarded coats and blankets for warmth. Cordelia had never heard them complain, despite the toll the streets took on their health—two people who'd given their careers to educating society's children. Gratitude filled her heart.

"Cordelia, love." Lucy Cobbett's weathered face brightened as she opened the door, her silver hair pinned back with the Italian tortoiseshell combs Cordelia had given as a birthday gift. "You're early. If we'd known..."

"I wanted to see you before we left for Scotland." Cordelia stepped into the small flat, breathing in the robust Irish tea that

1

filled their modest living room with citrus. The space was tiny, smaller than her bedroom, but Lucy had livened it with crocheted throws and Jasper's art projects. Little did they know, he had a hidden talent, and the community painting classes helped him blossom.

"Royce apologizes for not coming. He has a meeting this morning, but said he'd visit when we get back."

"He's a sweet young man. We understand he's busy." Lucy rested her hand on Cordelia's arm as they settled onto the sofa. "Don't let that one go. He's a treasure." The crack in her voice had softened since moving into the apartment, revealing a melodic accent.

Jasper emerged from the kitchen, drying his hands on a worn tea towel. "Look who we have here." His Irish accent still carried hints of Cork despite forty years in London. "Bearing biscuits as usual, I see."

"Macarons. And your favorite shortbread." Cordelia handed him the box, feeling more like herself than she had in days. "Lavender honey, orange cardamom, and strawberry jam with a dusting of Christmas-fairy gold. Oh, and I got you two something else too." She pulled two wrapped packages from a shopping bag. One was wrapped in white paper with colorful christmas trees and the other had laughing Santas and reindeer. "It's early I know, but Merry Christmas."

Lucy carefully unwrapped a pale blue cardigan with pearl buttons. "Oh, Cordelia, you shouldn't have...it's beautiful." She wrapped it around her shoulders, admiring the soft mohair. The color enhanced her smoky-blue eyes. "It's much too nice, dear, but now I have an excuse for Jasper to take me on a date."

"It'll keep you warm on your walks to the market." Cordelia said.

"You know I never need a reason to take you out on the town." Jasper chuckled and ripped the wrapping paper open, revealing a thick emerald green cardigan with toggle buttons. "Spoiling us rotten, my dear. You shouldn't have." He slipped it on, beaming as he performed a catwalk for them. "I'll put the kettle back on so can have a proper tea with these treats." The sweater brightened his countenance as he walked taller.

Cordelia's stomach lurched at the thought of a bold tea and sugary cookies. "Actually, I can't stay long. Royce and I have to get to the airport soon."

"Where are you goin' again, dear?" Jasper asked from their tiny kitchen that consisted of a two burner cooktop, a toaster oven, sink, and a sofa-length counter.

"Scotland. We're visiting his family's cottage north of Edinburgh."

"Oh, the highlands in December. I haven't been there since I was a girl." Lucy reclined and pressed her shoulders against the back of the sofa. The springs creaked in protest.

"When I get back, we're ordering you a new couch. This one's seen better days."

"We couldn't ask that of you." Jasper said, keeping a close watch on the copper water kettle as it softly bubbled. "Scotland, eh, cold as a witch's teat up there this time of year."

"Jasper. You're in mixed company." Lucy said.

Cordelia laughed, "I don't mind." She perched on the edge of the sofa, fighting the wave of nausea that lately seemed to strike at the most inopportune time. "And don't worry, Jasper, we have snow boots and coats packed." The radiator groaned and suddenly the warm air stifled, making her feel dizzy.

"You look a bit peaky, love," Lucy said. "Jasper, bring the girl a tissue."

"No, it's fine. I'm just hot in this sweater." Cordelia said.

"Not coming down with something, are you?"

Not exactly. "Just tired. I was up late working."

Jasper carried the tea pot and an extra cup to the coffee

table, and then settled into his chair with a grunt. "I'm afraid my joints creak like a ghostly house in the winter. Did I tell you about Mrs. Henderson's boy? The one who works at that fancy hotel?"

"The one in Kensington?" Cordelia smiled, even as her stomach performed an uncomfortable flip.

"That's the one. Well, he found me some volunteer work at the charity shop near here, if I'm interested. Said I might enjoy meeting new people. And give Lucy some peace."

"I'll go to crochet class with the girls." Lucy poured Cordelia a cup of tea and handed it to her.

"Wow, that's exciting. Are you going to walk there alone or will he pick you up." Cordelia heard the strain in her voice and cleared her throat. The smell of cookies and tea overwhelmed her senses.

"He said he'd walk with me, but I told him not to bother. I still have two functioning legs and I intend to use them for as long as I can." Jasper slurped the hot tea and let out a satisfied sound.

Cordelia pulled at her sweater, faning it against her skin. "I really should go...Royce will be waiting...But do you mind if I use your bathroom?"

"Of course, dear. Are you sure you're well?"

"Just the sweater, thank you." Cordelia fled to the bathroom just as her stomach rebelled. She flushed the toilet, patted water onto her face with a tissue, and shouted out to Lucy, who'd knocked on the door. "I'm fine. Just a food reaction, that's all." Her pale reflection stared back at her. *You can do this. It's normal.*

When she emerged, both Lucy and Jasper hovered by the door.

"I'm fine, just last night's dinner. But I feel much better." Cordelia said.

4

Lucy's eyes narrowed, "Food poisoning. Is Royce sick, too?"

"I doubt it." Cordelia hated lying to them, but she wasn't ready for anyone to know. Not until after she told Royce. "I should go." She gathered her things, avoiding Lucy's penetrating eyes that read people well. "But I promise we'll visit after Boxing Day."

"All right. You take care of yourself, love," Lucy said, pulling Cordelia into a fierce hug that smelled of lavender soap. "And tell that young man of yours, Merry Christmas."

Cordelia squeezed feeling Lucy's fragile frame. Her emotions thickened and flowed, like cake batter poured into a pan. The two of them had become the first of her London family, and in some ways, Lucy filled a void her mother had left behind. "I love you both."

"Love you too, dear girl," Jasper said gruffly, patting her shoulder. "Now off with you before Royce comes searching for ya."

As the lift descended, Cordelia pressed her forehead against the cool metal wall. Eight weeks. She'd only known for two weeks, but every day the secret grew heavier. The constant nausea, the endless excuses, and the exhaustion left her longing for bed, pj's, and a solid night of sleep.

Three days till Christmas. Just three more days, and then Royce'll know. She rested her hand on her belly, smiling and envisioning his happy reaction.

The elevator doors opened and outside the building Cordelia merged into a frenzied crowd, all going somewhere. All keeping some kind of secret. It was Christmas afterall.

Chapter Two

9:30 AM

The bank's viewing room smelled metallic and musty, a combination that defined the historic institution and its wealthy clients—traditional, reserved, and private. Every aspect of the room, from the black stone flooring to the heating system that monitored humidity to security protocols, it all represented the bank's dignified and serious reputation.

Royce adjusted his cufflinks, a habit he'd inherited from his father whenever he anxiously waited. Mr. Pember, the elderly vault manager who'd been there since Royce was a boy, slowly unlocked the box with ceremonial precision.

"Here we are, your lordship." He lifted the burgundy velvet box as if he were unpacking the Crown Jewels. "Just as your grandmother left it for you."

Royce paused before opening the box, cradling it between his palms. On its sides, the velvet had been worn smooth from the countless times fingers had opened it, desiring its contents. Strange how something so small, so delicate could carry the burden of a family's history and unwritten future.

He cracked back the lid. Inside, sat a navy velvet ring box.

And inside that was his grandmother's ring. An art deco design that reflected the room's subtle light—the symphony of precious stones captured and amplified every ray. In the center nested a flawless two-carat round brilliant sapphire flanked by baguette diamonds. They cascaded down the platinum band like glacial frozen tears. It was sophisticated without being ostentatious, elegant without being cold. It was unmistakably Cordelia.

Even though he'd seen the ring thousands of times, the reality took his breath away. Never before had he imagined it on someone's hand, other than his grandmother. Now it's the only thing he could envision. Yet, he wondered about the timing. Was Christmas too predictable? Was he rushing the next step? They'd been inseparable since Venice, deeping their relationship and feeling solid together. *Some things you just know, and I know it's time.*

"Your grandfather had exquisite taste," Mr. Pember said. "Cartier, I believe?"

"Yes." Royce lifted the ring from its silk bed, realizing he felt two weights simultaneously—physically and emotionally. That one piece of jewelry represented more than his love story or promises he'd make to Cordelia. It held memories of commitment, laughter, and tears. Giving it to her meant he honored their love and his grandparent's love.

Two months earlier, he'd driven to Hayton Manor to meet with his parents. He'd told Cordelia it was a meeting with his father and the estate's manager. A partial truth. The memory rushed back with clarity.

When he arrived that morning, the family living room glowed from the early October sun. Golden rectangles cast across the Persian rug, the same spot where Royce and Marcus had played as children. His mother sat at her writing desk, responding to a stack of invitations. Her yellow fountain pen swiftly checked off yes or no, only pausing for her to double check the calendar. His father sat in his usual armchair, dressed in his standard attire of khakis and white polo, reading the newspaper with a cup of English tea, sugar, and no cream.

"Good, you're both here. I need to discuss something with you." Royce's heart hammered against his chest like a caged animal.

The Earl never looked up from the headlines. "If it's about the roof repairs on the east wing, I already contracted—"

"I'm going to ask Cordelia to marry me."

The fountain pen dropped onto the mahogany desk, and the newspaper rustled to a stop. Silence. The grandfather clock ticked three times before they spoke.

"Well," his mother said joining Royce and the Earl in the lounge area. "It's about bloody time."

"Alia." There was a hint of amusement in the Earl's tone rather than chastisement.

"You know I'm right, Charles. We've been waiting for this boy to come to his senses." She slid closer to Royce, side hugged him, and cupped his face. Her hands smelled of rose hand cream, the one she imported from India. "She's perfect for you, darling. Just perfect."

His father folded the newspaper into precise quarters. "You're not asking our permission."

Royce noted the distinct tone of the Earl's voice—flat yet acknowledging. "No. I'm telling you my plans."

"Well, you know how I feel about it."

"I think I do. But just to make sure, why don't you go ahead and tell me."

The Earl smoothed the surface of his trousers, removing any folds or creases from his crossed leg. "Very well. She makes us all look incompetent in the kitchen. She argues politics and challenges my views. She's delightfully unguarded when she thinks no one's looking. But...she's smart, talented, and most importantly, it's obvious she loves you."

"Thomas." The Countess laughed. A bubbly sound, as bright as champagne bubbles.

"What? It's true. Remember when she corrected my pronunciation of bruschetta in front of the Penley's after your Venice trip?" He chuckled and sat forward on the edge of the chair.

"And she was correct," Royce said. "You made it sound like you were sneezing."

"Exactly my point. She's not intimidated by any of this, and she bloody well didn't hide from Lady Penley either. That's rare."

"That's special." His mother said, squeezing him around the shoulders. "I'm so happy for you."

His father stood and extended a hand, "I'm proud of you. And I approve, wholeheartedly."

"Thanks, Pop. I can't imagine life without her."

His father's gruff exterior cracked, offering a hug that extended to Royce's shoulders. "That's all we needed to hear. That and a prenuptual in place."

"Thomas." Alia said from her desk.

"A legacy must be looked after, and even you signed one."

Mr. Pember cleared his throat, dragging Royce from his memories. But somehow, the warmth of that October morning lingered, even in the sterile bank vault.

"Do you require anything else, Lord Brownell?"

"No. This is it." Royce snapped the small ring box closed and tucked it into his monogrammed satchel.

Outside the bank, Christmas shoppers hurried past, their breath visible in the crisp air. Music played carols from the nearby department store, and charity bells rang from street corners.

Royce hailed a taxi, tucking the satchel close to his side. As the car pulled away from the bank, he checked his watch, remembering Cordelia planned to visit Jasper and Lucy before they left for Scotland. *She's probably fussing over them right about now.* He smiled, thinking about her nurturing tendencies with everyone. *It's time for her to be cared for.*

After weeks of planning and selecting the ideal spot at Waileigh Lodge, Royce chose Christmas Day evening, just as the sun set to propose. He'd reflected on what to say and how. All that remained was executing it.

A flutter of nerves accompanied his confidence. Marriage would change everything between them, creating new expectations and responsibilities. He pictured her face, and any nerves dissolved into pure anticipation.

As the taxi navigated toward Mayfair, Royce smiled. His cheeks hurt, but he couldn't stop smiling. By Christmas night, if everything went according to plan, they'd return to London engaged, and planning their future.

Chapter Three

3:oo PM
Cordelia fidgeted with the touchscreen of their rental car. "I'm convinced this radio is stuck in the nineteen-eighties," she said, just as another synthesizer-heavy ballad filled the car with British new wave. "All I need is big bangs and black eyeliner. What do ya think, sexy look for me?"

Royce grunted, "Mmhmm." The rental car had a faint smell of the previous driver's coffee with a hint of pine air freshener.

He merged into Edinburgh traffic, cutting his eyes from the road to Cordelia, "I'm listening."

She adjusted her seatbelt. A few rays of afternoon sun warmed her face. "Are you sure about that? Because I just proposed revital—."

"Proposed? What did you propose?" Royce's heart leaped as he glanced at his rearview mirror. "Why would you propose this moment?"

"Royce, relax." Cordelia placed her hand on his shoulder and massaged it. "You drive in traffic all the time."

"Who said anything about the traffic?"

"I did."

"What gave you the idea I was stressed over traffic?"

"Your reaction." Cordelia deepened her voice and imitated him, "Propose? What did you propose?" Her giggle had an amusing tone, as if she did the voice more for her own entertainment than for his clarification.

"That's not how I speak." Royce navigated the congestion, proving he didn't need voice assistance to guide them out of the city. "I don't say pru-poze, I say, propose."

She threw her hands into the air, "It's the same thing. That's how I said it."

"Darling, I will never say, pru-poze. No matter how many drinks I've consumed."

"I disagree, but I think I know better."

The music faded and another synth-pop song launched into a catchy beat despite the broken hearted lyrics.

Cordelia swayed to the music, interjecting her own words. "This really isn't that bad."

"I think we need to change the station." Royce tapped the screen.

"No, this is fun."

"At least one of us is enjoying it."

Her hands glided through the air, feeling invisible waves drifting past. "I wonder if your parents ever danced to this at a club."

"I doubt Pop knows what a club is, unless you're describing somewhere that has porcelain china and his consommé."

"Too bad. I bet he's got some groove in there, somewhere." She turned the volume lower and rested her hand on his thigh.

"That's an image I don't care to see." Royce laughed, fighting the image of his father with gel-spiked hair dancing and bouncing like a pogo stick. The car downshifted and slowed as they approached a roundabout, causing the brake pedal to tighten under his foot.

Cordelia laughed, "I bet your mom could tell us what he was like."

"Are you that curious?"

"Yes...Oh, can we stop for the restroom?" She pointed at a sign, indicating a service area five km ahead.

"Sure. I'll grab us some waters. Do you want anything else?"

"No. Well, maybe some salty chips."

"Chips or crisps?"

"Crisps. And get the salt and vinegar ones. That sounds good."

Royce squeezed her hand and laced their fingers together. "Anything else?"

"No. Just the bathroom."

"I thought you went at the airport."

"I did, but I really need to go again."

She sounded anxious, so Royce drove faster, weaving between two cars. They arrived at the station and Cordelia hurried inside. The area hustled, with cars maneuvering in every direction and parents yelling at their kids to slow down. Diesel fumes mixed with fried food from the café, leaving an unappetizing smell hanging in the air. As Royce stood outside the car, the constant whoosh of passing lorries created wind tunnels that sent bits of dust flying.

He took the opportunity to look in his black leather travel bag before going into the store. His hand felt around, searching. *There it is.* He gripped the velvet box, peeked at the ring, and then tucked it underneath his clothes.

When they left the service station, Christmas music played in the background. Cordelia snacked on her salty crisps and sang carols in between crunchy bites. The traffic heading north had increased and continued to get heavier after passing through Perth.

The Scottish Highlands stretched before them in shades of

gray and green, the air so crisp it seemed to hover and shimmer just beyond the windshield. He cracked his window and breathed in the smells of wet peat and winter herbs, a clean scent that made London's exhaust-heavy air feel far away. Surrounding them, the rolling mountains felt ancient and wild. He bumped up the heat, watching as the window's fogged edges dissipated.

Cordelia stashed her empty crisps bag and gulped her water.

"Eat too many?"

"No, just thirsty." The usual rosy glow of her cheeks had faded. She picked at the bottle's label, occasionally resting her head back and closing her eyes.

"Are you feeling alright?"

"Just getting a bit carsick." Her hand pressed against her stomach. "I'm fine." She shifted in her seat. "And what about you? You keep smiling to yourself like you're miles away. What's going on in that head of yours, Mr. Brownell?"

"Nothing. I'm looking forward to having Christmas here with you. Aren't you?" Royce's fingers drummed against the steering wheel.

The delicate Murano glass necklace he'd given her after Venice reflected the light from a lone ray that burst through the clouds. It rested beneath her collarbone, highlighted by the edges of her cream sweater. He remembered the morning he gave it to her, just before they left the palazzo. Everything had shifted between them there—a new kind of love.

"There's something I should probably mention about the cottage," Royce said as they crested a hill that revealed miles of heather-covered moors.

"What? Is it off grid? Don't worry, I won't judge you for having a rustic cottage. We used to camp at a hut—."

"Why would you think I'd take you to an off grid hut in winter?"

She finished drinking another sip of water and replaced the cap. "I don't know. That's what I think of when someone says cottage."

"Well, Waileigh Lodge is a bit more than that."

"Oh my god, it's a castle, isn't it? What you call a cottage is actually a massive castle."

"It's not exactly that either."

"Then what is it? Just a house?"

"Compared to a castle, yes. It's more like Hayton."

"Royce, that's not a house. That's a manor, a palatial estate."

"True. But Waileigh is smaller. Our cottage. It only has ten bedrooms and—."

"Ten bedrooms? That's not a cottage." She twisted in her seat to face him fully, the seatbelt pulling taut across her chest. She stared at him. "Have you ever stayed in a real cottage? A one to three bedroom houses where everything's wood with rockers and fireplaces?"

"I don't think so, especially if it looks that rustic."

"It's not bad, really, except for the composting toilet. I assume yours are porcelain?"

"Yes," he chuckled, "Ours are real flushing toilets."

"Good. I have a feeling I'll use them a lot."

"Right. Planning to drink a lot?"

"No. Uh, no, I only meant that while we're here, over several days, I'll probably use flushing toilets. That's all." She plopped her head against the neck support and stared out the window.

"Are you nervous about being here, because I assure you, it's a fully functioning house."

"That you call a cottage."

"Right."

She looked at him and laughed. "Very well, then, I propose we pull off somewhere so I can pee." Her British accent still had a slight Southern US drawl, as if the two articulated words the same.

Before long, the car bounced up and down as the road narrowed and wound through a valley. They rounded a bend and exited onto a nondescript dusty, paved road. After a few curves, they reached a gated fence, where he input a security code and drove through. The leather seats, warmed from their bodies, cushioning them against the occasional rattle from a rough patch on their private drive.

The first glimpse of the estate appeared through bare winter trees, a sprawling silhouette of white and grey stone against a darkening sky. The bare branches framed the house, revealing there was more to Waileigh than one private residence. In the distance, were several smaller homes and out buildings. The entire scenery looked like a small village—an ideal spot for a proposal.

As they drove closer, the smoke from multiple fireplaces curled and faded into the night.

"That's definitely not a cottage," Cordelia said. "Now, I understand why you said, Marnie and Maisie wouldn't be a bother. You've got room for a basketball team here."

The car pulled to a stop in front of the house. Wood smoke drifted from the chimneys, mixing with the crunch of pea gravel underfoot. The distant sound of wind moved through bare Highland oaks and whistled. Wreaths with oversized red bows hung from each window and on the front door. A giant ball of mistletoe hung above the three steps that led to the porch, where they'd strung red, green, and white christmas lights.

Cordelia pulled Royce back, before getting out of the car. "Thank you."

"For what?"

"For this? It's magical." Her lips against his were soft and tender. "First Venice, now this. What'll you think of next?"

"This for starts." He wrapped his hand around the nape of her neck and kissed her. She tasted salty and sweet—a perfect representation of Cordelia.

When they stepped from the warm car into the sharp December air, their breaths became visible and they stretched, excited for Christmas festivities to begin.

Chapter Four

5:oo PM

The massive oak door closed behind them with a click, as if history sealed itself between the high ceilings, wood, and stone. The entry echoed. A witness to countless Scottish winters, and a reminder of the lives that had passed through there, feeling safe within those walls.

Cordelia stood in the entrance hall, and scanned the massive oak staircase that rose three stories, at least that's how many she counted. Yet, she imagined it rose higher, hiding an attic that once housed ladies maids and valets. The vast space could've housed her entire London flat twice.

Surrounding them the heavy iron chandelier cast pools of pale light, and merged with the portrait spotlights. Stern-faced ancestors and Highland landscapes adorned the staircase walls, breathing life into each landing. And touches of lighted Christmas garland draped the banisters. Portraits peered at them, as if they watched their arrival and waited for secrets to be revealed.

Throughout the entrance hall, temperatures mingled, a swirling mixture from the chilly night air and a radiator that hissed on a nearby wall. It created small currents of air, stirring the Christmas garland above. Through her shoes, she felt the cold dampness of the flagstone floor. A chill that sent a shiver up her spine.

And like Hayton Manor, it smelled of floral-beeswax, a fragrance of time and elegance. Oddly, Cordelia felt as if she'd arrived home.

"Welcome to Waileigh Lodge, miss," said Mr. Smyth, the estate manager. His Scottish accent, softer than she expected, carried a warm rolling brogue. He finished the sentence with a wide toothy grin. He must've been in his sixties but had a head of white hair thicker than Royce.

In one motion, he relieved them of their coats and luggage, a movement that appeared second nature after decades of managing households. She watched how he folded her wool coat across his arm, making sure the shoulders aligned, before wheeling her suitcase away.

"Thank you, Mr. Smyth. Good to see you," Royce said. His posture straightened and a stiffness would always emerge whenever he stepped into a formal world: squared shoulders, lifted chin but just a fraction, and a well-trained, unconscious air of authority.

"You too, Sir. It's nice to have you back after so long." He placed their coats inside a paneled door closet.

"Yes, it's been over a year, I believe." Royce patted Mr. Smyth's arm, a noble sign of affection.

"Yes, Sir, it has. Can I get either of you anything to eat or drink before dinner?"

"Not at the moment, but thank you."

"Your family's in the den, Sir."

"Great, thank you. And Merry Christmas, Mr. Smyth."

"You too. And Ms. Dyer, if you need anything, please ask myself or Mrs. Smyth. She's around and she'll be happy to assist you."

Cordelia thanked him, and turned to Royce, "Your mom does a beautiful job decorating." The air, fragrant with the aromas of pine, cinnamon, and clove drifted in from several hallways. It created a symphony of delight—one of the first odors of the day that didn't cause her stomach to do somersaults.

Royce looked around, noticing the fresh holly and deep red velvet ribbons that accented the dark green pine garland. "I guess she does. It's like this every Christmas." He shrugged and squeezed her hand. "Leave it to you to notice."

"Is that a compliment?"

"Of course," he pulled Cordelia closer and kissed her cheek.

Mr. Smyth disappeared up the grand staircase with their luggage, shuffling his feet across the plush red rug that ran up the stairs. When he reached the first landing, he set their bags down, and paused.

"Should we help him?" She whispered, watching his lean frame struggle with their bags.

"Smyth? No. If we did, he'd probably take offense."

"But he's having a hard time. Look at him. Royce, you really should help him." They kept their voices low, avoiding an upward echo.

"You don't understand, that's his job. If we offer, he'll assume I'm suggesting he's too old."

"But he kinda is." Cordelia fidgeted with the glass necklace, rubbing it between her fingers like a comforting talisman.

"Well, as the future Earl, it's not my place."

"That's illogical. It's definitely your responsibility to look after him."

Royce wrapped his arms around her waist, exploring her eyes. "Always challenging the rules. You'll understand better when you're—one day you'll understand." His finger traced the gold chain of her Murano necklace, a gesture that usually lead to his lips leaving little kisses on her collarbone.

"Maybe." Cordelia rested her head on his shoulder, "I just realized, I'm tired."

"Why don't we say hello, and then you can rest before dinner. Sound good?"

"Sure. But can we stay like this for a moment? It's nice." Cordelia leaned her body into Royce, feeling his hands move across her back in slow circular motion. She could feel his back muscles flex beneath her palms, and the steady rhythm of his breathing against her cheek. The warmth tickled her skin.

The entry remained peacefully quiet, other than the faint sounds of a ticking clock and mumbled voices. The smell of crackling fireplace from somewhere added to the festive holiday aromas.

"This is like stepping into a Christmas card," she said.

"You'll get used to it."

"Gladly." She pulled back and looked into his eyes, "I love being here with you." The flutter in her stomach had settled, and she felt the gurgle of hunger pangs.

"Me too." He brushed his thumb across her cheek. "Ready?" Royce stepped back, sliding his hand down her arm and entwining his fingers with hers.

Through an archway to their left, she caught glimpses of multiple doorways, like a neverending path of rooms. The first, a formal gallery glowed with firelight that bounced off the wood paneling and danced across the faces of former lords. A single table lamp provided extra light to a blue floral wingback chair. The second, clearly a library, was warmed by a fire that snapped, startling Cordelia. She sighed, admiring the bookshelves that lined three walls and were illuminated by ceiling spotlights, casting shadows on the books.

But as they approached the den, the sounds of laughter

drew them into the heart of the house, where formalities and grandeur gave way to comfort. Ada Rose giggling each time Marcus said, "Whoosh," followed by clapping. Royce squeezed her hand as they stepped into the threshold where a room of warmth and christmas tree lights embraced them. *This is Christmas.*

5:10 PM

The den's intimacy reflected his mum's personality— softer, warmer, and inviting—far less formal than the entrance hall. The tall Christmas tree in the corner had become a collage of memories and childhoods, rather than a design theme.

Ada Rose squealed with delight as she demolished Marcus' block tower, and the Earl casually joked as he poured Royce a whisky. Emma and the Countess chatted by the fire, while Cordelia settled onto the sofa with a cup of herbal tea. Within minutes, Ada Rose had climbed into Cordelia's lap. Her tiny fingers played with the Murano necklace, fascinated by its texture.

Royce watched Cordelia and Ada Rose from his club chair near the oak bar. *One day that'll be our daughter she's holding.*

Outside the windows, a few snowflakes floated down, reminding him that it would be a Christmas to remember.

Chapter Five

6 :20 PM

Royce's bedroom was nothing like Cordelia had expected. Instead of restrained antique decor, the suite felt warm and lived-in, masculine without being heavy. The walls were a combination of raised wood panels with navy cotton fabric, all offset by cream moldings. Accenting the buttery wood tones was a marble fireplace, where light spilled out and danced images across the walls. The cozy fire crackled from behind a black screen, providing soothing sounds from the well-seasoned oak.

Tall windows hid behind off-white velvet curtains, and according to Royce, provided spectacular views of the loch that stretched across the glen while rugged mountains framed it like gatekeepers to the far side.

"Not a shabby cottage to spend your summers at." Cordelia ran her fingers along the smooth mahogany footboard of an over-size bed, where the carved headboard stood as its own piece of art. The wood was smooth, polished and inviting. Nearby, racks held their luggage with a chest of drawers in between. Another feature to the room, a stately wardrobe with four doors, brass handles, and trim details that looked Gatsby-inspired.

"No, I guess not." His voice had a thread of tension. "Why didn't you tell me you were getting car sick? We could've stopped for a cup of tea." He unpacked his bag, carefully placing a stack of neatly folded clothes into drawers. He kept his back to her.

"Honestly, it wasn't that bad. And I know you, if I'd said anything, you would've worried."

"Is that so bad?" He fussed with the clothes in his drawer, situating them to perfection.

"No." Cordelia walked up behind him and rested her hands on his shoulders, "But do I need to tell you every time I feel uncomfortable?"

Royce shoved the drawer closed and faced her. "Of course not. I'm only surprised you didn't mention it."

Through the soft wool of his grey sweater, she felt his biceps flex with tension. His shoulders had hard knots of stress, that usually appeared after twelve hours hunched over research books. "Seriously, we're not going to tell each other every time we have some minor ache. For example, you're not telling me why you're tense..." Her fingers located the pressure points at the base of his neck and worked gentle circles until he groaned with relief.

"I'm relaxed."

"Mmhmm."

"Probably from the flight and drive. Nothing for you to worry over."

"That's exactly my point." Her hands continued working the tension in his shoulders.

"But...the doctor says a hot shower with you will always cure my tight muscles."

The heat from his body seemed to radiate through the

fabric, and she could smell the faint scent of his cologne—the complex scents of leather and pepper—a reminder of their Venetian excursion. But another aroma made her pulse quicken, a heated note from his skin. Undeniably Royce. "Talking to the doc about me?"

His hands eased around her waist and gripped her glutes. "Only because you're my favorite form of therapy."

She laughed, "Is there some cheesy seduction hotline you call to come up with these?"

"No, does it sound like it?"

"Yes."

"Is it working?" His eyes darkened and dilated.

"Possibly." Desire spiraled upward, creating a throb in her chest. She wavered about telling him *the surprise*. She could reveal the news right then and there or stick to the plan. The words were ready to spill out, but she hesitated. *Christmas, wait till Christmas.*

"That's exactly what I want to hear."

"But I'd like to unpack first, unless the doctor said it's an emergency."

Royce lifted her onto her toes. "Oh, it's an emergency."

She ran the back of her hand across his cheeks. "You seem alright to me."

"Trust me," His voice lowered, getting rough around the edges. "it's an emergency." He feigned heartache, "So, put your clothes away later?"

Her pulse quickened. His moody gaze and soft lips on her skin made her body tingle. "Go, I'll join you in a few minutes. She pushed him toward the en suite bathroom. Her hands wanted to linger, to explore the hard planes of his body, but unpacking had to come first. "And wait for me...doctors orders."

He groaned, "Ms. Dyer, you torture me."

The bathroom door closed behind him with a soft click that

echoed off the marble hearth. Soon she heard the rush of water as the shower came to life, followed by the subtle sounds of his clothes hitting the floor—the soft thud of his sneakers, the metallic sound from his jeans button, and a whisper of wool and cotton hitting the marble.

Cordelia opened her suitcase, forcing herself to concentrate. She methodically hung shirts in the wardrobe that smelled of cedar and lavender, organizing them by color and fabric. But her attention kept drifting into the bathroom where a steady cascade of water would be washing down his back and tumbling past his buns. His hands would thread through his wet hair, and then he'd turn into the water and let it stream down his body. She paused, hung a silk blouse between two different shades of blue shirts, and rested her hand on her belly. *Your father is very distracting.*

Royce hummed some half-remembered song. His unguarded voice became louder, and he added words to the parts he couldn't recall. She imagined his eyes closed, head tilted back under the water, and steam rising around him like incense.

Cordelia flushed, and it had nothing to do with the crackling fire or pregnancy. She unfolded and folded a sweater, placing it on a shelf in the wardrobe. As he sang, she pictured the water streaming over his broad shoulders, running in rivulets down the defined muscles of his chest and then onto the ripples of his stomach. His skin would be warm, inviting her touch. He'd smile, and those dimples that first caught her attention in Paris would welcome her closer.

Despite the morning sickness and exhaustion, overwhelming desire rose with intensity. She felt beautiful. She felt powerful. She felt utterly feminine. The emotions transcended any physical discomfort. This was about wanting him, wanting to embrace the man she loved with her whole self.

Without hesitation, Cordelia undressed. She kicked her shoes under the suitcase, dropped her cashmere sweater onto the thick wool carpet and quickly followed with her jeans and undergarments. The fire-warmed air sent tingling sensations across her bare skin.

She moved toward the bathroom, but paused when she caught sight of herself in an antique mirror hanging on the wall. Her profile looked the same as it had a year ago. Looking back at her wasn't a woman who felt tired, or queasy, or different. It was a woman who fully found herself and Royce in Venice. The reflection smiled as her hand drifted to her stomach. She stared at the face of woman who knew exactly what she wanted—a woman in love.

When she stepped into the bathroom, it was thick with steam. The heavy air fogged the mirrors with moisture that carried the scent of moody, masculine soap. Through the glass shower enclosure, she watched Royce's silhouette. The lines of his body, broad and tapered, moved with finesse. He had an unconscious physical confidence that made her core tingle.

She opened the shower door and stepped inside.

His eyes flew open and he stopped humming. "Took you long enough."

"Shh," she whispered, moving into the torrent of water. The heat hit her skin, moistening it as it streamed down her shoulders and past her breasts. She stepped closer to him, pressing her hips against his muscles, and sighed as his hand grazed down her back. "I want to tell you something..."

Her hands found his chest, fingers splayed and gripping the muscles that jumped under her touch. His skin was slick, flushed from the heat. She could feel his heart pound beneath her fingertips like a caged animal clawing to be free. The water tumbled over them, creating an intimate world where nothing else existed. "I—."

"You're beautiful," he exhaled.

"So are you," she murmured. "I wanted to..."

His hand cupped her chin, pulling her mouth closer. He traced the curve of her neck, her collarbone, the gentle slope of her shoulder.

Every touch electrified her system. Somehow the pregnancy heightened the physical sensations, awakening desire. She wanted to consume passion. Her lips found the pulse point on his neck. It throbbed against her mouth. She felt desirable, in control. Cordelia backed him against the cool marble, and let her hand follow the trail of water. His body craved her.

Their kiss was fierce. It claimed them. After Venice, she knew how precious their connection was. She knew what it meant to love and almost lose, to almost let it slip away. She felt the crescendo of time—the depth of fearless authenticity. Royce responded, tangling his hands into her drenched curls. He spun her around and pressed her back against the stone.

Wedged between the cool marble and his heated body made her gasp. She breathed in the steam and arched her back as his mouth trailed kisses down her throat to the hollow between her breasts. Her pulse fluttered. She wanted more.

Cordelia guided his mouth to hers, letting her tongue seduce him. His back rested against the glass. Water flowed down her cheeks as she gazed into his eyes and held their attention.

Her hands mapped the shape of his body, memorizing him through touch. Her mouth followed. And soon, he groaned with pleasure, the sound low and intimate in the steamy air.

"I love you," he whispered in her ear as she arched her back under the water and let it tumble across her face. His arms wrapped around her waist, "I love everything about you. Your strength, your passion...you fill my life in so many ways."

"Show me," she said, her hands gripping his shoulder

muscles. The space between them dissolved until only the water seeped between their bodies.

Royce bumped the faucet hotter. "Is that a challenge?"

"Show me, Royce. Show me."

His hand slipped between her thighs and the shower became a dance floor for desire and devotion. Their bodies moved together like souls reuniting. The water and fog muffled their gasps and whispered longings. Their breathy words of endearment faded into a physical manifestation of passion as her legs wrapped around him.

They were lovers who knew exactly how to please each other, and his touch created an intense sensation within her body, more than normal. It transported her beyond the bathroom walls.

Her fingers dug into his shoulder as a breathless release rose from her core. His moan rattled against her ear and they clung to each other, merged as time stood still.

Lukewarm water poured over them, causing a shiver up her spine.

"Are you cold?" Royce bumped the faucet as far as it would go. "I think we drained the hot water." He chuckled, "I think that's a first for this house."

Cordelia rested her face against his. "I hope no one heard."

"If they did, I bet they're jealous." His voice rough with amused satisfaction. "You're going to be the death of me."

"Don't say that."

"Not literally." Their eyes connected.

"I know, but don't even joke about it." She nuzzled in his arms as the lukewarm water massaged her back. "That would be horrible."

"Not for me."

She tapped his bum, "Seriously."

"Alright, alright." He squeezed his arms tighter, "It's cold. Come on." He flipped the faucet off.

As they dried off, their hands continued touching each other. A simmer, beneath the surface seemed ready to spark into a full blown fire again. *Man, if this is what pregnancy does for ya, I'll take it.*

Wrapped in thick Turkish robes that had been hanging on the towel heater, Cordelia caught sight of their reflection as the mirror unfogged. Their faces, flush with fulfillment, and eyes bright with love moved toward each other—one last kiss before emerging out of their steamy cocoon.

Her head leaned backwards against his chest as they watched their reflection. His hands rested on her belly, unaware that he caressed their baby—their little nugget of love.

"I...I wanted to tell you...I love you." Cordelia couldn't tell him just yet. Her Christmas night surprise included an engraved silver spoon that read *You're going to be a dad,* and a leather-bound journal with her personal notes to him since she learned of the pregnancy. She had to wait.

"We should probably get dressed," he said. Although he made no move to release her from the comfort of his arms. "They'll wonder where we are."

"Probably." Yet, she felt reluctant to break the spell of intimacy. "I'm sure they're smart enough to assume we needed some time to settle in."

"They're surprisingly perceptive, especially right now." Royce stepped away, cleared his throat, and tightened the sash of his robe.

"What do you mean, right now? Do they have some magical powers here I don't know about?"

He led her into the bedroom, "Wouldn't that be interesting?"

"Do you think they know?"

"Know what?" He stoked the fire that settled to glowing embers while they were occupied. It cast soft light around the room, and crackled against the hot iron poker. Outside, the faint sound of the loch lapped against its shores.

"About us, in the shower."

"No, no, I doubt it." He added a log to the fire and closed the screen. "But we should hurry."

As they readied for dinner, stealing kisses and touches as they navigated around each other in the bedroom, Cordelia sensed a deep contentment settling in her core. Whatever challenges they faced, from navigating family expectations, to the beautiful chaos of raising a child, they'd do it together.

She swiped mascara onto her lashes, knowing it would be an eventful Christmas. *Definitely memorable.* She dropped the tube into her makeup bag, distracted by Royce pulling on a V-neck tee. Over top he buttoned up a cable knit cardigan. *Those hands...* Those hands that caressed her hips and drafted creative stories would soon be rocking a baby to sleep. He glanced up and caught her watching.

"Come on, we need to get downstairs."

"Right."

"Besides, if you keep looking at me that way, I'll be forced to lie about why we never joined them for dinner."

Cordelia smiled, nodded, and grabbed a burnt orange sweater from the wardrobe. "Ready in five."

"I'll give you fifteen." He laughed and dodged the Turkish robe that flew his direction.

Chapter Six

8:oo PM

The family dining room, a space the Countess deemed as unpretentious. A space where required attire was casual and comfortable. Although it was two rooms away from the formal dining room, to Royce it felt like a world apart.

The round oak table offered a closeness that they didn't get in the formal spaces, not even at Hayton's casual dinner table. At Waileigh, they sat close enough to pass bread and share platters without effort. It's one of the reasons he loved visiting the estate. It gave them a chance to feel like a regular family.

Royce settled into his chair beside Cordelia. She leaned against the green wool highback, relaxing her hands on the edge of the table. He rested his hand on her thigh, and soon she interlaced her fingers with his. Intimacy lingered from the early—her pulse throbbed against his palm and she traced delicate circles with her thumb.

She'd been to enough Sunday dinners at Hayton to know their routine, but at the lodge, even his parents softened. No stately portraits glared at them. Only a suit of armor suggested something unusual about the family. Otherwise, the decor encompassed family photos from summers at the estate, to his mum's collection of antique porcelain plates that hung on one wall. Some from India and France, but most were English.

Mrs. MacLeod entered with two platters, a lamb roast and another one piled with root vegetables glistening with herb butter. The aromas of rosemary and garlic filled the air as she placed them on the sideboard. A photo of Royce and Marcus, with broad smiles and freshly caught fish stood nearby.

Mrs. Smyth placed a basket of fresh bread, steam still rising from the crusty loaves, onto the table. "Anything else, M'Lady? Mr. Smyth is getting the mint sauce, as we speak."

"No, Mrs. Smyth, thank you." The Countess said.

Cordelia served herself a slice of the lamb. "This looks incredible." She reached across him for the vegetables, adding a larg portion of them to her place. Her shoulder brushed his, and he caught the faint scent of his woodsy soap on her skin. "I can't believe how hungry I am."

The aroma lingered, a reminder of water trailing down her body, and his mouth against her skin.

"Mrs. MacLeod you outdid yourself tonight." Alia said, pouring sparkling water into everyone's glasses.

"It was a piece, Ma'am." She paused before pushing the kitchen swing door open, "I hope everyone enjoys their dinner."

Cordelia leaned into Royce, "Piece? What does that mean?"

"Simple. She's telling mum it was an easy meal to prepare."

"Gotcha." She dropped a potato piece onto her plate, "I would've never known."

"You begin to understand them after a while...except when they're drunk. It's like deciphering a foreign language."

Cordelia returned to her seat, laughing. "Maybe that's how they feel about you when you've had one too many."

He guffawed. "Probably so."

The Earl stabbed at a thick cut of meat, "Cordelia, dear, did you get a slice from the inside of the roast? That's where the juiciest bits are."

"Well, if I go back for seconds, then I'll try a piece."

Cordelia cut her eyes at Royce. They winked at each other —their silent message of *I love you*. She licked her lips and pressed them together. The simplest things she did caused an inner burn.

"Don't let him influence you too much," The Countess said with affection, "He'll try to convince you he's the connoisseur of the family."

"And you disagree?" He said, joining everyone at the table, and grabbing a slice of warm bread.

"I would say you have unique preferences, darling." Her amused tone diplomatically emphasized his finicky tastes.

Under the table, something cold and wet pressed against Royce's thigh. He glanced down and noticed Piper, the estate's golden retriever, sat at attention. His soulful brown eyes begged for food. "No, Piper, go lay down."

Piper circled the table, before sitting beside the Earl, fixated on his fork.

"Piper," the Earl said without looking down, "you know the rules."

She wagged her tail, swishing it against the carpet.

"Thomas, don't even think about it," Alia said, as her lips twitched in suppressed amusement.

"What? It's all her. And she's a member of the family."

"Right."

Royce caught the private look between his parents—something mischievious, that had nothing to do with Piper. His father's eyes sparkled in response to her gentle gesture to his hand.

They're so obvious. Royce cleared his throat and gave his father a stern look. *Not now. You better not give anything away.*

Thomas blinked, smiled, and gave his meat a precise cut. "Wine, Cordelia?" He passed a bottle to the Countess.

"Oh, no thank you. The staff decided to participate in a charity event and we all agreed to be alcohol-free over the holidays. It's to help raise money for a program to help those that are homeless in London."

"How admirable," The Countess said. "What a thoughtful way to support the community."

"You never mentioned this."

"I guess I forgot. We decided last week."

Royce watched Cordelia take a large bite of lamb. She chewed, "Mmmm." Her hand reached into his lap and squeezed his thigh. *Why isn't she mentioning this to me? It's not insignificant.* Usually she shared work-related initiatives with him—her passion for humanitarism was one of the things he loved about her. Somehow, the omission felt odd, but perhaps he'd been too distracted with proposal planning to notice.

"Did Marcus tell you what happened with Odalin Max this week?" Emma said, helping Ada Rose navigate her applesauce spoon to her mouth.

"Oh, it's hilarious," Marcus said. "So you know he's 29 years now..."

"Thirty. I think he's thirty," Royce interjected.

"You're probably right. Anyway, you know he's massive—fifteen hands, strong bones—big horse. Well, last week, a squirrel, this tiny little one, ran across the stable yard. Right in front of Odie. The old guy spooked and bolted straight out of the stable doors. He knocked over two wheelbarrows trying to get out. Bridles went flying out of one of them, and he just ran. And it's as if he knew exactly where Denny was repairing the fence, because he went straight there, jumped the low railing, and went to the far side of the pasture."

"Is he alright?"

"Yeah, other than having a shock and shortness of breath. He's okay."

The Countess leaned toward the Earl, "Did you just feed Piper?"

"No." The Earl adjusted his plate and dessert spoon, lining them up with the edge of the table.

"I distinctly saw your hand disappear under the table."

"Then why did you ask?"

"To see if you'd tell me the truth."

"That's entrapment."

"Only because you're guilty."

"She's been waiting patiently, so I rewarded her good behavior."

"Thomas Brownell, you're incorrigible."

The Earl kissed the back of her hand, and then tossed a small piece of lamb to Piper.

"Alright, spoil the dog."

Royce glanced at Cordelia and stared at her soft smile. She had an affectionate giggle—an appreciation for his parent's quirks. She genuinely enjoyed them.

The conversation briefly returned to Marcus and the family horse, Odalin Max. The Earl fed Piper a few pieces of bread and then told her to go lay on her bed. Mr. And Mrs. Smyth came to clear the plates, while Mrs. MacLeod served butterscotch pudding for dessert, the Earl's favorite.

As spoons clinked against the bowls, Cordelia asked, "Is that armor real?" She pointed to the suit of armor that stood in the far corner behind the Earl. It's dull metal gleamed in the firelight. "Can you actually wear it?"

Marcus and Emma exchanged grins.

"Oh no," Emma said dramatically. "You've opened Pandora's box now."

"That's Sir George Brownell," the Earl said. His voice took

on a theatrical quality that Royce recognized from his childhood summers at the lodge. "My ancestor, Earl of Hayton Manor, a Yorkist supporter and friend to the Earl of Warwick, but proudly, he never betrayed King Edward IV, unlike some folks."

"If legend is to be believed," Royce said.

"That's amazing. Can you wear it? I mean, have you ever tried it on?"

"I wouldn't recommend it. The poor fellow's held together by little more than wire and determination at this point."

A gust of wind rattled the windows, and the ancient armor groaned. The gauntlet shifted, causing the entire suit to lean sideways.

"Okay, that's creepy," Cordelia said.

"That reminds me," Thomas continued, "Has Royce told you about Lady Margaret?"

Royce suppressed a groan. His father's ghost stories were legendary, and slightly redundant. But he loved how theatrical his father sounded when telling the tales.

"No, who's Lady Margaret?"

"The former Lady of Waileigh Lodge and Loch. Seventeenth century. Beautiful, by all accounts, but rather... particular about housekeeping standards. And exacting when it came to her staff's attire."

"Pop," Marcus said, "Again?"

"I'm simply sharing the estate's history. Besides, Lady Margaret is perfectly harmless. Although, Mrs. Smyth says she is particular when the linens are stored inappropriately."

"Seriously? A ghost cares about that?" Cordelia said.

"Exactly. Ask Mrs. Smyth, she'll tell you what happens when new staff do things incorrectly."

"You're joking, aren't you?"

"Not at all."

"She's especially active during Christmas," Alia said. "We

don't know why, but things are moved more during the holidays."

Marcus leaned forward. "Mum's right, last year, all the stockings were rehung." He'd joined in the scheme against Cordelia. "Every one of them had been moved. And I'm not joking."

Royce scanned each one of their faces, well aware of the smirks that lurked behind their words.

"Royce, are they for real?" Cordelia looked at him, her fingers rapping on the table.

"They know better than I do."

"Mmhmm." She looked at each one, trying to gauge the truth. "Emma? Tell me the truth."

"They know what they're talking about." She said, keeping her eyes on Ada Rose, while wiping the little girl's face with a wet towel.

A sound rattled in the wall. Everyone froze. The noise moved in the wall behind the sideboard, growing louder.

"What's that?" Cordelia said, keeping her voice just above a whisper.

The rattling intensified. The sound of chains dragging across stone grew louder.

"Oh dear," Alia said in a concerned but calm tone. "She must know were talking about her."

"She doesn't like being discussed," Thomas said. "It always seems to anger her."

The rattling moved through the wall—a grating sound. Piper moved under the table.

"She doesn't like it, whatever it is," Emma said.

Cordelia's eyes widened as the sound reached the corner where Sir George stood. The armor creaked, and one gauntlet shifted with a metallic groan.

"It makes the armor move?" Cordelia asked. Her hand

squeezed Royce's pinching the blood flow from his fingers.

"Lady Margaret enjoys theatrics." Royce said. He chuckled to himself, knowing Cordelia would be disappointed when she learned the truth, and hopefully wouldn't hold the fun against him.

A loud clang echoed through the room. Cordelia jumped. Even Royce felt his pulse startle, despite knowing what had happened.

"Perhaps we should move to the den," Alia said, with perfect timing. "Until she calms down."

"Why don't they have her removed?" Cordelia whispered in Royce's ear.

The room silenced, only broken by the crackling fire and Piper's panting.

The Earl grinned and began to laugh, "I'm sorry my dear, it's only the dumbwaiter and old pipes making that noise." He laughed, joined by the snickers of the others. "We didn't mean to frighten you."

"Yes, we did," Marcus said.

"The dumbwaiter," Cordelia said flatly. "That was pipes?"

Royce tried to ease her frustration by rubbing her back.

She glared at him. "I can't believe...ya got me."

To soothe her playful annoyance, he reached for her hands and pressed them to his lips, offering a silent apology. She pulled one away, but let him linger a bit longer in a groveling kiss.

"Don't worry, they did it to me the first time I visited, too." Emma said. "You're lucky though, they dragged it on for two nights with me."

Marcus burst into laughter, "You were so gullible. We debated not even telling you."

Emma elbowed him.

"Although," Thomas added with suspicious seriousness,

44

"the pipes don't explain the armor moving. That might actually be Lady Margaret."

"Thomas, that's enough," Alia said.

"I'm simply pointing out..."

Cordelia shook her head, but Royce noticed a smile tugging at her lips. "You're terrible, Royce Brownell."

"I prefer committed."

"Committed to what? Scaring me?"

"Tradition." He laughed.

"As your mother said, incorrigible." She rested her elbows onto the table and hid her blushing cheeks.

Conversation on topics other than Lady Margaret resumed and Royce watched his parents—their playful mannerisms, gentle touches, and soft gazes. They represented family, despite the confinements of duty and tradition, they represented home. *In two days, that'll be us. Some traditions are worth maintaining.*

Under the table, Piper's tail thumped. Her eager eyes were hopeful. Royce watched his father discreetly drop a piece of bread. Cordelia giggled and rested her head on his shoulder. Out of the corner of his eye, he glimpsed his mum looking at them. She nodded and stood, suggesting them take tea or coffee in the den while they wait for others to arrive.

Chapter Seven

9:10 PM
The family had just settled into the den when the sound of car doors slammed out front.

"That'll be Cassandra and Richard," Royce said, checking his watch.

Through the tall windows, Royce saw Cassandra's petite silhouette beside two oversized suitcases. "You'd think she was staying for the entire season."

Seconds later, voices carried from the hallway as Cassandra cooed over the entrance hall Christmas tree. "So, lovely. Oh my, it's fabulous...Richard, let's check the den."

"Cassandra, people might be sleeping," He said.

"Nonsense, it's too early."

"Not for Ada."

"Right, babies go to bed early, don't they?"

Cassandra appeared through the library doorway, "Hello, darlings." She crossed directly to Cordelia with arms outstretched. "You look wonderful."

The pair hugged and became lost in conversation while

Richard greeted the Earl and Countess. Soon after, he joined Royce who'd already poured him a Scotch. And within minutes, Cassandra and Richard debated across the room over her obsessive need to stop and admire every holiday decoration between Edinburgh and the house.

"I'm expanding my cultural knowledge of Scotland." Cassandra said.

Thomas situated himself into his favorite chair, and sipped his tea. "Cassandra, you've been coming here since a girl, and I've never known you to care anything about Scottish customs."

"One can change, Sir, can't they." She giggled and playful curtsied at him, lifting a non-existent skirt into the air.

She continued to hold Cordelia hostage, talking about a man she'd met on a flight back from Brussels. "He was charming, intelligent, but he lives in Shoreditch."

"Well, if you'll excuse me, I need to check in with Mrs. MacLeod before retiring," the Countess said. She disappeared into the kitchen, not waiting for the round of 'good nights'.

A few minutes later, Luke MacGregor, the estate gamekeeper came in from the kitchen, wearing a navy Barbour jacket and jeans. His dark windswept hair tumbled across his face. Luke was quintessential Scottish ruggedness, and when he said 'hello', Cassandra and Cordelia both smirked.

"Your lordship," Luke said. "Sorry to interrupt. I just wanted to let you know the turkey's delivered and in the pantry freezer for Mrs. MacLeod."

"Excellent. Luke, thank you." The Earl offered introduction, beginning first with Royce and Cordelia, introducing her as his partner.

Luke extended a hand, his socks shuffling across the rug. He had a confident air about him, unphased by the more formal environment. When he was introduced to Cassandra, something shifted in his demeanor—a spark, an attraction that left him grinning.

Cassandra beamed, her white teeth sparkled against her broad lips.

"Countess," Luke said. His Scottish accent deepened.

"Mr. MacGregor." Her voice held a breathless quality. Their handshake lingered a moment longer than socially necessary.

What the hell? Royce sat down next to Cordelia, who curled up beside him, resting her head on his shoulder. She elbowed him every time Cassandra giggled at something Luke said, which was frequent. He glanced at Richard, who sat near the fireplace, cutting his eyes between emails and Cassandra's flirty voice.

His father yawned. "Well, I'll leave you young people to it. Luke, enjoy the whisky." He excused himself, and retired for the night.

Within minutes, Cassandra, a title-conscious, bored by anything that didn't involve London society, hung on his every word. She questioned him about his life, intrigued when he mentioned wildlife photography. Her usual sophisticated detachment melted into genuine interest. Likewise, Luke never let his attention drift too long from her.

"I'll be right back, need to make a call." Richard said. He slipped into the library, shutting the door behind himself.

Cordelia leaned her weight against Royce's side. Their fingers threaded together as they watched Cassandra flirt.

"I don't know whether to feel awkward or proud of her," Cordelia whispered, her soft breath warmed his ear.

"I lean toward awkward."

"I think she just blushed. Did you see that?"

"It's like two species mating, and I can't look away."

Cordelia burst into laughter, temporarily interrupting

Cassandra and Luke. "Sorry. Royce was telling me a childhood story."

"Wow, you thought up that lie fast. Should I be worried?"

"Hey, it's a skill, and comes in handy sometimes."

"Right, like a party trick."

Royce watched as Cassandra began touching Luke's arm or hand when laughing. "In my wildest, I never imagined she'd—."

"Maybe they thought that about us—beautiful American pastry chef and a haughty British author. Bet they didn't see that coming."

"Haughty? I thought we eliminated that from our vocabulary back in Paris." He turned to look at her, mock offense in his voice.

"Oh, you're very proud, but..." her eyes sparkled, a warmth that sent energy coursing through his veins. The same look she'd had earlier, when the rest of the had world disappeared and it was just them—heat, steam, and passion.

Richard returned and caught Royce's eye as he took his seat. He shook his head at Cassandra, smirked, and mouthed, "What the hell?"

Royce shrugged. Whatever unfolded between Cassandra and Luke caused him to reflect, and become acutely aware of Cordelia's presence beside him—the way her body fit against his, the casual intimacy of her touch, the silent knowings in their glances.

Cordelia yawned, covering her mouth with her free hand. "I think the drive and dinner are catching up with me."

"Bed?"

"No, I have to wait for Marnie and Maisie to arrive. I can't let them show up and not be here."

"Right. I guess it would be rude to invite them, and sneak off," Royce pressed his lips to her ear, "for selfish reasons."

Cordelia shivered. "Selfishness is sometimes beneficial. But not tonight, not until later." She turned to face him, "Besides we don't want them walking into Mr. Lonely over there and animal kingdom here."

Royce laughed. "Richard, up for a game of chess?" He stood, kissed the palm of her hand, and joined Richard by the fireplace.

Chapter Eight

1 1:30 PM

The library had become a sanctuary for Cordelia after an evening of arrivals and introductions. She enjoyed the solitude, as the house slept—a reprieve to gather her thoughts. Keeping the secret until Christmas night was proving more difficult than she'd imagined. Every time she felt his hand at the small of her back, or caught him looking at her smiling, she wanted to blurt it out, to share the happy news.

Cordelia watched the glowing embers settle in the fireplace with shadows flickered patterns across the ornate marble hearth. What was left of the wood hissed and popped. A contrast to the stillness of the room—a cozy vibe inviting her to linger until it dissipated.

Her perch, a tartan club chair, provided the perfect spot to curl up and consider her options. *Three days...less than that.* Maybe she'd wake early on Christmas morning, have coffee in bed and a roaring fire, and then surprise him. *But is that romantic enough?* Her plan included a decorated tree, a glowing fire, and no morning sickness. That was key. She imagined being halfway through the words, 'Royce, I'm...' and then needing to bolt for the bathroom. Not romantic. Not exciting. *That settles it. I'm waiting.* She watched a cinder break apart, tumble into fresh ash, and pulsate a deep orange.

"I thought I'd find you here," Marnie said, startling Cordelia. Her best friend peeked through the doorway, wearing red plaid flannel pjs. Her midwestern accent had evolved, adding a distinct Australian sound to the end of her sentence.

"What are you doing up?"

Marnie curled into an armchair across from Cordelia, tucking her legs beneath herself. "I could ask you the same question."

"Just needed to think for a bit."

"I knew it. Even after two years I could tell you were somewhere else. Everything alright with *Mr. Lush?*"

"Everything's fine, actually perfect...a lot going on at work. But life's great." The chair's woven fabric created rough friction under her restless palm, an irritating sensation. *I wish I could tell you, but Royce comes first. And I'm sticking to my plan.*

"So, why the late night mind sesh?"

"I told you, work. There's just a lot going on." Her firm tone sliced. *God, you're making this difficult to keep quiet.*

"Sure, I get it. But, it's Christmas, and you're in a place like this, and you're losing sleep over work?"

"I have a lot on me." Cordelia fidgeted with the throw blanket across her feet, straightening and shifting it to lie in a precise way.

"I guess some things never change."

"Meaning?"

"I thought you'd changed since New York, started to live a little."

"Wow, I'd forgotten how you don't hold back."

Marnie leaned closer, "And I never will, because I love you." She dragged the chair closer to Cordelia, "You know you're obsessive still, right?"

They shared a look, holding each other's gaze, and scanning one another's face.

Cordelia scrunched her nose at Marnie, and playfully stuck her tongue out.

"Oh, very countess-like."

"Shhh, I'm not a countess."

Marnie propped her feet onto Cordelia's chair, and sighed. They sat in silence listening to the pipes rattle in the wall.

"I can't believe you're here, after two years. You guys are finally here." Cordelia said with an enthusiasm that elevated her tone.

"I know. Remember when I told you I was going to Sydney? You blew a gasket over three months." Marnie ran her fingers through her pale blonde hair. "Who knew it'd be two years?"

Cordelia rested her elbow on the chair arm, propping her head up with her hand. "It's crazy. Things have really changed for both of us. I mean, my god, Maisie's grown up and now she's this hip little Bondi beach girl."

Marnie laughed, "Yeah, I wonder what Dar—." The air thickened. Marnie looked down, biting her lip.

Both began to speak, but Cordelia told Marnie to go ahead, hoping she'd say his name.

"You know, Royce isn't at all what I expected."

"But you've met him on video."

"Yeah, but it's not the same."

Cordelia shrugged, "And?"

"I thought he'd be stuffy and cold in person."

"Marnie, why would you think that?"

"I don't know. He's a British lord with two mansions."

"They're not his."

"Yet...Maisie adores him, said he looks at you like he's staring at the stars."

"No, he doesn't."

"He totally does," she threw her hands into the air. "The guy's crazy in love with you."

Cordelia stretched out, propping her feet on Marnie's chair and nuzzled under the blanket. "Yeah, me too."

"It's good to see you happy, Cordy. You seem settled." There was a catch in her voice—a hesitation that matched the distant look that had settled like a fog across her blue eyes.

"Marnie? You're not the only one who senses when something's off. What's going on?"

She was quiet. For at least sixty seconds Cordelia watched as Marnie stared at the painting above the fireplace, seemingly captivated by the portrait. During that time, she cleared her throat twice, and dabbed her watery eyes. "It must be smoky in here."

"I hadn't noticed."

She coughed. "Edmund and I split."

The words tumbled like a boulder down a mountainside.

"When?" Cordelia asked gently.

"Last week. Apparently, two years is his cutoff," Marnie laughed—a hollow sound that echoed with pain. "Wish he'd mentioned that before I moved us all the way to Sydney and sacrificed my career. Asshole."

"Oh, honey." Cordelia sat on the edge of her seat. "Why didn't you tell me?"

"Because. I knew you had a lot going on at work—."

"Whatever, you should've called me."

Her eyes watered, "I couldn't let Maisie see me looking like a hot mess. She needs stability." Marnie used her sleeve to wipe away a tear. "I already had to lie to her and tell her we're visiting granpa after Christmas. I couldn't tell her all of our stuff's being packed up as we speak."

"Marnie—."

"I know. I'm shitty for getting involved with my boss and moving her half way around the world."

"That's not what I was going to say. He put you in this predicament. And at the holidays." Cordelia swiped a tear off Marnie's cheek. "He's at least going to give you a reference, right? He owes you that much."

Marnie plopped her head into her hands. "Yeah, he said he still admires me professionally, and personally. But he gets restless after two years in a relationship." She gestured, emphasizing 'restless'. "He wanted me to keep my job, for us to continue working together. Can you believe that? I told him to 'go to hell.'"

Cordelia resisted laughing, "I hope you got your reference first?"

"Oh, don't worry, I did. He knows he owes me that much."

"I'm sorry, Marnie. I'm sorry I wasn't there for you."

"It's okay."

"Did you, did you love him?"

Marnie paused and held her breath for a moment. She picked at her red fingernail polish. "I don't know. We had fun, and all. Great sex. But I honestly don't know. It's just..." She cut her moist eyes at Cordelia. "It's just crappy. The whole thing, but at least he's paying to ship our stuff back, once we get settled. Wherever that'll be." Marnie groaned and flung herself backwards, "I'm sorry. I really didn't want to dump this on you, not tonight."

Cordelia put her hands on Marnie's knees, "Are you okay

financially? And what about Maisie's education? Are you going to go back to New York or closer to your dad's?"

"I don't know, so many questions." She sat straight up, placing her hands on top of Cordelia's "I just don't know." A tear rolled down her cheek and landed on the back of her hand. "I need to do what's best for Maisie...but I thought that was Edmund."

Cordelia and Marnie held a gaze, both attempting to smile at the other.

"What if you started over here?"

"Here? Like here the estate or here Scotland?"

"No, London."

"I don't—."

"Hear me out. You're a highly trained, international pastry chef with more than five years working for Edmund, and before that you worked under others who all give you glowing recommendations. I know you could get a job here."

Marnie's eyes widened. "Wow, I hadn't thought about it." Her fingers tapped against the backs of Cordelia's hands. "I don't know. That's risky."

"No, think about it. You'd be in London. We'd be in the same city again, and you could build a new life here for you guys. Maisie could start school right away, and we can help you get settled. And she could be—."

"Right, that's risky. We'd be in the same city as him."

"That's my point. You can finally tell him about Maisie, and she can get to know her father."

Marnie stood and paced. She held her thumbnail between her teeth and clicked her teeth together. "Maybe it's time to stop being scared, right?"

"Yes, exactly." Cordelia said, repositioning and her crossing her legs.

With each step, Marnie's shuffling feet created static electricity sounds on the rug, "Maybe you're right...maybe he should know."

"They both should." Cordelia rested her hand on her belly. "He has a right to know."

"Darius," Marnie whispered, stopping to look at Cordelia. "You said, he's asked about me?"

"Every time we see him. He gets that sad, puppy dog look whenever he asks about you."

Her face lit up, "What if he...what if he hates me after I tell him?"

"It's not going to be perfect, or even ideal, but I know Darius, he'll listen. It's time Marnie."

"I don't know."

"He deserves to know, and this is the perfect opportunity."

Marnie plopped onto the chair's arm, "Can you imagine, Maisie and me in London?"

"I'll make some calls when I get home, and we'll get interviews lined up for you. Can you delay your flight to the states?"

"Yes. Yes, I can." She slid down onto the seat and propped her feet up beside Cordelia. "You'd really do this for me?"

"Oh, my god." Cordelia flopped her legs up beside Marnie's. "Has it really be that long? You know I'd do anything for you and Maisie."

Marnie blew her a kiss.

"Besides, it's purely selfish. I'll get to have you two near me and—."

"And *Mr. Lush?*"

"Yes, near me and Royce." Cordelia arched her back and stretched, feeling as her breasts had added five extra pounds.

"Does that mean you'll babysit whenever I ask?"

"No."

"Then what's the point?" Marnie let out a chuckle.

They talked until almost two am, running through varied

logistics and possibilities. The fire had burned out, and become a pile of ash, leaving a crisp chill in the air.

Cordelia stood, stretched, and yawned, "We'll talk more tomorrow. I'm exhausted."

"Thank you," Marnie said, offering a tight hug. "You're the best, Cordy. I don't know what I'd do without you."

The warm, familiar hug reminded Cordelia of their years at culinary school—the late night supportive chats that became the foundation of their sisterly bond. "I'm always here for you, Marnie."

As they climbed the softly lit staircase, Marnie whispered, "Everything's changing for best."

Cordelia's hand moved across her still-flat stomach. *You have no idea.* She smiled, nodded, and yawned.

Lying to Marnie was difficult, but she had to share it with Royce first.

December 23rd

The Scottish Highlands

Chapter Nine

7:30 AM

A soft light streamed through the tall windows of their bedroom, painting everything in shades of cream. It glimmered off the full-length mirror and surrounded Cordelia's reflection with a glow.

In the bathroom, Royce whistled a Christmas carol, as he massaged cream on his hands. His black terry robe gaped open, exposing the trimmed trail that ran southward from his muscular chest. "Any plans this morning?"

"I think we're going to the village Christmas market. Aren't you coming?"

"Depends on what time you're leaving. Luke's giving Marcus, Pop, and me a tour of the forest."

Cordelia examined her profile in the dark oak mirror, noticing the slight bodily changes. "Oh, you're going on a hike? I'd love a good walk in nature." She adjusted the red lace underwear that stretched across her bloated stomach, and sighed.

"Ah, well, it's not that kind of a tour. He's showing us some spots...it deals with deer management." There was a hesitation in his voice, almost as if he didn't know why they were taking a tour.

"Oh. You're not planning to kill any are you?"

"No, no. Just looking."

"Promise me you won't hunt deer today. It's the holidays." Her stomach churned. A queasy discomfort she dismissed, hoping to keep the morning sickness from surfacing.

"I will not be hunting any deer today, or tomorrow. I promise." Royce joined her in the bedroom. "Everything alright?"

Cordelia sat in the chair beside the mirror, catching her breath. The nausea had increased. "Last night's lamb was rich and I don't think it settled very well. Or maybe I ate too much mint sauce." She pressed a hand to her stomach, stood, and reached for her bra that dangled on the back of the seat.

"I've never known you to complain about rich food. Are you sure it's not something else?" Royce dropped his robe and dressed.

"It's not." The lace bra dug into her swollen breasts like a torture device. She glanced at her image, glaring as her chest spilled over the sides. "I'm not sick, if that's what you're suggesting." Well aware her tone snapped, Cordelia quickly softened her voice and smiled at him "Sorry. I'm just tired, we were up until two-thirty."

Royce zipped up his brown sweater jacket, revealing a spot of orange from his T-shirt. "Was it that late?"

"Yes, I don't think you heard me when I came in." Cordelia pulled a chunky brown sweater with a roll collar over her head, "Normally, you roll over and spoon." She smoothed the sweater, looking at herself in the mirror. "I'm deprived now."

The bra had fit perfectly two weeks prior. *Ugh, why now?* She adjusted the back hooks and tucked her aching breasts into the sides. *It doesn't fit anymore. I'm not even showing but they're already the size of melons.* The combination of her queasy stomach and inflated boobs made her increasingly irritable. "This is ridiculous," she mumbled, reaching around to adjust the band for a third time.

"What's ridiculous?" Royce asked, slipping on his house shoes.

"This bra. It doesn't fit anymore." She froze, realizing the words had tumbled out before she could filter them. *Great. Think Cordelia. Think.*

Royce walked over and examined her reflection. "Looks okay to me. What doesn't fit?"

"Just okay?"

"It's a figure of speech. You're beautiful." He kissed the back of her head, resting his hands on her hips.

"You're only saying that because I asked." Heat flooded her cheeks.

"Someone's hangry this morning." His hands slid around her waist and settled on her belly.

She felt her breath catch. *Does he suspect?* Cordelia gestured at her chest, "No, it's the wrong bra. I'm having a complete wardrobe malfunction."

"Really?" He pulled her closer and rested his lips beside her ear, "I have to say, I think it's doing a *smashing* job at showing them off."

"Royce," she said with mock exasperation, feeling a smile emerge her frustration. Her stomach churned when she smelled the vanilla in his cologne. It sent a wave of nausea upward. "Seriously. I'm not in the mood to be a buxom beauty today." She reached under the sweater and adjusted her breasts.

"For what it's worth," he said, dropping the tone of his voice. The smoothness sent shivers down her spine. "I'm quite fond of them, exactly as they are."

"What?" She turned in his arms to face him. "Are you saying you didn't like them before?" The movement caused a queasy wave to erupt in her gut. The blood drained from her face and she gripped his shoulders.

His eyes widened. "That's not, I didn't mean...of course I liked them before."

"But you like them better now?"

"I've always loved them." Royce paused, he looked away before making eye contact. "Darling, they're you, they're beautiful, past, present, and future."

"Future?" Cordelia raised her eyebrows. *Please tell me he doesn't...?* She shifted her weight between feet. "What do you mean by future? What are you suggesting? The pause lingered longer than she expected. She knew she'd cornered him in a game of words.

Royce's fingers tensed, tapping random beats on her waist. "Well, we all age, right? Everything changes."

Sooner than you think.

"Take my parents for example." He thumbed her cheek, "All I meant, all I want you to know is that I'll love your breasts no matter how they change over time."

"Really?" Emotions flooded Cordelia, like a tidal wave crashing into her. "Well, I need—."

"When we're old and grey, no matter how they look, you'll still be the most beautiful woman in the world to me."

"Royce." Her throat tightened, a jumbled ball of feelings blocked her words from revealing the surprise, as if the universe insisted she stick to the plan—her Christmas night plan. "That's so romantic, scary, but romantic." She leaned into the comfort of his arms, ignoring the way her stomach flipped.

"Scary? I confess you'll be the hottest granny in the neighborhood, and you say 'scary'."

"I thought I was the most beautiful in the world? You've already reduced me to the neighborhood?"

His fingers slid up and down her side, finding her ticklish

66

spots. "Ms. Dyer, you have been, are, and will be the most beautiful woman in the world to me, even when your breasts are less than buxom beauties. Does that clarify it?"

Her eyes scanned his face. "Now that's romantic." The irony of his timing wasn't lost on her. He offered reassurance about bodily changes, unaware of the truth—unaware that the breasts he said he adored were swollen, achy, and outgrowing her bras as each day passed.

"I've been told I'm very romantic," he said with a playful seriousness. "Supposedly, it's one of my most redeeming qualities."

"Is that right? What are some others?"

"I'm an excellent listener with a fantastic sense of humor." He kissed her neck. "And I have superior taste in women." His lips brushed the base of her neck.

"Clearly."

Royce laughed, warming her skin. And I know how to make a good cup of tea."

"That's debatable."

"Says the woman who drops a bleached bag into her cup, and calls that done."

Cordelia's stomach turned and rumbled. Ignoring her discomfort, she stretched up and softly kissed him. An acidic, dark coffee taste lingered on his lips. "I love you."

"I love you, too, my buxom beauty who—."

A sudden surge of nausea rose from her gut, sharp and undeniable—the combination of aromas overwhelmed. "Oh, god." She clamped her hand over her mouth and ran for the bathroom. Her knees hit the stone floor beside the toilet as Royce called out her name. "No, don't."

He stood outside the door, "Cordelia, are you alright?"

Her stomach surged. "No, but don't—."

When the worst had passed, she slumped against the marble

wall. A cool sensation from the stone seeped through her sweater, soothing as she counted her breaths. *One...two...* A habit she'd learned as a teen to manage panic attacks—now a useful tool for alleviating any embarrassment as the scenario replayed in her thoughts. *Perfect. How do I explain this one?*

"Cordelia?"

"Yeah?"

"Are you alright?"

"I will be."

"I'm coming in."

"No, don't."

It was pointless to argue, Royce entered, moistened a washcloth, and handed her the warm towel.

Cordelia thanked him as he slid down the wall beside her. Her secret, their little surprise was becoming more difficult to hide. *Just two days, that's all I need.* She wiped her face, letting the water soothe her skin. They sat together for a few more minutes in silence before she looked at him. "Still think I'm the most beautiful woman in the world?"

He smiled, brushed a strand of hair off her face, and said, "Always. Although, I'm pretty sure this won't make the annual highlights reel."

She smirked and rested her head on his shoulder. "You never know."

8 :30 AM
The dining room windows faced a small mountain range and flooded the room with natural light, even on cloudy days.

Cordelia sat beside Royce, quietly eating a bowl of porridge, drowned in milk. "I can't believe how beautiful it is here."

Royce finished chewing a bite of sausage, "Mmm, it's one of the best views in the house." He cut another bite and washed it down with a gulp of black tea. His mind raced over a list of items for Mr. Smyth. *I should've written it down.* He bit into his toast and realized he'd only buttered half the piece.

"What's going on with you?" Cordelia whispered.

"Just eager to get outside, I guess." He gulped his hot tea, feeling a slight burn on the back of his throat. "Like you said, it's a beautiful morning."

"Right, but...."

Marcus fed Ada Rose pieces of biscuit. "Since when have you been excited for morning walks?"

"I'm reformed," he said, draining his cup and immediately refilling it. The lid of the tea pot faintly rattled in his hand. "And you'd better hurry, we've got a lot of ground to cover."

Cordelia stirred her porridge, crinkling her nose.

Royce leaned closer to her, "Sure you're alright?"

"Yes, I'm fine." Her voice clipped the words, "don't worry."

Royce sipped his tea, burning the roof of his mouth. *Christ.* He set his cup down rougher than intended, causing it to clink in the saucer.

"Seems like someone's feeling worse than me." She took a large spoonful of porridge and chewed.

Royce stood and dropped his napkin into the chair. "Well, Pop...Marcus, are we ready for some fresh air and exercise?"

"Right, fresh air." He winked at Royce and then glanced at the Countess, "We'll be back. Going on a hike with Luke."

Just then, Cassandra burst into the breakfast room, looking as if she were headed to a brunch in the city. "Good morning." She breezed past the platters of food on the sideboard, "My lovely, Mrs. Smyth, what's on the breakfast menu for today?"

Royce shook his head and whispered in Cordelia's ear, "I'll

see you soon, love," brushing his lips across her cheek before walking towards the back hallway. "Ready, Pop?"

The Earl stood. "Of course. Marcus."

Royce waited by the door. He repeated a list in his mind. *Champagne. Outdoor lights. Heat, we need heat out there.* They had forty-eight hours to make it perfect—even less when he excluded Christmas morning.

"Royce?" Cordelia's voice pulled him back.

He turned. The window light illuminated her. "You're coming to the Christmas market, right?" She was completely unaware that in two days he'd propose.

"Yes, of course." Royce hurried into the hall with the Earl and Marcus directly behind. Once he'd put distance between himself and the dining room, he pulled out his phone and confirmed delivery for a dining pod that afternoon.

Chapter Ten

4:45 PM

The western path weaved away from the main house toward the loch and stables. The towering trees provided a buffer from the cold wind, and lush moss lined the sides of the trail.

After a day of ice skating and reindeer farm chaos, he needed down time in nature with Cordelia. As an excuse, he'd suggested they walk Piper, letting the family know they'd return by dinner.

"And did you see, Luke actually blushed when she asked about his photography," Cordelia said as they walked the estate's western path. Piper bounded ahead through a dusting of wet snow. "I haven't known Cassandra long, not like you, but I've never seen her so animated."

Royce laughed and wrapped his gloved hand firmly around hers. "I have to say, she never behaved this way with Jason."

Their breaths created small clouds in the winter air. He'd suggested the walk, which would give Piper her daily exercise. But after a hurried day of ice skating, crowds, and reindeer he really needed alone time with Cordelia.

"Luke doesn't strike me as a blushing kind of guy," Royce said, watching the dog investigate something near a fence post. He knew if they followed the path, they'd end up at the loch where plans were in operation, so he turned and guided them toward the stables. "I suppose having Countess Cassandra Shaw hang on your every word about deer migration patterns would come as a shock."

"I don't know, she seemed genuinely interested." Her lips twitched with amusement. "I mean, as interested as she can get about anything that doesn't involve social events or Italian handbags."

The cold air stung his lungs, invigorating after the stuffy van ride back from the reindeer farm. "I give it three days before she remembers she's allergic to mud and Scottish solitude."

"Wow, you're extremely confident." Cordelia squeezed his hand. "I wouldn't be so sure. Did you see that dreamy sparkle in her eyes when he described hiking out to nowhere to photography birds? It was like she was listening to someone explain their fashion collection."

"Wait, I missed that. Where was I?"

"I don't know. You were staring out the window a lot." She paused and called Piper back from exploring a rabbit hole. "Anyway, she seemed hooked—seriously hooked on him."

He was about to respond when her phone buzzed.

She pulled it from her pocket, "It's Marnie. They're having drinks in the study whenever we return." She replied and scrolled through her messages, stopping to click on Jessica's thread. "I haven't heard from Jess or Sam in twenty-four hours." Her eyes darted side-to-side, "Twenty-nine to be exact."

"That's a good thing, right?" He guided them down a path that looped toward the stables, away from the main house and family. "Means they're managing everything with no problems, right?"

"Or they've burned the place down and are afraid to tell me." Her voice held a mix of humor and anxiety.

"Cordelia." He stopped and faced her. The fading sunlight settled on her hair, shimmering in shades of honey. "They're not children. They're trained professionals who've been working with you for two years, and even longer with Bastien."

"I know, but—."

"No, darling. I don't believe there are 'buts' this time." He cupped her chin. "I know you want to check the numbers and make sure Jessica hasn't created a scheduling fiasco, but you planned everything perfectly for your absence."

"I would feel better if I just checked in, just to make sure everything's alright."

"Why? So you still feel in charge?"

Her shoulders dropped. "Maybe. I am the boss." She buried her face into his jacket. "Am I that obvious?"

"Like a Piccadilly billboard." He pulled her close, aware the cold made her shiver. "Trust me, they're well. You've trained and shaped their leadership abilities. Now, you have to trust them."

"I'm trying." She moved closer, resting her cheek on his shoulder. "It's just hard to let go. It's my reputation with Bastien on the line, and he's trusted me with his."

"I understand." He pressed his lips to the top of her woolly hat, breathing in the scent of her mint shampoo. "But you can't micromanage from Scotland. You either trust them or you don't."

"I do." She pulled back to see his face. "Intellectually, I completely trust them. But the perfectionist in me, never got that memo."

"Well, send it a message and tell it to take the holiday off." He brushed a strand of hair from her face, his thumb lingered on her cheek. "You realize you're in the Scottish Highlands with someone who's madly in love with you, even when you're obsessing over pastry production schedules."

She laughed, flinging her head backwards. "You're such a charmer."

"That's my goal." He gave her a quick kiss, noticing a chill on her lips. "Let's keep moving and warm you up."

He called for Piper, who ran back down the path and happily greeted them as if it had been years. As they walked, their conversation grew more intimate, as if the cold made their bodies and words reach for a deeper connection.

Royce's awareness narrowed—the brush of her hip against his, the subtle inhale of her breath for walking uphill, and her tongue moistening her lips.

By the time they reached the stables, his body responded to the sensations of her touch, to her laugh.

"Should we head back?" Cordelia said, looking around to see if anyone else was nearby.

"In a minute." He opened the stable door, gesturing her inside. "I want to have a look around while we're here. The horses might need fresh water."

He knew she saw through his excuse—the way she dropped her chin, tilted her head sideways and smiled. She had a way of reading him.

The heavy door bounced shut. They were alone in the dimly lit barn, where the heating system offered a reprieve from the wind. The air smelled earthy, a blend of hay and leather.

Piper rushed to the far end of the barn, to the main tack room and disappeared.

"Royce." Cordelia's voice dropped to a lower register.

He turned, she unzipped her jacket, and his pulse spiked. "Yes?" He moved toward her, ignoring rational thought.

"We should probably—."

He backed her against a nearby stall door, sliding his hand underneath her coat. "Should probably what?" His mouth located the sensitive spot just below her ear, brushing his tongue across her skin.

"We should get back before—." Her hands zipped his jacket. Royce nibbled on her earlobe.

"Before they notice we're gone and send a search party."

"They think we're walking Piper." He pushed her coat out of the way, dropping it off one shoulder. "We could be gone for an hour and no one would question it."

"An hour?" She laughed. "Someone's confident."

"Someone," he said, removing the woolly cap from her head and dropping it to the ground. "Has been thinking about this since we started the walk." His hand stroked her side, feeling the curve of her hips.

"Only since then?" She pushed his jacket off his shoulders and watched him toss it onto a fresh pile of hay. "And here I thought I was on your mind this morning." Her cold hands inched underneath his sweater and T-shirt.

He flinched.

"Oops. You'll warm them up."

He explored her eyes, searching, silently knowing her. A heat flooded his body and he lifted her onto his hips.

"This is insane," she whispered, letting her head drop backwards. She slid down, resting her toes on the ground and looking up him. Her hands caressed his chest.

"We're on holiday." His mouth followed her jawline, leaving

a trail of kisses that lingered as her pulse throbbed beneath his lips. "It's an adventure."

"What about the horses?"

"Other end of the stables." Royce's hands moved underneath her sweater. "It's just us." He guided her sweater up and over her head, his fingers traced the bra covering her breasts.

"This is madness."

"We can stop if you're feeling shy."

Her heart pounded against his palm. "No." She kissed him urgently, unzipping his jeans. Her cold fingers found his warm skin.

He groaned, hypersensitive to her touch, and within seconds, his mouth found the swell of her breast, teasing her through the red lace.

"This is...the hell with it." In one seamless motion, she kicked off her trainers, eased her jeans past her hips, and dropped them to the ground.

As the cold air and his lips moved across her body, the tiny hairs on her stomach raised. He savored the taste of her, provoking her appetite—encouraging it to surrender to the pleasure.

Cordelia's hands threaded through his hair, unable to keep them still. She bit her lip, trying to muffle her moans, but when his tongue found the right pressure and rhythm, she gasped. Her sounds drove him. He pursued her sweetness.

When Cordelia came, she released a sharp cry that startled a horse in a distant stall. Her body arched against him and as she trembled through the aftershock. Royce held her, feeling desire course through his body as her breath tingled against his skin.

She seemed lost in the sensation of touch, as her fingers glided and moved around his body—mapping him for her own pleasure. "You won't be needing these right now," releasing his jeans to the ground. Her fingers drifted down and across his taut skin.

A phone ding startled them. "Ignore it," he said.

The heat of Cordelia's breath mingled with his as they kissed, she held him close.

A few seconds passed and Royce's phone rang. The tune echoed in the quiet barn, causing the horses to become restless.

"Someone's anxious," she said.

"I'm sure it's not important."

But less than a minute passed when it rang again. *Not now.* Reluctantly, he fished the phone from his jacket pocket, noticing it was Luke trying to reach him.

"Go ahead," Cordelia said, slipping on her undergarments.

"Yes?" His voice came out rougher than intended, holding his phone against his shoulder while tugging on his jeans.

"Sorry to bother you, Lord Brownell." Luke sounded genuinely apologetic, as if he knew what he was interrupting. "McLeish and I have a question about the setup for Christmas night."

Royce closed his eyes, hyper-aware of Cordelia dressing beside him, of the hay stuck to his knees, of his nakedness. Not to mention, his body longed for satisfaction even as his brain attempted to engage with logistical questions.

"He wondered if you needed him to build a fire pit outside the structure? If you do, he wants to—." Luke said.

"Yes, that works. I trust your judgment." Royce zipped his jeans. *Bloody hell.*

"Right then. We'll get it sorted. Sorry again for interrupting, enjoy your walk." There was something knowing in Luke's voice —an uncomfortable tone that made Royce suspect he understood more than he said.

When he hung up, Cordelia grinned with flushed cheeks

and kiss-swollen lips. It took every ounce of willpower for him not to back her against that stall door again.

"An emergency?" she asked.

"Just estate business." Royce finished dressing and slipped on his trainers.

"I see." She stepped closer, her hands resting on his chest. "I think I owe you." Her lips drifted over his neck.

"I'm not complaining."

"We'll finish what we started later tonight?" Her fingers trailed down his stomach, causing his breath to catch.

"It's a date, Ms. Dyer." He pulled her in for another kiss, a taste of promise and want. He hesitated releasing her from his arms, enjoying the stillness of the barn.

"I guess we should head back before they get curious or worry."

"Probably," he said, adjusting the wild strands of hair that draped onto her cheek.

But neither moved—knowing family interactions would invade their intimate bubble.

As they made their way back to the house, Piper trotted ahead as if she knew to keep their secret.

Royce glanced back at the stable lights that filtered through the trees. *Any moment is the right moment with her.* Anticipation rose for what lay ahead. Mud squished under his feet as they walked hand-in-hand. There was nothing polished or planned about what had happened, just spontaneous abandonment—two people who fit together and soon, under an orchestrated moment, would commit to their future.

Chapter Eleven

6:30 PM

The family study had become one of Cordelia's favorite spots in the house. Smaller and more intimate than the grand entertaining spaces, even smaller than the family den, the study felt like an oasis with its bookshelves that stretched to the ceiling. A crackling fire added to the ambiance as it cast golden light over the brown leather furniture and invited long conversations. Blue and white stockings hung from the stone mantel, an understated reminder that it was the holidays.

Cordelia curled up beside Royce on a leather sofa, warming her hands with a cup of spiced cider. It smelled of cinnamon and nutmeg, a soothing fragrance that blended nicely with his vanilla cologne. *Finally. No more excuses.* Cordelia tucked herself under Royce's arm, feeling the vibration of his laughter against her ribs as Marnie recalled stories from the reindeer farm.

"That child is fearless. I swear I thought that beast was going to faint when she tried to climb it like a horse."

"Where is she now?" Richard said. The lines around his eyes softened when he looked at Marnie.

Sprawled in a club chair with pink fuzzy slippers dangling from her toes she grinned and paused. The last time Cordelia had seen that coy smile was the night Marnie met Darius at their classmate's barbecue party. He happened to be one of the housemates.

"She's in the kitchen with Emma, helping prepare Ada Roses' dinner." Marnie crinkled her nose and lifted an eyebrow at him.

She did not just do that. Cordelia recognized her flirtatious pattern.

Richard sat beside Cassandra on the opposite sofa. He cleared his throat and repositioned himself. His body leaned forward while they engaged in comfortable banter and held each other's attention.

Cordelia elbowed Royce, who didn't appear fazed that their best friends were sending each other signals. She wanted to say '*Look. They're hitting it off,*' but even a whisper would've been in earshot of the pair.

Besides, she wasn't sure how she felt about two of her closest friends becoming bedmates.

"Yes, I'm serious. she told Mrs. MacLeod the scones needed 'more drama,' which I think means more butter and jam. But who knows what goes through the mind of a five-year-old," Marnie's eyes brightened with laughter.

"Sounds like she's following in her mum's shoes," Richard said.

"Or becoming the world's youngest food critic."

Richard burst into laughter, "Right."

Cassandra shifted sideways, "Darling..." She rolled her eyes. "So, Marnie, do you prefer Sydney more than New York? It seems very far from home."

Royce's arm settled around Cordelia, giving her a tug that felt protective and possessive in a loving way. A lingering satisfaction from the stable intimacy mixed with the warmth of friendship. Glowing firelight perfected the moment.

"Both cities are great, for different reasons." Marnie cut her eyes at Cordelia, "But I'm thinking it's time to move from Sydney—look for opportunities elsewhere."

"Will you go back to New York?" Richard asked.

"Actually, I thought I might see what's available here," she winked. "It's time Cordy had some competition again."

Cordelia smiled at Marnie's declaration. "Competition? Who won best rising pastry chef in New York?" She leaned forward across Royce's lap, playfully challenging her. "And one of the top thirty under thirty?"

"Blah-blah-blah...you gotta step up your game." Marnie popped a peppermint candy into her mouth and offered one to Richard, who accepted it.

"Oh, it's on. We'll do a bake-off tomorrow and they'll blind taste." Cordelia glanced at Cassandra, "Care to be a judge?"

"You know I love a good match." She tucked her feet underneath her, sitting up taller and elbowing Richard. "Come on Darling, join the fun."

He chuckled and cleared his throat. "That sounds like a precarious position to be in."

Royce's phone buzzed against the leather sofa. He shifted, pulled it from his pocket, and glanced at the screen. His thumb moved quickly over the keyboard.

"What are you afraid of, Richard?" Cordelia said.

"Having to choose."

Royce's phone buzzed again. Marnie said something—a muffled sound followed by laughter. He typed out a reply, shifting his shoulders away from Cordelia. He tucked his phone under his leg.

"Everything alright?" she whispered.

"What? Yes. Just—." He vaguely gestured. "Nothing urgent." He wrapped his arm around her, brushing his fingers across her arm.

Richard and Cassandra debated over where Marnie should submit her CV, suggesting they knew better than the other. Then, three minutes after the previous text, Royce's phone buzzed. And again, he checked it.

Cordelia frowned. "Who's that?"

"My agent." He didn't meet her eyes. "Questions about my next manuscript." His jaw tightened.

"But it's the holidays."

"If I recall, that never stopped you, Ms. Dyer." With a light tone leaned in to kiss her cheek.

She pulled away, looking him in the eyes. "Because I'm a chef."

Cassandra asked Marnie about Maisie's school situation if they moved to London. She said she hadn't thought that far, and Richard offered to help out. The conversation bounced between the three of them, but Royce remained distracted. His eyes darted around the room, and despite his fingers on her skin, his touch felt distant.

The phone buzzed two more times in less than ten minutes and each time he replied in cryptic messages.

"Who's Sammie?" Cordelia whispered, her tone reserved as a lump stuck in her throat.

He snapped his eyes at her. "What?"

"I saw the name on your phone. Sammie."

"Oh." He coughed. His mind raced for an answer. "It's Donnelly. You know, my agent. It's...what we called him at uni."

"I've never heard you call him that." Cordelia felt a flutter of anxiety in her chest.

"Right—." He stopped, caught Richard's eye, and exhaled.

"Yeah. Well, we were reminiscing the other day and it came up. And I'm sure you've heard me call him Sammie."

"No, I don't think so." She cut her eyes to the side, trying to remember a time she'd heard Royce call his agent Sammie. "But his first name is Donnelly, where did Sammie come from?"

"So, Cordelia, what are going to bake for tomorrow's bake off?" Richard said.

"I don't know." Her eyes remained on Royce.

"Cordelia." His finger tapped against the phone. "Can we not discuss this right now?"

"Is there something to *discuss*?" She lowered her tone.

"I'm handling some things. Trust me. Do I need to explain every message?"

Cassandra and Marnie paused mid-conversation, and then continued, politely pretending not to notice the tension.

Cordelia sat back, creating space between them on the sofa. She kept her voice soft, "I wasn't interrogating you. I was just curious."

"And I answered." His phone buzzed again. He silenced it and shoved it between sofa cushions.

Cordelia sipped her cider. The warm drink had lost it comfort—tasting like a thick cold syrup.

Richard broke the silence by suggesting he and Marnie check out some of the books on walls, while Cassandra found her fingernails more entertaining than talking.

Who the hell is Sammie? The question burned in Cordelia's mind. A university nickname made sense—they did seem to like random ones. But the frequency of texts, the secrecy, and his defensiveness felt off. *Whatever. I trust him...although odd.* A yawn pressed its way out, releasing a wave of exhaustion.

Royce reached over and pulled her close. "Tired?" His voice had softened into a genuine warmth.

"A little." Cordelia felt overtaken by fatigue. The day had

been packed with activities, and coming up with nausea excuses had drained her. Her body craved sleep.

"You look like you haven't slept in days." Marnie chimed in from the bookshelves behind the sofa.

"That's nice to know." Cordelia said as another yawn threatened. She stifled it, pressing her lips together.

"I'm just saying..."

"Got it." She curled up alongside Royce.

Royce adjusted, giving her an opportunity to rest her head on his shoulder. "Do you want me to bring you some dinner up to our room?"

"This isn't a hotel with room service. No, I'm okay, I'm just tired."

"It's no trouble. Mrs. Smyth can bring us a tray."

"Oh my god, no. I'm not going to make her haul a tray upstairs." She tilted her head back, "I think the walk earlier, tired me out."

He smirked and kissed her forehead. The sofa cushion vibrated as his phone buzzed again.

"Let me guess, it's Sammie."

Royce silenced it.

"You can check it. I'm not going to bite your head off."

"I know." He flipped the phone upside down. "Sammie can wait." He strained to look at Richard, "When you talk with Sammie, can you let him know I'll get back with him?" His voice hesitated over the words.

"Yeah, sure, mate." Richard winked.

Sammie. If it's Donnelly, then why does Royce appear so uncomfortable? A list of ideas ran through her mind: a missed publishing deadline, slow book sales, dropped by his publisher.

"Cordelia, you and Marnie should collaborate on a cookbook—British desserts with an Australian twist. What do you think?"

"Yeah, sure." She rested her head against Royce's shoulder, half-listening as her mind circled back over the list of secrets. Their days of evasive responses had passed. It wasn't them anymore, and yet secrecy stared her in the face. *What was he hiding?* Her thoughts spiraled, causing her chest to tighten. Tears moistened her eyes.

This is irrational. It's not us. A twinge of guilt flickered over her own secret. *I'm overreacting. Damn hormones.* Her eyelids became heavy as she listened to his heartbeat—solid, comforting, loving.

Royce's fingers pressed against her sweater, tracing patterns on her shoulder. The warmth of his breath breezed past her hair.

His phone remained silent and she felt herself settling into the cocoon created by friends, the crackling fire, and knowing she was safe in his love.

Chapter Twelve

7:15 PM

Burning wood popped in the hearth, casting shadows across the book-lined walls of the study. Garlands of pine draped the mantel, releasing their fragrant scent as the fire's heat warmed the room.

The weight of Cordelia's head rested against Royce's chest, her breath stretched long as she slept, a soothing sound of ease. The laughter had settled into whispers between Marnie and Richard, who sat on the floor near the fireplace, sipping the last of their ciders. Her pink fuzzy slippers stuck out from beneath her—oddly oversized like elephant's feet. Richard picked at the fur but his eyes lingered on her mouth. *Interesting.* Everytime she laughed, he mirrored her smile.

His best friend had always been private with his feelings. Even at university, Richard preferred to keep his feelings closed off, but Royce recognized the signs. He was falling—and quickly. His body leaned towards Marnie whenever she spoke. He sought out her companionship, listening when she laughed. Despite Richard's warmheart outlook on life, he kept his emotions well-hidden. But she drew them out.

"Royce, how long has Luke worked here?" Cassandra stretched out across the opposite sofa, smoothing the edges of her sweater. "He seems quite dependable."

"Luke?" Royce kept his voice soft, hoping he wouldn't wake her.

"Gameskeeper, Luke?"

"Right, him."

"The tall, dark haired, broad shoulders—."

"Really? Is that how you describe him?"

"The dashingly handsome Scottish guy?" Richard added.

"Alright, yes. Him." She rolled onto her side, facing Royce, "I'm only saying, he seems very professional."

Royce grinned and murmured. "Is that what we're calling it?"

Cassandra blushed. "Yes, he seems very professional... educated."

"If you're interested, then why don't you ask him yourself?" Marnie said.

"Darling, unlike you Americans, I'm not assertive."

Royce and Richard simultaneously said, "Yes, you are."

"Only with you guys—."

Royce's mobile vibrated, causing Cordelia to stir. He silenced it and slid it across the sofa cushion.

"Speaking of assertive. Someone's desperate, Royce." Cassandra glanced down at him. "Haven't angered someone have you?"

"No." His sharp tone caused a pause of silence.

"Well," Richard said. "Marnie, it sounds as if you're prepared to move to London." "No more warm beaches and sun everyday."

"I like a challenge." Marnie grinned. "And Cordelia can't dominate without a bit of competition."

" I don't dominate," Cordelia mumbled, peeking an eye open.

"You have two bestselling cookbooks and a third on the way. You're practically a household name here. That's close to dominating."

"That's Bastien, not me." She sat up, fluffed her hair, and gulped the last of her cider. "Ugh, cold. He's the household name."

Marnie waved this away. "Don't be modest. You're brilliant and you know it."

Royce contemplated checking his mobile, but Cordelia watched him—her head titled sideways with one brow lifted. She waited, ready to verbally pounce. "Enjoy your nap, darling?"

"I guess I did." She rubbed her face, attempting to remove the makeup smears from under her eyes. "I'll be right back." Her kiss landed on the side of his mouth, just before dashing out of the room.

The smell of roast chicken and potatoes drifted in when she opened the door, triggering a conversation between the other three about hungry appetites and food cravings.

Royce scanned through the text messages, frantic to reply before Cordelia returned. Sammie—the nickname he and Marcus had given to Mr. McLeish when they were boys. Royce only called him McLeish in formal situations or when other staff might overhear. The latest messages dealt with lighting layouts and generator placement. *I thought we'd discussed all of this.* He typed out a quick response, "Generator, backside. Lights, you make the call. Will discuss later." He flipped his mobile upside down on the sofa.

"You're very obvious." Cassandra sat up, sitting on the edge of the sofa. "I thought you were better at secrets."

"Why don't you just tell her who it is?" Richard said.

"Who is it?" Cassandra said.

"No one." He looked toward the door.

"Sammie is no one?" Marnie tucked her hair behind her ears and straightened her shoulders. "Now you've got my curiosity up."

"Just tell them. If you don't they're not going to stop and before you know it, you'll have three women on your back or worse, angry at you." Richard had a way with words—convincing others with his predictions.

Royce looked back at the door again, "It's Mr. McLeish... Sammie is McLeish."

"That's it? Your mysterious messenger is your grounds-man?" Cassandra threw her hands in the air and flopped back.

"Wait, something doesn't add up. Sammie's that sweet old man that works in the yard?" Marnie tucked her knees into her chest.

"Yes." Royce crossed his leg over the other and interlaced his fingers.

"He's planning a surprise and he didn't want anyone to know yet." Richard stood, stretching his back and offering to help Marnie off the floor.

Royce felt the weight of it all—elaborating, evading, and each day he seemed to add another layer of secrecy. All for a proposal that was supposed to be romantic and uncomplicated.

"But you knew," Cassandra said.

"Right, but—."

Royce cut Richard off, nervous about telling Cassandra and Marnie more than necessary. "It's a surprise for the family and Sam...Mr. McLeish is assisting." Royce lowered his voice, glancing at the door. "We all know Cordelia is persistent when it comes to surprises, like a sleuth, so I need it kept quiet. For now."

He'd hoped they would end prying, but both women quizzed, forcing he and Richard to fabricate a lie about a horse-drawn sleigh ride and a Christmas eve bonfire with toasted mallows. *Great, more to arrange.* He informed McLeish.

"Alright, I promise not to say anything to our *little snoop.* Although, I still don't..." Cassandra trailed off as the metal door handle turned. "And you said he knows land management..." She mouthed 'Luke'.

"Yes, medieval land management." Royce glanced at Cordelia as she joined him on the sofa. "He studied wildlife biology in Edinburgh."

"Fascinating," Cassandra said dryly.

"Who are you talking about?" Cordelia asked, tucking her legs underneath herself.

"Luke." Royce's mobile buzzed. "Excuse me for one second." He squeezed Cordelia's hand, feeling the grease of fresh lotion. *Two more days. Then it'll all make sense.* He paced in front of the smoldering fire, waiting for McLeish to answer his call. "Yes, Mr. McLeish, what can I do for you?"

The group sat silent, listening in to his call.

"Wonder what that's about?" Cordelia said, glancing at the ticking mantel clock. "No wonder I'm so hungry, it's almost eight."

Everyone agreed, mumbling about the savory smells drifting in from the kitchen. The aroma of fresh bread seemed to be the one that excited them the most.

"Right...no, I'll meet you in a few. Give me five minutes?" He gripped the mantel, rapping his fingers as he listened and grinned at Cordelia. "Okay, right. Yes." Royce hung up, wildly gesturing that Mr. McLeish needed someone to sign off on some...some invoices. *And I don't want Pop disturbed. So, I'll* go." He walked to the door, meeting eyes with Richard, Marnie, and Cassandra. "I won't be long." He blew Cordelia a kiss. "I promise. See you at dinner."

He clicked the door behind himself and leaned against it. *Sorry, Sammie.* Royce massaged his temples. "A sleigh ride and toasted mallows? What was I thinking?" On paper his plan looked simple with only a few components—a starry night dome, champagne, and the ring. Somehow, it continued to grow into bon fires and perpetual lies.

7:50 PM

Royce and Mr. McLeish rushed out of the bootroom and cut across a field towards the loch. Their torch lights lit the path in front, creating a whitish glow. "What do you mean 'larger?'" Royce said as they reached the patch of forest where the dome structure stood. "How much larger?"

"I guess, three times the size of your dimensions."

"Does it fit the space?" Feeling the chill against his neck, Royce zipped his coat higher. His breath fogged in front of him.

"We did a wee bit of clearing to make it work, but it's in there," Mr. McLeish said, pointing his torch to the left. "This way."

Positioned between two tall pine trees, the dome filled the clearing, leaving little room for a generator. Two-thirds of the walls were opaque, rather than the full transparent dome he'd ordered.

"That's significantly larger," Royce said.

"Aye, you said you wanted 3.6 meters but this one's 6."

Royce shined his torch onto the dome, examining its position in relation to the far path. "Can we shift it slightly, so the door is closer to that trail and faces the loch?"

"I can try, but at one-hundred-seventy kilos, I'll need the lads down here helping me."

"And they can't deliver a smaller one tomorrow?" Royce walked slowly around the dome, realizing the proportions could comfortably host a dinner party, diminishing the intimate ambiance he'd envisioned for the proposal.

"The delivery lads apologized." Mr. McLeish's accent thickened as he delivered the news. "They have your proper size, but it's back in Glasgow and isn't available until Boxing Day...if ya pay the rush fee."

"Are they joking?" Tension settled between his shoulder blades. "I need this ready for Christmas Day night." Royce circled the dome, envisioning a larger, more romantic setup. "We'll scale up. I'll give Mrs. Smyth some ideas for the inside." He walked to the front of the dome. "Why don't we string white Christmas lights over here, and run them from that path to the door. And we can forgo the firepit."

"Yes, Sir." Mr. McLeish shined his torch toward the backside, "Do you mind if I put the generator here?"

"Wherever you need it." Royce stepped inside, examining the expansive space.

Mr. McLeish joined him. "I had a thought, we have lots of plants in the conservatory. I could bring some down and we could fill the space with ferns and boxwoods."

"That's perfect...let's turn it into a garden." Royce said, enjoying the flood of ideas. "And string lights around the topiaries. But I don't want it to look like Kew Gardens. It needs to be integrated with the furniture...she'll prefer a natural setting. As long as it's romantic."

Mr. McLeish nodded, writing a few notes on the palm of his hand. The black markings appeared illegible.

"We need some furniture in here too." He pointed off to the side, "Speak with Mr. Smyth and find a side table for here, something larger than what we'd originally planned. We'll use that for the charcuterie and champagne."

Royce circled the inside of the structure, reimagining everything. He'd have Mrs. Smyth lay several overlapping Persian rugs on the floor. "Also, check with Mrs. Smyth about blankets and pillows. I want them here, with a mixture of wool and fur, with pillows stacked three to four deep." The ideas flowed. "I'll text Mrs. Smyth a list, and she can print a copy for you. I need to get back to the house before she suspects anything."

"Right. We'll handle it, sir." They shook hands. "Don't worry. Ms. Dyer will be surprised."

"Thank you, Mr. McLeish." He turned to leave, paused, and wrung his gloved hands together. "One more thing. I need a bonfire set up on the terrace. Tonight, if possible."

Mr. McLeish's eyebrows rose. "Tonight, sir?"

"If possible. I know it's a huge request," he glanced at his watch, "but I sort of mentioned to our friends that we'd be having one."

"Sort of mentioned, did you?" There was amusement in Mr. McLeish's voice.

"More like fabricated under pressure."

Mr. McLeish burst into laughter.

"They were curious to know who kept messaging, and it's the first thing that came to mind." Royce managed a self-deprecating smile.

"My boy, you never were any good at telling lies."

"I'm terrible at it. But it's been that kind of week." Royce scanned the dome and lights. "So, can we make that bonfire happen?"

"Aye." Mr. McLeish chuckled, "I'll get Luke and Mr. Smyth to help me. We'll have something arranged within the hour."

"You're a lifesaver. Truly." Royce patted his arm, "I owe you after all of this."

"An invitation to your wedding would be nice."

"Of course. You're like family to us." He rechecked his watch. "Gotta go, thanks for everything." Royce hurried up the trail that led to the house. The wind coming off the loch howled, sending bitter cold air nipping at his neck. It seemed everything about their relationship continued to hold surprises—some exciting, like meeting on a random street in Paris, and some that challenged their feelings. But he'd learned to find beauty in the unplanned moments.

8:20 PM

The kitchen provided warm relief from the cold night air. The lingering scents of roast chicken, homemade bread, and fruit pie gave an inviting fragrance. Mrs. McLeod stood at the worktable, briskly wiping down the butcher block counter.

"Mrs. McLeod," Royce leaned against the doorframe and off his moist boots. "Is everyone still in the dining room?" He aligned them beside another pair of muddy shoes in the boot room.

"Aye." She cut her eyes at him. "Your food will be cold by now."

"I'm aware, but I had urgent business." Hot water from the side sink washed over his hands, "I wondered, do you happen to have any mallows that we could have for tonight's bonfire?"

She paused mid-wipe. "Mallows?"

"Yes, for tonight's bonfire on the terrace." He hoped his charming smile would ease the last minute request.

"No one told you were having a bonfire tonight." She dropped her cloth onto the counter. "Or that you'd be needing mallows."

"I realize it's last minute—."

"Last minute would be this afternoon, sir. This is hardly a moment's notice." Her eyes twinkled, adding a bit of humor to her aged eyes as she walked into the pantry. Mrs. MacLeod emerged with a bag, "All I have are these wee ones. I'd planned to use them for tomorrow night's hot cocoa bar." The bag squished as she set it onto the wood counter.

Royce stared at the bag, "Those are...tiny."

"Aye, they are." She patted the bag.

He inspected the bag, "Take what I can get, right?"

"It's what I have available on the night just before Christmas Eve when someone decides they need mallows immediately."

"Alright, yes, well..." Royce tossed the bag gently into the air, caught it, and handed it to Mrs. MacLeod. "We'll make them work, thank you."

"I guess you'd like them prepared for your bonfire?"

"That would be fantastic, thank you." He gave her a kiss on the cheek.

"I'll settle up with you later." She chuckled. "Now go and eat your cold dinner."

Royce returned to the boot room, slipped on his house shoes, and headed for the dining room.

Chapter Thirteen

8:30 PM

The formal dining room glimmered from two crystal chandeliers that cast prismatic patterns across the long mahogony table. Its reddish-brown tone complimented a floral-wallpapered wall. Garlands of pine and holly draped the over-sized mantel and sideboard, where flickering candles cast shadows onto antique portraits. Silver serving pieces caught the light, and the scents of roasted hen and rosemary hung heavy in the air, mixing with the freshness of evergreen.

Classical Christmas music played softly in the background, piped in through small speakers that hung in each corner.

Cordelia shifted in her chair, trying to find a position where the waistband of her jeans didn't dig into her belly. *Why didn't I change before dinner?* Each day, the bloating intensified. Sitting at a formal dining table, in a hardback chair that provided no support felt like a torture device. She tugged at her waistband, catching the attention of the Countess.

"Everything alright, dear?" she asked.

Suddenly the empty chair between them, the one that

should be occupied by Royce, exposed Cordelia's belly to attention. She pressed her back against the seat and sucked her stomach. "Yes, of course."

"I'm afraid this furniture wasn't designed for comfort...or tight fitted clothes." She smiled and winked.

What is she implying? Cordelia took a sip of water, catching Marnie's gaze. "I guess that's why they wore so many skirts." She attempted to laugh but it sounded more like a gurgle, causing everyone to look her direction.

"Yes, well, can you imagine how binding it would've been?"

Marnie darted her eyes between the empty chair and Cordelia.

She shrugged. *Tomorrow I'm wearing those sweater leggings all day. I don't care how hot I get in them.* Cordelia ate the last two spoonfuls of the winter thyme-squash soup, a creamy compliment to the herb chicken. Despite the bloating her stomach craved more.

"I'm surprised Royce isn't back from meeting with Mr. McLeish," she said, glancing at the Earl. "He said he had to sign some invoices." Her voice raised, almost asking a question and fishing for more information.

The Earl and Countess exchanged looks. Quick and almost imperceptible.

"Oh, well." The Earl aligned the spoons sitting beside his plate, "I believe he also needed to help with the horses."

"The horses?" Cordelia frowned.

"Right," Marcus said. "One of them...looked unwell. Royce's favorite, so he said he'd check on it while out."

"But we were..." Her words faded into a mumble. "But I thought you knew more about horses than Royce? You're the one that rides them daily."

Marcus opened his mouth and closed it. He had a fleeting plea across his brow as he looked from the Countess to Richard.

"Royce knows more about horses than he lets on," Richard said. "He hasn't told you?"

"I've never seen him overly attentive to them." Cordelia said. She knew one of the older horses meant a lot to him, but earlier in the barn he seemed oblivious to their presence.

"Yes. And me and Richard were busy researching." Marcus nodded. "It had to do with the horse's health."

Cassandra set her soup spoon down and raised an eyebrow. "The two of you...Richard researched horse medical advice?"

Richard sliced off a bite of chicken and popped it in his mouth. "Mmhmm." He nodded, but maintained eye contact with Marcus.

"We did. Mr. McLeish suggested a technique his...grandfather used. You apply a herb paste on and wrap them in blankets." Marcus said.

"And you and Richard did the research instead of Royce?" Emma wiped soup from Ada Rose's cheeks as the little girl banged her spoon on the highchair tray.

"Yes." Marcus clanked his fork against the plate. "We researched while Royce signed—."

"We know, invoices." Cassandra leaned back in her seat. "Richard, tell us what you discovered."

They're terrible liars. Cordelia unbuttoned her jeans and pulled her sweater on top. *My god, relief.*

The Countess tapped her fingernail against her wine glass. "Yes, well, I'm sure Royce will join us as soon as he can. Richard, please help yourself to more chicken." She stretched to look down the table, "Maisie, did you enjoy your dinner."

"Yes." She said, using the back of her hand to wipe her mouth.

"Yes, thank you," Marnie whispered to her.

Maisie immediately copied her mother, giving the Countess a wide smile—framed in a chocolate milk mustache.

The dining room door opened and Royce appeared. His house shoes created friction across the rug. "Sorry I'm late." His rosey cheeks and breathless voice suggested he'd hurried in from outside.

He kissed Cordelia on the cheek, causing a chill from his cold nose to run down her spine.

"Mr. McLeish needed longer." He settled into his chair, unfolding the napkin perfectly in half and placing it in his lap.

"I heard. Including the horses."

"Right. The mare..." Royce kept his eyes on his empty plate. "The bay mare is unwell."

"We don't have a bay mare." Marcus murmured into his soup spoon.

"Sorry, obviously. I meant the chestnut mare. The bay mare is at Hayton, not here." He adjusted a fork that had become unaligned with the rest of his silverware. "Yes, the chestnut mare is here."

Cordelia watched his tell-tale signs—a faint rise in his voice's pitch, eye contact avoidance, and the tug of his left earlobe. *What are you up to Royce Brownell?* But whatever his secret was, she trusted he'd confess later that night in the privacy of their room. "Is the chestnut mare feeling better now?"

"Much better. Yes. The vet's medicine worked wonders."

Richard cleared his throat. "Medicine? Didn't you see the text I sent about the herb paste?"

Ada Rose squealed, fighting having her face and hands cleaned by Emma.

"Ah, right. I did, but the vet had already arrived."

"That's some fast medicine."

Royce buttered a dinner roll, "It is."

Mrs. Smyth entered from the kitchen and began clearing

bowls and plates. "Lord Brownell, would you like for me to prepare you a plate?"

"No, I'll do it, thank you." After taking a bite of bread Royce fixed himself a plate of food, skipping the soup.

I'm burning these jeans tomorrow. Cordelia fluffed her sweater, feeling the heat from the chandeliers.

"This looks wonderful, Mrs. Smyth," the Countess said warmly. "Please give our compliments to your husband."

"Mister Lord Earl," Maisie said, sitting tall and leaning over the table, "does Santa visit you here?"

The Earl's expression softened. "Of course he does. Santa is remarkably good at finding us wherever we are at Christmas."

"Even in Scotland?" Her accent spun the words with an Australian flair.

"Especially in Scotland. This is practically his neighborhood."

Maisie's eyes widened. "It is? Are we near the North Pole?"

"Oh yes. That's why we have reindeer farms." He shifted to the edge of his seat. "Did you have fun today visiting Santa's reindeer?"

"Yes!" Maisie bounced in her chair, beaming with enthusiasm. "But, if he knows we're here, then which chimney will he come down? That one?" She pointed toward the formal living room where the fireplace was large enough for Cordelia to stand in.

"He prefers it, probably because it's much easier to get packages down it. Especially for good little girls and boys."

Royce sliced a bite of chicken, "And we always hang our stockings there, so Santa doesn't have to search for them."

"Did you bring a stocking, Maisie?" The Countess smiled, resting her fingertips on the edge of the table.

"Mummy, did you bring our stockings?" Maisie asked.

"No, baby, I forgot. But I bet they have one we can borrow."
Marnie fiddled with Maisie's cocoa-colored curls.

"Well, of course we have extra stockings. How about, if
tomorrow morning you and I go into the attic so you can pick
your favorite one?" The Countess looked from Maisie to
Marnie.

"Mummy, can I?"

"For sure." Marnie whispered in Maisie's ear, "What do you
say?"

"Thank you, I would like that." Maisie grinned, scruching
her shoulders up to her ears. "Santa will be so excited."

Everyone burst into laughter, causing Ada Rose to startle
awake. Her little cheeks turned red and her lip quivered. She
scanned all the faces watching her as if she searched for something. As soon as she saw Emma, tears rolled down her cheeks.

Emma stood and lifted Ada Rose from her high chair. "I
think someone needs to go to bed."

"I'll come with you," Marcus offered, pushing back his
chair.

"No, stay. Finish your wine." Emma kissed him on the
cheek. "I'll be back shortly." She carried Ada Rose over to the
Earl and Countess. "Say goodnight to Poppy and Nan." Ada
Rose buried her face in Emma's shoulder. "Well, nevermind."

"It's fine, darling. Goodnight, Ada," the Countess said,
patting her leg.

The Earl partially stood and kissed Ada Rose on the top of
her head, "Sleep well."

Emma left with Ada Rose dozing off against her shoulder.

The dining room fell into a soft, quiet moment as everyone
finished off their dessert—everyone except Royce who swiped
his dinner roll across remnants of chicken juice and mashed
potatoes. Mrs. Smyth removed his plate and served dessert, a

warm apple pie. The steam rose, releasing an aroma of cinnamon and nutmeg. The warm smell enticed everyone to indulge, despite the complaints of being stuffed.

A sadness lodged in Cordelia's chest. She watched the Earl, someone who prided himself on formalities and legacy, display a gentle kindness with Maisie. He revealed his playful nature with her, and laughed in a special way—one reserved for children.

Cordelia longed to hug her father, to introduce him to Royce. *He would've loved being a grandfather.* She blinked as tears stung her eyes. *God, more emotions. I can't be like this for seven more months...I'll drive myself insane.* Yet, beneath the hormones was real grief for the happy events her father would never see in her life: the child she carried, a someday-wedding, her cookbooks. All the in-between moments he'd miss.

In the shadows of her mind, her mother lurked. *Gillian.* The complete opposite of her father. The opposite of the Countess. And definitely the opposite of Cordelia's growing maternal feelings. The lodged pain in her chest swelled. She focused on the pie, flaking the crust into tiny pieces.

"Don't you like it?" Royce murmured.

"Oh, yeah...sorry, I was thinking about something."

"Are you okay?"

"Yeah, yeah. I'm fine. Just thinking about stuff."

"Stuff?"

"Work. My dad. Stuff."

Royce brushed his hand down her arm, squeezing her fingers. "Tell me tonight?"

"Yeah, sure." Cordelia smiled but her heart lingered on her father as two emotions tugged at her heart. One for him and one for Royce. Grief vs joy. Letting go vs new beginnings. And the bloating made everything more stiffling—except Royce's touch.

Conversation flowed around the table as Marnie shared a funny story about Maisie's 'very stern' art teacher. Which somehow reminded Cassandra about an artist in the village she wanted to visit before leaving. And to no surprise, the Earl knew exactly the one, giving her pointers on how to negotiate rates with him.

"I think your button is undone." Royce pointed at Cordelia's jeans.

"Oh, right." Cordelia adjusted her sweater, covering the exposed zipper. "I think all this delicious food is catching up with me."

Royce chuckled, "Then how about a morning run?"

"I should, as long as it's not too early. And I'm not too tired."

"I've never known you to turn down a morning jog. What've you done with Cordelia?"

"Ah, wouldn't you like to know?" She and Royce held a gaze —a quiet reminder of hours before in the stable. His hand rested on her thigh. In her peripheral vision she caught the Earl watching them. His smile was thoughtful and affectionate as if he wanted to say something but withheld the words.

Everyone finished their dessert and Mrs. Smyth cleared all the dishes from the table, while the Countess suggested tea and coffee in the formal living room.

"Maybe if we sing carols it'll get Santa to arrive early," the Earl whispered to Maisie.

Royce cleared his throat, glancing at his mother. "Actually, I have a better idea. Why don't we all grab our coats and meet on the terrace."

The Countess looked surprised. "It's rather cold this evening. And dark."

"I know, which makes it perfect, because..." Royce grinned, giving extra attention to Maisie who eagerly waited to hear his news, "I've arranged a bonfire, with toasted mallows."

"Mallows. What's mallows?" Maisie emphasized each syllable of the word, scrunching her nose tight.

"A bonfire?" The Earl raised his eyebrows. "When did you arrange this?"

"Tonight. When I was with Mr. McLeish."

"When you were signing invoices or looking after the horse?" Marcus chuckled.

Royce shifted in his seat and glared at his brother, "Does it matter? We're having a bonfire."

Cassandra stood, dropping her napkin into the chair. "Well, I'm not missing an authentic Scottish bonfire. Even if it's as cold as the North Pole." As she headed for the door she stopped and whispered to Cordelia, "I wonder if Luke will join us."

"I'd bet money that he will be," Cordelia said.

As everyone shifted away from the table they thanked the Countess and Mrs. Smyth for a lovely dinner. Marnie instructed Maisie on which scarf and gloves to bring down from their bedroom, while Richard hovered around Marnie, waiting for her cue. The two had become obviously interested in each other, even though they attempted to hide their casual glances and physical touches.

"Surprise." Royce's breath tickled Cordelia's ear.

"So, this was your secret? All those texts were about this?"

"What else would it be about?"

The room had emptied, other than Mrs. Smyth coming in and out to remove dishes.

"I don't know. But I'm glad you're a bad liar." Cordelia stood and fastened her jeans, glancing at each doorway.

"You had no idea what I was putting together."

"Not the details, but I knew all that texting in the study was something." She patted his chest, "Babe, you don't even text me that much. So, I know you're not going to do it with *Sammie*."

Royce pulled her close, "You know me too well. Means I'll have to do better next time."

"Better? What happened to no secrets?"

"Ah, but there's a difference between surprises and secrets."

So true. Her jeans pressed against her belly and when they turned for the door, she unbuttoned them, hiding it beneath her sweater.

Chapter Fourteen

9:15 PM

Royce opened the terrace door, revealing a blazing bonfire within a stone foundation. Flames leapt and crackled off the standing circle of logs, creating ghostly patterns on the foggy night sky. The strung patio lights danced on the wind like playful fairies. And the cold air whistled through nearby trees, shaking the glistening baubles.

Luke tended the fire, while Mr. Smyth arranged a holiday themed table with mallows and traditional Scottish cookies. In less than an hour they'd transformed the terrace into a wintery magical scene.

"Well done," Richard murmured beside Royce as they stepped onto the terrace. "You actually pulled it off."

"You mean they pulled it off." Royce adjusted his leather gloves. "I don't know how, but they did it."

"Wow, it's beautiful." Cordelia stood in front of Royce and tucked her scarf under her chin. "This was all your idea?"

"Of course." He wrapped his arms around her waist. "You're surprised?"

"A little. I mean, it's a good surprise...but very impractical of you." She giggled and warmed her gloved hands by the fire. "I love it."

Richard leaned closer and whispered, "the webs we weave..." He snickered.

Royce elbowed him and watched as the group spread out around the fire, drawn to the its warmth.

Maisie broke free from Marnie's hand and ran toward the flames with five-year-old enthusiasm.

"Careful." Marnie snapped, catching up with her. "We don't touch hot things, remember?"

"I know, Mummy. But look how big it is." Maisie's milky skin glowed from the soft orange light. "It's like a dragon." She roared and stomped, giving her interpretation of a fierce beast.

"Well, thanks to Luke, it will remain a very controlled dragon," the Earl said, peeking over at Maisie and smiling. "But it might toast us some delicious mallows if we're careful around it."

"Yes!" Maisie gave him a firm nod.

Luke's attention drifted to Cassandra who stood back, watching the flames jump around, sending sparks onto the stone.

"Darling, you outdid yourself. I'm impressed."

Royce and Luke both replied 'Thanks' causing Cassandra to shift her stance and give each an awkward smile.

"What's with the tiny mallows?" Marcus held one up, pretending to pierce it with a steel stick.

Leave it to Marcus to notice first. Royce explained that there had been a miscommunication in size, and it was too late to send anyone to the market. Richard's laughter echoed across the terrace.

"Then we shall roast the wee ones," Marcus impersonated Mrs. MacLeod, elevating his voice until it cracked. "Help yourselves, laddies." He held up the bowl so everyone could grab a handful.

Maisie was the first to reach in, "The baby dragons will love these."

"Wait, Maisie. Let me help you with that." Marnie grabbed the stick out of her hand, "How does five sound for a start?"

"No. It has to be six." Maisie handed her a mallow. "Here Mummy, it has to be six."

"Why six?" Richard asked, threading a long row mallows.

"Because, that's how old I'll be on my birthday."

Cordelia's laugh vibrated against Royce's chest as she leaned back on him, slowly rocking side-to-side. "But tell them, when's your birthday?"

"January. The eleventh," Maisie held up two fingers. "Like this."

Richard mimicked to her delight. A glance between him and Marnie held more than a simple look. Royce had never seen his friend so anamored with someone before, especially someone with a child.

"Alright, I have twenty on mine. Who thinks they can beat me?" Marcus boasted.

"Sweetie, it's not a competition." Emma quickly threaded mallows onto her stick. "Twenty-one, twenty-two..." She giggled and continued shoving more on.

"Come dear, let's see how this works." The Countess tugged the Earl closer to the table, handing him a stick.

"We need to make sure they won't fall into the fire. Or should I say, the dragon." The Earl centered his stick on each mallow before pushing it through. He counted thirty, and according to Maisie, become the mini-mallow champion.

The group gathered around the bonfire and ceremoniously inserted their sticks into the flames, playing a guessing game of who's would fall into the flames and who's would char first.

"No, no, no." The top section slid down Cassandra's stick. She tried to catch it, burnt her palm, and watched the ooze fall into the fire. "Da...darn."

Luke immediately attended to her, wiping the sticky mess from her hand and cheek.

"I told you something's going on there. That's more than just flirting," Cordelia whispered. She retrieved her crusty mallows from the flames and carefully touched them, "Perfectly golden." She slid a few off, dropped them in her mouth, and licked the warm sugar from her lips.

"But are they the tastiest?" Royce inspected his, picking at the charred ones.

"Why wouldn't they be?"

"I would argue that mine have more flavor." The smoky taste settled on the back of his throat.

"So you're the marshmallow expert?" Cordelia snuck a bite and scrunched her nose, "Why do you like it burnt?"

"It's fantastic."

She shook her head, "This is—."

Maisie squealed, "Mine fell off. Mummy." Her shoulders and head slumped, staring at her empty stick.

Richard quickly responded, helping Marnie console her. "It's alright, we can get more. Besides, you said you wanted to feed the dragon." Marnie's hand brushed his shoulder, and he gave her a sideways grin. "Here, you take mine and have your mum help you near the fire."

I hope you know what you're doing, mate. Royce caught Cordelia watching their interaction. "Everything alright?" He whispered close to her ear, smelling the faint scent of cedar on her neck—a subtle reminder of their night after the masquerade ball.

She mumbled, her expression darkening into a frown. "Sorry, whatever they're doing, isn't my business. But I don't

110

like it."

Royce chuckled and wrapped his arms around her waist. "Forget about them. This is about us."

"I agree." She kissed him and her mouth tasted sweet, with sugar bits on the edge of her lips, waiting to be savored.

"Marcus! Honey, you nearly set me on fire." Emma's voice broke the momentary silence.

"Sorry, love. I was trying to blow my flaming mallow out." He extinguished the last small flicker with his fingers. "I didn't mean to spray you with sparks. Are you okay?"

Emma inspected her clothes, noticing a small black spot on her coat. She sighed and took a step away from him. "This is why I don't let you cook. You're dangerous in the kitchen."

"That's why I have you." Marcus said, placing his hand on her lower back. "And look, it's perfectly charred."

"Darling, that's not charred, that's carbonized." Emma laughed and pulled a bite of warm mallow off her stick.

"Do you realize, there's a proper technique to this?" The Earl positioned his stick at a ninety degree angle to the flames. "You want to rotate it, but slowly, and maintain consistent distance from the fire, watching how the flames shift."

"Yes, darling." Royce's mother affectionately rested her hand on his arm. "But are you aware, your stick is bent."

"Bent? It's perfectly straight." He examined it, ignoring the crescent shape.

"I'm afraid your method is flawed. That is bent."

He held the stick higher, letting the fire glow create a shadow and prove his mother was correct. "It's defective. Well, now I need to start over." He scraped the mallows onto his finger and tasted them, "Not bad." There was a humor, a playful modesty in the way he nibbled at the cooled mallows. A youthfulness resided behind formality.

Royce's chest tightened in admiration. *He's the best. Rigid, but the best.*

"Here." Luke handed Cassandra a napkin.

"Brilliant, thank you." Cassandra wiped her face, smearing sticky white mallow across her cheek. "It's in my hair."

Luke laughed, "Here let me help you." He wet his fingers from a nearby bucket of water, and ran them through her hair. "Is this your first time?"

"Me? Oh, no. I love outdoor activities like this—getting into nature, cooking over fire, camping. All this stuff." Her hand rested on his, and neither moved.

Royce caught Richard's eye, indicating he should look at Cassandra.

"Thank you." Cassandra's face flushed, yet she stood more than six feet from the fire.

"My pleasure." Luke towered over her, his body inches from hers.

Richard looked back at Royce and rolled his eyes.

"You two are behaving like children," Cordelia said, pressing her back into Royce's chest. "Let her have fun."

The Earl cleared his throat. "I believe bonfires call for singing. Shall we start with something festive?" He hummed the opening notes of "We Wish You a Merry Christmas," and then broke into song, encouraging everyone to join in.

Voices mingled with varying degrees of musical ability, including Maisie who sang the loudest with complete enthusiasm. She even found words to interject when she didn't know the song. And Marcus and Emma balanced out the off slightly key singers with a natural harmony. At one point, Richard raised his voice, displaying his deep baritone voice that made Marnie smile.

This is what I'd hoped for. What I'd imagined. He watched the softness on Cordelia's face—the way she radiated a beauty and joy. The fire's shadows danced across her smile, and she looked back at him. Her gaze revealed a deep longing. *It's all for you, my love.* What began as chaotic ruse had been exactly what was needed, a prelude to their future.

"Thank you," she mouthed.

Their voices trailed off and his mother cleared her throat. Her voice rose softly and grew louder as she sang "I'll Be Home for Christmas". She always sang soprano, but the crisp air seemed to lift her voice higher. It traveled on the wind and seemed to reverberate around them.

The fire crackled and sent sparks upward. Everyone listened, their gazes lost in the flames. As friends and in some ways, sisters, Cordelia and Marnie gravitated to one another, hugging against the backdrop of Scottish fog. She'd been in London for two years, alone in some ways—missing her father, estranged from her mother, distant from her brother. But she'd made a home with him, and soon, his family would be hers. Yet, there was Marnie, a friend who flew across the world to be with Cordelia.

This is us.

The fog grew thicker and wrapped around the terrace like a blanket as his mother finished her song in soft applause.

"Beautiful, darling." His father slid his hand around his mother's waist and pulled her into his chest. He held her with a rarely seen warmth—a glimmer of intimacy that made Royce wonder if he should look away.

Cordelia rejoined Royce and curled her body up to his. Her knitted hat smelled of wood smoke. She pulled a bit of mallow from her stick and smeared it across his lips, laughing as he nibbled the remnants from her finger. In the background, Emma laughed, teasing Marcus about his second round of mallows. And Maisie debated with the Earl over Scottish shortbread versus Australian, insisting there was a flavor difference.

"Years from now, decades even, this'll be us." His breath bounced off Cordelia's ear.

"Will it? Awful sure of yourself, Lord Brownell."

"Yes, I am."

His parents, married for over thirty years, still found ways to make each other laugh. Their relationship seemed to expand rather than diminish over time. It appeared rich in love and respect. *Marcus and Emma are navigating parenthood and still devoted to each other.*

He'd have that with Cordelia—one day, but first he needed to finalize his proposal speech. "One day, Ms. Dyer, one day."

She buried her face into his chest, tucking her hands beneath his coat. "I don't need anymore than this, right now. I love you."

Emma's phone buzzed and she checked the notification. "Ada's waking up," she showed Marcus the baby monitor app.

"You know she does that sometimes. Just let her fall back asleep."

"I know, but—" She watched the screen as Ada Rose shifted in her crib, making sounds.

"I'll go check on her," Cordelia said, turning in Royce's arms. "I'm exhausted anyway, and I desperately need to get out of these jeans."

Royce smiled, remembering she'd complained about the waistband at dinner. "Okay, I'll be up shortly. I need to speak with Luke about upcoming plans."

She kissed him, leaving a warm mallow taste on his mouth. "Ooh, you're cold. Don't freeze out here."

"I won't."

He watched her say goodnight to everyone and then disappear as the fog formed a curtain as she entered the house.

Royce and Luke met beside the fire, as he situated the logs with large tongs. "Thank you for everything."

Luke grinned. "Sure. Just doing my job, but I appreciate the hospitality."

From across the terrace, Cassandra eyed them, partially engrossed in conversation with Emma. The bonfire crackled and popped against the iron poker, startling everyone who stood near it.

"Well, I think if Cassandra has any say in the matter, you'll be joining us for Christmas dinner."

There was an uncomfortable sound in his laughter, but the way his hands sheepishly tucked into his jacket pockets, followed by a stream of fumbled words communicated he wanted nothing more than to spend more time with her. Royce patted him on the shoulder, said good night, and joined his parents at the table, where his Pop snacked on shortbread cookies.

Chapter Fifteen

9:45 PM

The bedroom reserved for Ada Rose was a haven of pastel yellow and plush fabrics. An antique bed was draped with a woolen duvet and unfurled cashmere throw blankets. Across from the bed was Ada Rose's crib. She stood with outstretched arms and a tear running down one cheek.

"Oh, sweetheart," Cordelia murmured, lifting her out. "What's wrong?" As she picked her up, she noticed their shadows moved across the cream wallpaper, designed as a forest with foxes, deer, and an owl.

Ada Rose buried her face against Cordelia's shoulder and hiccupped. Her soft skin smelled of lavender lotion and that elusive sweetness that was distinct to babies. She breathed it in. *I can't believe...me, a mom.* For a moment, she stood and moved side-to-side, holding her close. She hummed a nursery song her mother would sing when she was little. *At least I got something useful from her.*

A few minutes later, they settled into a padded rocking chair near a window where the open drapes allowed faint light to filter into the room. A handknit throw blanket had been tossed across the chair arm, providing warmth to Cordelia's socked feet. She cradled Ada Rose against her chest and rocked. A soothing motion for both of them.

"There we go," she soothed and rubbed circles on Ada Rose's back. "No more hiccups, no more tears."

As Ada Rose's breathing evened out, her little body relaxed and her hand affectionately patted Cordelia's collarbone.

She felt a mellowing effect from the rocking, combined with a hush in the room. The only sound came from a machine clipped to the crib that played a soft rain pattern.

"I have a secret," Cordelia whispered, her voice barely audible, "Not even your Uncle Royce knows yet."

Ada Rose widened her dark cocoa eyes as if she understood. She focused on Cordelia's face, her gaze exactly like Marcus when he concentrated.

"In about eight months, you're going to have a cousin," Cordelia continued, her free hand brushed across the little girl's cheek. "I'm pregnant." The word felt strange and magical as she spoke it—a surreal feeling that bubbled in her stomach. Holding Ada Rose brought the future into reality.

"To be honest, I'm nervous." She slowed the rocker's pace. "I hope I'm good at it, like your mummy." She watched as Ada Rose's eyes fought to stay open. "I really want to be the kind of mother who shows up for everything important. And makes her child feel safe and loved." Her voice caught in her throat and she felt a surge of tension. "What if I can't be..."

Ada Rose's hand tugged at Cordelia's sweater, and her eyelashes fluttered as she gazed up.

"I didn't have a good example growing up. I only had my dad, he was the best. But I didn't even have a grandmother nearby. So I might need your help."

She cooed and babbled.

"I promise, your cousin will always feel loved. But your

Uncle Royce can't know until Christmas, so you have to help me keep the secret." Cordelia whispered, her hand settled on her belly. "And it'll have you as a friend. Who could ask for more?"

Ada Rose's eyes drooped and her body grew heavier. Her fingers that had gripped Cordelia's sweater relaxed, resting on her chest.

Cordelia continued, knowing the little girl had drifted far from their conversation. "Do you want to know how I'm going to tell your Uncle Royce?" She brushed her hand across her feathery hair. "I have a gift for him—something that tells him he's a dad, that marks the date. I want to wait until Christmas night, by the fire, when he's not suspecting anymore gifts."

"You're going to be a beautiful mother." The Countess stood in the doorway with her hands clasped together and smiling.

How long has she been listening? Shit. Cordelia's heart pounded.

"I didn't mean to startle you," the Countess said, softly walking into the room and cracking the door behind her. "I thought I'd check on you two before I went to bed."

Cordelia's mind raced, replaying everything she'd reveal.

The Countess clicked off the baby monitor that was attached to the crib, causing the camera's green light to fade. "Now we can speak freely."

"About?" Cordelia continued to rock Ada Rose, even though she'd fallen asleep.

"What's troubling you." She sat on the edge of the window seat. Soft light from a lamp fell on her face, highlighting the strands of silver in her hair. The lines around her eyes lifted, matching the warmth of her smile. "About your secret."

"I'm not sure I know what you mean. Countess, I'm not wor—."

"How far along are you?" There was a nurturing, anticipatory tone to her voice.

Do I deny it? She swallowed hard and stood, placing Ada Rose in the crib. The little girl stretched and relaxed underneath the pink blanket. "Nine weeks." Cordelia smoothed the creases out of the blanket, avoiding eye contact with the Countess. Her admission stirred relief and fear—a ball of emotions ready to unravel. "Almost ten." She looked at the Countess, resisting the smile that pushed its way onto her face.

The Countess gestured, "I knew it. That's wonderful news, my dear."

"Really? You're excited?"

"Of course." Her open arms embraced Cordelia. "You have no idea how happy I am."

"But you can't tell anyone." Panic thumped at her chest. "Please, don't. I haven't even told Royce yet."

"He doesn't know?"

"No. I'm planning to tell him on Christmas Day. It's a surprise."

"Don't worry, I won't say a word." The Countess squeezed Cordelia's shoulders, her grip gentle yet enthusiastic. "Of course it's your news to share. Are you sure he doesn't suspect?"

"I don't think so. I've tried hiding my symptoms. And he seems to believe me."

"Well, men are pretty naive on these things." Holding Cordelia's arm, the Countess guided them back to their seats. "But I knew you had to be...it was the only thing that made sense."

"How? Emma doesn't know, does she?"

"Possibly, but she maintains discretion, more than you realize. She kept her sister's marriage to a footballer from her parents."

"Really?"

"Calle asked her not to tell them, even after they'd read about it in the press. Emma can be a 'vault' as Marcus says."

"I knew she was trustworthy, but that's another level." Her cheeks flushed, feeling the room's air warm as if someone had lit a fire.

The Countess giggled, "One of Emma's hidden talents."

Cordelia fidgeted with her sweater, relaxing as her fingers rubbed across the soft fibers. "I'll remember that." She pulled her sweater further down, hiding her unbuttoned jeans.

"How are you physically handling things?"

Cordelia laughed, causing Ada Rose to stir. "Where to begin...daily nausea, exhaustion, and I never know what smell is going to trigger one of the others." She shifted in her seat, easing the pressure on her stomach. "One day the cedar trees make me sleepy, but the smell of coffee makes me ill. Then, today, it flips. So, that's exhausting on its own."

"That's how I felt with Royce. For three months I played a roulette game with my senses, which drove me insane. I even made Thomas question my sanity on more than one occasion." She had a far away gaze, "The best things rarely happen according to our plans, but that's what makes them extra special."

"This definitely wasn't planned. We've talked about children in the future, like several years from now. After my career was more established."

"Your goals won't change, maybe adjust, but they don't have to change. Look at Marnie."

"I don't know. I watched her career move slower than mine, because she had to sacrifice to be a mom."

"Have you asked her if she sees it as sacrifice?"

"No. She's amazing. I don't know how she's managed to become an executive pastry chef and be a mom."

"It's built in. You'll do the same thing, if that's what you decide to do." The Countess held Cordelia's hand, "You're going to be a wonderful mother. I've watched you with Ada Rose and Maisie. You're patient, kind, and calm. Those qualities matter."

"Thank you. That means a lot." She felt her eyes moisten. "I think I'm just worried about how everything will change besides my career—my relationship with Royce, my body, my identity..."

"You're very self aware, aren't you?"

"To a fault."

They laughed, letting the silence linger between them for a moment.

"Everything will shift, but you won't lose yourself, Cordelia. You'll expand." She tilted her head, letting the light illuminate her eyes. "You'll find more room for love than you ever imagined. And Royce will be there to support you." She walked over and tucked the blanket around Ada Rose's feet. "He's ready for this. Don't doubt his commitment."

The words settled and swelled in Cordelia's chest. "Thank you," she whispered. A sense of ease washed over her. Maintaining the secret, along with the heightened exhaustion and moodiness, had been a greater load on her body than she'd realized.

"Any time, my dear. You and Emma are daughters to me. I'm always here for you." She turned her attention to Ada Rose, whose cheek rested in the Countess' palm. "Sleep well, sweetheart," blowing her a kiss. With one tap, she turned the monitor on and the green light came back to life. "Goodnight, Cordelia."

"Goodnight." Cordelia sat alone for a long moment, listening to Ada Rose's breathing. It had a soothing rhythm that blended with the rain sound, giving her a glimpse into the future. In less than a year, they'd have a decorated nursery with a baby that trusted them to keep it safe.

Her breasts throbbed. *First I have to get through this.* She adjusted them in her bra, seeking relief from the swelling discomfort. Her stomach pooched, pushing sweater and jeans slightly forward. She'd always prided herself on a lean core, but this was outside of her control. *Time to get comfortable.*

Cordelia took one last look at Ada Rose, "Sweet dreams, Ada, sweet dreams."

Chapter Sixteen

10:45 PM

Amber light from the bathroom spilled across the carpet and merged with the glow of dying embers, casting shadows at the foot of the bed. There was a crispness in the air, softened by the heavy drapes pulled across the windows.

Cordelia blew out a cinnamon candle on the mantel, watching the smoke curl and rise. Her red flannel pajamas covered in tiny reindeer drooped onto her bare feet, their softness a comfort to her bloated belly.

"I knew we should've added more wood to the fire." Her feet left prints in the blue wool carpet as she scurried back to bed.

"Are you that cold?" Royce fluffed his pillows and crawled into bed.

"I don't know, you tell me." She buried her feet under the covers and slid them against his leg.

"Bloody hell, you're ice." He jumped. "Why don't you put some socks on."

"Then I'll get hot." Her feet continued to seek warmth from his body. "You're a better option."

"I'm not going to win this, am I?"

"Nope."

Royce wrapped himself around her, moving his fingers in steady strokes, slowing to a tranquil circular pattern.

"Do you ever think about the future?" Cordelia grounded herself in his heartbeat.

"In what context do you mean?"

"Us. Our future?"

"All the time." His voice rumbled and vibrated throughout his chest—strong and certain.

"What about children?" She cringed when her voice elevated with a tentative pitch. "I know we've discussed it before, but do you...have you thought about it lately?"

"Yes. It's hard not to when Ada Rose is around."

"I know, she's adorable." Cordelia interlaced their fingers. "Do you worry about how it'll change your routine or work schedule?"

"No, I can't say I have. Are you worried about it?"

"Sometimes..." Her mind resisted formulating words into coherent sentences. How could she explain without revealing the truth? She sought a response that satisfied without disclosing their future. "It's, uhmm, it's a big decision, you know?" Her fingers walked up and down his arm.

"True. But look at Marcus and Emma, look at Marnie. They've made adjustments and their careers are okay." He rolled on top of her. "Ms. Dyer, are you worried about losing your career because we decide to have children?"

"No. Yes." She felt her body sink into the mattress as she succumbed to the truth. "Maybe. It's just a big decision. When-ever it happens. I was only curious. I was curious about what you were thinking. If you even thought about it."

"All the time, but there's no rush or pressure. Do you think I'm pressuring you?"

"No, no. Not at all. With the holidays and the two little girls around, I started trying to imagine myself as a mother." A twinge of guilt sat in her stomach. *Just dig that hole deeper, girl.*

"Cordelia, when you're ready we'll make adjustments."

"I know, I'm overthinking it. I don't need to stress about our careers." The Countess' words echoed in her mind, *'He's ready for this.'* She wrapped her legs around his, "Royce, I hope you know, I want a family with you. In the future."

"Me too." His mouth hovered above hers. His hands glided down her side, "Babe..."

"Yes?"

"Do you know how sexy you are in these pajamas?"

Even in the darkness, Royce's smile warmed her heart. "Really? In these?"

"Definitely. Who wouldn't be turned on by flannel with nursery animals?"

"They're reindeer, thank you." She flopped her legs to the bed. "Comfy Christmas pjs. And you think they're sexy?"

"You could wear cling film and be sexy."

"You mean, basically naked."

"Exactly." His lips brushed across her neck. "But I think you'll be the hottest mum to ever wear Christmas pjs."

She playfully pushed him off and pressed her cold feet into his leg, "How's this for sexy?" Internally her mind panicked, wondering if he'd figured out her surprise. *Dammit, you better not know. Not yet.* She wedged a foot between his bare calves.

He jumped. "I tell you you're beautiful and all you can think about is turnin me into an ice cube." Royce grabbed a throw blanket and spread it across the duvet. "Come here, darling. Let's freeze together."

Cordelia nested against his chest, seeking warm spots on the sheet. Her feet rested beside his, and she listened to how his breathing flowed in tandem with his heartbeat. It was steady, calm, reassuring. She closed her eyes, feeling exhaustion spread throughout her body. Their lives stood at a crossroads—a new journey was beginning for them and he had no idea, not yet anyway. She smirked, thinking about his 'hottest mum' comment. *Guess that means I already am.*

Royce's fingers brushed through her hair. "Still awake?"

"A bit."

"Now let me ask you a question." His hand traced the lines of her waist and hips, but there was reservation in his voice. "Were you one of those little girls that dreamed about their wedding?" He hesitated on the last word.

Cordelia lifted her head, trying to see his face and understand his intentions. "That's a random question. What are you asking?"

"Nothing. No reason. I overheard Cassandra and Emma talking earlier and I wondered if American women daydreamed about their wedding." Royce adjusted his pillow, causing Cordelia's head to bob against his chest. A silence lingered as he repositioned. Outside, wind rushed past the window, breathy, like an old man pursing his lips to whistle.

After adjusting her hair, she said, "Babe, American women invented the idea of daydreaming about over-the-top, big weddings. We stockpile magazines over it." She chuckled. "And yes, I admit, I did it. But it doesn't mean I obsess over it now. That was back then...when I was twelve or thirteen."

"And?"

"You want to know what I imagined?"

"Sure." His hand slipped under the covers and pulled her thigh on top of his. "Let's compare yours to Cassandra's."

"My god, you must be really bored or wide-awake to want to hear this." She scooted up and rested her head on his pillow.

"Call it curiosity."

"Okay." The memory felt like someone else's fantasy—a

little girl's dream that no longer fit the woman she'd become. She exhaled, releasing the embarrassment. "I always thought I'd get married on a cliff overlooking the ocean. Somewhere dramatic, with waves crashing and the wind blowing through my hair. But somehow the floral crown stayed put," she smirked and waited to hear his response. "And my dad would give me away to a very handsome guy." She giggled emphasizing her words and remembering the fragrance model cutout. "Who had tanned skin. Very modelesque and rugged—an athlete meets eco-farmer."

"That's very specific."

"Oh wait, it gets better. I wanted a sunny yellow mermaid dress."

"Yellow?" His voice wavered between shocked and amused. He laughed, causing his chest to shake beneath her head.

"Hey, don't judge. Back then I thought yellow was sophisticated for a wedding dress, not plain old white." She rested her hand on his, feeling the tiny hairs on his skin. "But my groom would wear a white suit—a Miami Vice type suit."

Royce burst into laughter. "Are you joking?"

"No, I'm serious. I used to watch the show with my dad and I thought any guy who could pull off a white suit with a tan, he was my kind of man."

His laughter increased and he tried to speak. Incoherent.

"Well, you asked." She poked him in the stomach, "Do you want to hear the rest?"

"Yes, yes. But if you tell me there were zoo animals, I can't promise I'll be quiet."

Cordelia rested her hand over his mouth. "No, there weren't zoo animals. There was a pink wedding cake with rose icing and real flowers waterfalling down the side." She removed her hand when he laughed.

"Waterfalling?" His warm breath landed on her cheek as he kissed her. "Darling, you're very creative."

"Draped. And thank you."

Royce slid his hand up and down her thigh. "How long did this fantasy last?"

"A year, maybe two. I'd get together with my friends and fill notebooks with pictures from magazines."

"Please tell me your ideals have changed?" He cleared his scratchy voice, letting a few hopeful chuckles linger.

"God, no. I literally woke up one day, dumped them in the garbage, and decided marriage was an inconvenience."

"Really? An inconvenience?" His hand tensed on top of her leg and his finger rapidly tapped.

"Royce, relax. That was then. This is now." Her hand trailed down his chest and past his stomach. "You're my future." She yawned. "So, how does my fantasy compare to Cassandra's?"

He sighed, "Yours is more...girlish. Adorable, but girlish."

Her hand explored his body, causing his breath to catch. "People change."

His hand cupped her face and he leaned in for a kiss. He moaned.

Cordelia turned her face away as a yawn overtook her, interrupting the moment. Hoping to conceal her exhaustion, she kissed him—soft and unhurried. A fireplace log crackled, releasing a gentle hiss that almost mirrored Royce's sounds as her hand glided over his skin.

"I love you, Royce." She fought another yawn that dragged out her sentence. *Stay awake*. He pulled her closer and she felt as if they were suspended in a timeless bubble.

"Tired?" His warm fingers slid beneath her pj bottoms, causing her skin to flutter.

"A little."

He froze. "Would you prefer to go to sleep?"

"Maybe...not yet." Cordelia slid under the covers, letting out a sighed yawn.

"Babe." Royce lifted the covers. "We can do this another time, when you're awake."

"No, I'm fine."

"Fine. Cordelia, that's less than ideal." He slid under the covers. "Let's go to sleep."

She nodded, lifting her heavy eyelids. *I blew that one...no pun intended.* Cordelia agreed and they emerged from under the duvet, resting on their pillows. She felt him pull the covers around them, as disappoint and guilt skipped in her thoughts.

"Sleep well," he murmured against her forehead. There was a sigh behind the tenderness.

Exhaustion had won and she didn't have the energy to protest, to insist they finish what they started. Unfulfilled desire hovered over them. "I'm sorry. This isn't like me."

"I know. There's always tomorrow." He shifted, resting his palm over her stomach—unaware of the life that breathed in synch with him.

Cordelia held her breath and cracked an eye open. *Can you sense it?* She listened to his breathing and let her awareness drift from the lingering cinnamon aroma, to the irony of their conversation. *Good night, my loves.*

December 24th

The Scottish Highlands

Chapter Seventeen

9:30 AM

Royce jogged along the estate's eastern trail, his trainers crunching against the frost-hardened earth. With each breath, he felt the crisp air hit his lungs and morph into a fog that warmed his cheeks. The sun had crested the mountains, sending shafts of light through the fragrant pine trees that lined the path.

He'd wrestled nervous energy in his sleep and woke before Cordelia. He needed to see the dome. He needed to step outside the house's walls and rehearse his speech. He had one opportunity to propose, and he needed to express his feelings. *Tomorrow.* He glanced at his watch. *Thirty-two hours, give or take.* His pulse quickened and his feet moved faster.

The trail curved and wound through the trees. To the left, it meandered towards the hills. To the right, it veered towards a clearing where the dome stood near the loch. He'd mapped the route a dozen times. He knew exactly how long it would take from the house to the dome. *We'll come in from the far path. I'll take us—.*

Voices carried and approached. The sound of their feet

reverberated through the trees. Royce stopped and looked around.

Dammit.

Marcus and Emma appeared. Dressed in running gear, their faces flushed as they jogged in tandem.

She sees me. Shit. Royce stopped and angled his body toward the trees, hoping Emma wouldn't spot the dome. "Morning." His heart raced. "Didn't expect to see anyone else out here."

"Since when do you start doing morning runs?" Short of breath, Marcus rested his hands on his hips while Emma paced in circles.

"Felt like a change." Royce glanced over his shoulder and cut his eyes at Marcus. "How are the horses?"

"Beautiful." Emma said, catching her breath. "Didn't plan on being gone that long." A strand of hay stuck to her cap.

Marcus removed it and dusted his hands. "We stopped by the stables after our loop around the loch. That gray Highland pony seems ready for Hayton. Think Pop will bring her down?"

"Probably." Royce watched Emma widen her circles, stepping into a stream of light as it shot through the trees near the dome. "Is Ada Rose with Mum? I'm sure you need to get back."

Marcus' eyes widened, "Right. Yes, we should. Darling, don't you agree?"

"Yes, in a minute." She picked at a bush with winter berries. "Mrs. McLeod said if we pick them, she'll teach us how to make Christmas wreaths." Emma began collecting them in her pockets. "Won't that be fun?"

"Maybe later." Marcus attempted to guide her up the trail, wrapping his arm around her waist. "Didn't you say she was going to make handprints in dough this morning?"

"Do you mean the flour casting with Ada Rose and Maisie?"

"That's the one." Marcus held her hips, letting the sunlight fall across her back. "Besides, I'm famished and would like to warm up."

"I'm sure you don't want to miss that experience with Ada Rose." Royce helped Marcus guide Emma a few steps forward. "I'll grab some berries on my return."

"In a minute." She managed to rotate free from their grips and scurry to the bush. "Besides, she's not doing their prints until after lunch." Emma froze. Her eyes locked ahead.

Bloody hell, she sees it.

The sunlight shifted and hit the dome, creating a brilliant reflection. She stretched and squinted. "Marcus, Royce, what's that?" She stepped into the bush, leaning toward the light.

"What?" Royce said, knowing exactly what she was pointing at without turning around.

"It's the loch darling."

"No, what I'm pointing at is not reflective water." Emma gestured firmly. "Do you see that structure? Over there?" She stood on her toes. "Is it…"

"Oh, you mean the white building?" Marcus' voice sounded dismissive as he gestured boldly. "That's just an estate thing…a maintenance dome. Royce would know."

"Right. It's a maintenance dome." Royce tried stepping in front of her. "Why don't we all head back up to the house?"

"Maintenance structure." Emma studied their faces, placing her hands on her hips. "A transparent geodesic dome, for maintenance?"

"Yes." Royce gently guided her closer to Marcus.. It's for the winter equipment. Luke suggested it's more eco-friendly."

"And sustainable. Less energy." Marcus said, wrapping his arm around her shoulders.

"Nice try." She slipped out of his arm and walked toward a path opening that lead to the clearing. "That looks exactly like those igloos at the Coppa Club in London."

I'm screwed. Royce turned to walk away, but paused. "No you're mistaken, the ones at Coppa are glass. This is utilitarian."

"Emma," Marcus hugged her from behind. "I love your curiosity, but it's only equipment. Why don't we forget about it."

She ducked under his arm and jogged toward the clearing. "You two are terrible liars. Horrible." She giggled, waving goodbye as she turned onto the side trail.

"Shit." Marcus said.

"Damn, she's fast." Royce said.

"Don't let her little legs fool you."

By the time they caught up with her, she'd circled the structure and peered inside.

"See," she breathed, pressing her face close to the side, examining every detail. "I knew you two were wrong. What is this place?" She looked back at Marcus, "And be honest, darling. Or else..."

"We told you, it's for equipment." He brushed the hair off his forehead.

"And miscellaneous—."

"With throw pillows and blankets?" She spun around, examining the clearing. "And fairy lights? What the bloody hell are you two hiding. Marcus."

Inside, the dome looked exactly the way Royce had imagine. "She'll love it," he murmured.

Marcus sighed. "I tried," he said patting Royce on the back. "Emma, my love, my very intelligent wife...maybe we should let it be."

"Why won't one of you just tell me what's going on? Who put this here, and why?" Her eyes brightened with excitement, and she adjusted her cap. "It's far too trendy for your father. Too cold for your mum. And darling," she wrapped her arms

138

around Marcus' waist, "you're amazing, but this isn't your style. It's too romantic."

"I never knew I was married to a detective." Macus said.

Royce walked around the dome, avoiding eye contact with Emma. The cold seeped through his gloves.

"So, if it wasn't you three, then that leaves Royce."

"Darling, let it be."

"Royce, what are you up to?" Her gaze met his through the transparent section of the dome.

"Nothing," he snapped. "At the moment."

"You know, it's very romantic. Like a sexy harem's tent. Good job, whatever you're up to."

"A harem's tent? Are you suggesting it's tacky?" Royce tapped his fingers against his hip. *Maybe it's good to get her opinion.*

"Not at all. It's romantic."

Will she--." He scanned the thick pile of wool blankets spread across a rug, creating a plush bed with burgundy and gold pillows.

"Yes, she will." Emma bobbed on her toes and smiled. "She'll love it. I know I would." There was a playful look between she and Marcus, a wistful glance. She brushed stable dust from her leg. "Women love surprises."

Marcus kissed the top of her head. "This is why I can't ever surprise you, you're too smart."

"I know." Emma rocked on her heels. "Alright, why the secrecy, Royce?" A cloud of fog hung in front of her face.

Royce strolled around the dome, letting the silence linger. *I could tell her it's for Christmas. Or tell her the truth.* A bird chirped and the sun reflected off the dome, warming the air hitting his cheeks.

"She's not going to give up." Marcus chuckled. "Trust me. You know she's an unstoppable force."

"Clearly." Royce invited them inside. "But what I'm about to share has to stay between us. Mum and Pop know, but that's it. Understood."

"I get it." Her voice squealed, making eager sounds as she fluffed the pillows. "So tell me. I swear I'm a vault."

Royce stretched toward the ceiling. "I'm proposing to Cordelia." His heart skipped and excitement swelled in his chest. "Tomorrow night. I'm proposing tomorrow night."

The words echoed. A bird chirped. The wind pushed against the dome.

Emma's face widened, and her eyes filled with tears as her hand covered her mouth. "Oh, Royce. This is...this is incredible. She'll say yes. For sure, I know she'll say yes." Her arms flung around his neck. "You know she'll say yes. I'm so happy for you."

"Thank you. But you promised not to say anything."

"I won't. I swear."

"And you can't cry when you see her." Marcus said, hugging Emma from behind.

A tear spilled down her cheek. "I'm just happy. This is one of the most romantic things I've ever seen. It's beautiful, and the setting is incredible. She's going to lose it." She laughed through her tears and pulled her phone out. "I need to—."

"No!" Royce and Marcus said, loud enough to silence the chirping bird.

"I'm just telling my sister."

"Emma, that's the point. You can't tell anyone. If Cordelia finds out, then it's ruined." Royce pleaded with her to keep it quiet one more day. *The one time she's not a vault.* He reminded her that her sister and Cassandra are friends. "She's terrible with secrets."

"Okay. I promise. But Cassandra will know tomorrow night, right?"

"Yes. Possibly." Royce gestured for them to step outside. The warmth of their breaths began to fog the transparent wall. "I should head back before Cordelia comes looking for me."

"Us too." Marcus checked his watch. "I'm sure mum will wonder what's taking so long."

"True." Emma hugged Royce again. "I can't believe you met her in Paris." She hugged Marcus. "Why couldn't we have a love story like that?"

"What are talking about? We have a fantastic story. We have the Olympics." Marcus said.

She flopped her forehead into his chest. "See you at the house, Royce."

They strolled up the trail, heading back to the main path that lead directly to the house. He listened to them banter about Marcus' proposal at his flat in the city. Their voices grew faint until he heard Emma laugh and squeal. Through the trees, Royce saw Emma on Marcus' back, clinging to his shoulders. *Another success.*

Alone. The sun warmed his face. Natural elegance surrounded him. Something special. Something just for them.

I 0:00 AM
Cordelia reclined on the library sofa with a mystery novel stretched across her stomach. The room reminded her of her father's home office, providing a momentary escape and relief from breakfast odors. She watched the flames dance in the fireplace. They crackled, giving off a smoky pine scent that ironically had become the one constant for soothing her nausea.

The lamp beside the sofa flickered. *Lady Margaret?* As she

shifted, the book slid onto the floor. Cordelia dusted it off and inspected it, hoping she hadn't damaged the vintage book.

"There you are." Marnie clicked the door shut behind herself. "I've been looking everywhere for you."

Cordelia sat up, placed the book on the coffee table, and adjusted her oversized crewneck sweater. The color matched the cool grey morning clouds. A cozy fit for her stretch leggings and wool socks. "Hey, did you guys get breakfast?"

"We did. Maisie insists on eating two scones every morning now." Marnie plopped onto the sofa beside Cordelia. "I told her we're not making this a habit when school starts back. Too much sugar for her little brain."

"Says the pastry chef mom." Cordelia stretched her legs out, crossing them into Marnie's lap. "So, tell me, what's up with you and Richard?"

"Wow, you really don't pull punches these days." Marnie propped her slippered feet onto the coffee table.

"What? I'm curious." Her feet poked at Marnie's leg. "Spill."

"There's nothing to tell. He's nice to hang out with, and he keeps Maisie entertained."

"He's easy on the eyes too. Admit it."

"I never said he wasn't." Marnie swayed her legs side-to-side, causing Cordelia to sway.

"Oh my god, you're rebounding."

"No I'm not. Plus, you're the one who said he's *easy on the eyes*."

"I only said what you were thinking." The motion aggrevated the nausea. "Please stop, that's making me sick."

"This?" Marnie swayed her legs wide and fast. "This is making you sick?"

"Yes." Cordelia tucked her legs close. "I can't handle motion these days." She rubbed her belly, bargaining with her body to keep the one cup of coffee down.

Marnie's arched eyebrows flattened. "Are you sick?"

"No, just sensitive to motion." She remembered when Marnie was pregnant with Maisie—unphased with an iron stomach. Cordelia envied her, wishing she could still eat and jog without any reaction. "Hey, how was the walk with Richard? Did you guys make it to the loch?"

"Freezing. We turned back right before hitting the forest. Oh, we saw Royce with Marcus and Emma, but they were back in the trees talking."

"Yeah, he said he was going for a run." She fanned her sweater. "Tell me the truth, are you hooking up with Richard?"

"No." Her voice squeeked.

"Do you plan to?"

"I don't know." Marnie's milky complexion turned pinkish. "You're not going to let up, are you?"

Cordelia shrugged. "What about Gavin?"

Marnie examined her French polished nails and frowned. "My skin feels like sandpaper. Do you have any lotion in that magical bag of yours?" She reached for Cordelia's tote bag on a nearby footstool.

The test. Shit. Cordelia had placed the positive pregnancy test inside a velvet jewelry pouch, and carried it for two months without anyone find it. She leaned for the bag. "No, I don't. It's upstairs."

"Come on," Marnie laughed and stretched for it. "You keep everything in there—bandaids, mints, chocolate, and lotion."

"Marnie, I said no." Cordelia lunged for it just as Marnie grasped the handle. Without thinking she yanked at it.

"What the hell, Cordy?" Marnie snapped. "It's only lotion."

"I know...I said I don't have any." Her voice softened as she rummaged through her bag. "I have a lot of stuff in here."

"Since when do you care what I see?" Her eyebrows arched. "We've literally been open books—."

"Things change."

Their eyes locked. Cordelia swallowed, trying to maintain a stoic expression. Marnie's eyes squinted. She grabbed the bag and twisted away, laughing as if it were an amusing game.

"What are you hiding?" She teased, running over by the fireplace.

Cordelia chased after her and they dodged around the wing-back chair situated near a window. "Marnie, stop."

"Is it, love letters? Or photos?" Her hand dug inside the bag. "Do you have a toy in here?"

"It's nothing like that." Cordelia scooted around the chair. "There's nothing in there, no toys or lotion...now give me the damn bag." She jumped for it and grabbed one of the handles.

They wrestled and bounced against the chair. Marnie screamed and laughed. Despite her panic, Cordelia found herself giggling at the situation. It felt childish—a release of anxiety.

"You're being ridiculous." Cordelia sighed, giving the handle a tug.

"You're being suspicious." She tugged back. "Which makes me curious."

"It's my personal stuff."

"We don't do personal secrets, remember."

"Marnie, I swear to God—." Cordelia lunged, wrapping her arm around the bag. Contents spilled onto the floor, including thread from a sewing kit, lip balm, and the velvet pouch. It landed and bounced. The soft thud echoed into a deafening silence.

"What's that?"

Both scrambled for the test that had partially slid out of the pouch.

"Nothing." Cordelia grabbed it and shoved it into her tote, along with her wallet that had landed in the chair.

"That's not nothing."

Voices drifted in from the hallway.

"Cordelia?" Marnie emphasized every syllable in her name.

Rubbing her stomach she returned to the sofa. "Don't worry about it."

"You're pregnant." Excitement bloomed. She flopped beside Cordelia. "Oh. My. God. You're freakin' pregnant." Her hug became an explosion of joy.

Cordelia fought a smile, but she couldn't contain it. "Shhh. No one knows."

"Royce?"

"No. The Countess figured out, but she's not going to say anything, and you can't either."

"How far along are you?" She danced in her seat.

Cordelia looked toward the door, waiting for the voices to disappear. She whispered, "Eight or nine weeks."

"And you haven't told him?"

"I'm waiting until tomorrow—for Christmas. So, when I say you can't let on, I mean, you can't *let on*."

"Fine. I'll keep a lid on it. " Marnie patted Cordelia's belly. "Honey, this is so exciting. Are you happy?"

"Yes. I..." She repositioned, resting her feet on the coffee table. "I'm worried about how it'll change things. I mean, I we both have careers that are pretty intense right now, but this, this changes everything." Her fingers rubbed the glass necklace. "Our relationship will change, my job will have to slow down, and I'll be a mom."

"Yeah, so? That's a good thing, right?"

"Of course. But who am I without work? You know how hard I've worked for my position."

Marnie slung her arm around Cordelia's shoulder. "None of

that will change. I might not be at the top of the food chain like you, but I've done pretty good as a single mom. Plus, you have Royce."

"You've done better than just good." Cordelia exhaled, releasing the tension in her shoulders. "I honestly have no idea how to be a super mom like you."

"It's called multi-tasking and focus, which if I remember was what put you at the top of our class." She rested her head against Cordelia's. "Seriously, it's not as hard as you think. And knowing you, you'll probably do world book tours and culinary shows with that baby strapped to your back."

Cordelia chuckled, "I wouldn't go that far."

"Really? We're talking about you, Cordelia Dyer, the one who has achieved every goal on her list. Do you still have that checklist? I bet it's framed somewhere."

"It's in a box." She stretched and arched her back. "Promise me you'll move to London and see Darius?"

"Nice change of subject."

They stretched their legs out facing each other and rested against the sofa's roll arms.

"It'd be fun having all of us in the city together."

"Circling back to you, and this little bundle," Marnie made a bullseye motion at Cordelia's stomach. "You'll be incredible. I know you have nothing to worry about. Maisie thinks you're the coolest aunt ever, and she's brilliant."

Cordelia reached into her bag, retrieved the pregnancy test, and showed Marnie. "It's faded, but I wanted him to see it. I started to bring another one with me and pee on it Christmas morning, just so he could see the lines."

Marnie rolled her eyes. "You're such a romantic. Just tell him already."

"I will, tomorrow."

The library door flung open. Cordelia jumped and hid the test under her leg.

"Ladies, we're trying to decide, private dinner at the distillery or crepes and caroling in the village. We're split down the middle —the men prefer whisky, of course, and us women prefer the village. FYI, Luke didn't vote, but he's our driver and guide." Her eyes twinkled as she said his name. "Do you have a preference?"

"Village." Cordelia said.

"Fine, let's make it unanimous," Marnie sang her answer, "the village." She held the last note, exhausting all oxygen from her lungs.

Cassandra nodded and grinned, "Excellent. The men lose." She swept out of the room the same way she entered, letting the handle click behind her.

"Thank you for not saying distillery. If I have to lie one more time, I'll scream." Cordelia checked the time on her watch. "Crap, I've got to get ready." She shoved the test back into her bag.

"For what?"

"Hiking. Aren't you coming?" She stood, stretching her fingertips to the ceiling.

"No. Richard promised to give Maisie an ice skating lesson at the pond."

Cordelia locked her hands onto her hips. "What are you doing?"

"Well, she's been begging to skate since we arrived, and it gives me time to plan my recipe out."

"Plan all you want, I'm winning this bake-off."

Marnie tossed a throw pillow at Cordelia. "Think again, Princess."

She caught it, "That's Queen, thank you." Cordelia fluffed the pillow and placed it back onto the sofa. "Love you."

"Love you too, chicky." Marnie drew an air heart. "And don't worry, your secrets safe...in the vault, not a word until tomorrow night."

"Right. Tomorrow night." Cordelia felt around for the pouch, situating it underneath her wallet. She had twenty-four hours to wait, two allies guarding her secret, and a growing mountain of lies. "It's not going to get here fast enough, but at least, in the meantime, I have the satisfaction of beating you... again." Cordelia scooted for the door, feeling the breeze of a throw pillow on her back.

Chapter Eighteen

2:00 PM

The wind coming off the loch invigorated Royce and nipped at his skin. He adjusted his wool scarf and tucked it inside his coat. Marcus raced up the rocky path, assuring Emma he knew the trail so well he could guide her blindfolded. But it had been at least ten years since they'd walked that trail, and the loch had eroded closer.

"Sorry ladies, the terrain's trickier than we remembered." Royce held Cordelia's hand, guiding her past earth-colored patches of ice. Emma trailed behind, yelling at Marcus to slow down.

Marcus waved her off. "Don't worry, I grew up exploring every inch of this countryside."

"Right, but I didn't. Love—." Emma said.

"Bloody fucking hell." Marcus lifted his foot, examining the deer droppings that dangled from his shoe.

"Oh my God, Marcus." Her laughter echoed across the loch.

The three caught up with him as he scraped his boot against a rock and cursed the deer who left their piles on the trail.

"Anyone want a sip of water while we wait?" Royce leaned against a tree and handed Cordelia and Emma granola bars Mrs. MacLeod had made the day before. "Here, Marcus, I think you'll need these." He passed him a handful of wet naps.

"Thanks." Marcus wiped his hands. "Here."

Royce gestured at him, "You're the one who stepped in it, you're the one to carry it."

"You must be joking. I'm not putting this in my pocket. Where's the trash bag?"

"I couldn't tell you." Royce said, glancing at Cordelia. He attempted to hide his smirk but it forced its way onto his face.

"I see what you're doing. Let me see the pack." Marcus reached for it, but Royce kept it from his grasp. "Very immature."

"What? You're the one who stepped in droppings, not me. Why should I carry your trash?"

"Because it's Christmas, and that's what kind older brothers do." Marcus grabbed for the pack.

Royce stepped behind Emma and Cordelia. "Who said I was kind?"

"Seriously, you guys are behaving like children." Cordelia said.

Emma shifted sideways. "I agree. Marcus don't touch me with that." She spun away from them, almost losing her balance on a tree root. "Royce, give him the trash bag before he flings crap on us."

"Only if he agrees to carry it himself."

"You're so immature." Marcus said, taking a step closer to Royce.

He laughed and pulled a paper shopping bag from the pack. "Would you be any different?"

"Of course." Marcus popped the bag open and dropped the dirty wet naps inside.

"I doubt it." Royce slung the pack onto his back. "I don't want to smell your garbage. You carry it." He laughed and handed Marcus a granola bar.

"You guys are being ridiculous." Cordelia walked away, keeping her eyes focused on the ground. She paused where a downed tree had formed a lakeside bench. "Royce, come look at how beautiful it is."

Royce joined her, followed by Emma and Marcus. He scraped his shoe on another rock, holding the paper bag under his arm. The dark water stretched beneath the winter sun as a few thin patches of ice reflected the light. Snow dusted mountains rose in the distance, giving the air a shimmer of grey.

The wind whistled and Royce listened as it harmonized with their breaths, enhancing the magical feeling. It almost convinced him that monsters lurked beneath the water, hiding and defying his academic explanation.

"Right," Marcus said, folding the paper bag until it fit inside his coat pocket. "Anyone want to join me on a standing stone hunt? Emma?"

"You want to look for standing stones? Since when?" Emma blew on her hands.

"Luke told where to find them. Supposedly, it's a door to the fairy realm...when they want to visit Nessie."

"You still believe in fairies?" Royce wrapped his arms around Cordelia, who quietly stared out over the loch. "You know those are only fables, just like Nessie?"

"That's skeptical." Cordelia said, burrowing against his chest. "Have you always been this way?"

"Always." Marcus interjected. "He's tried to convince me magic that didn't exist." He patted Royce on the shoulder. "It never worked."

"I have to say, I'm on team Marcus with this one."

"Me too. Sorry, Royce." Emma's voice had a touch of pity.

"That's three against one, mate. Your tricks won't work on us." Marcus tousled Royce's cap, causing it to slip dip over an eye.

Royce swatted his hand and readjusted his cap. "We'll catch up with you at the car. Try not to get lost."

"Say hello to Nessie for us." Marcus took Emma's hand and headed toward a trail that veered away from the loch. Emma's laughter floated past them and drifted toward the mountains.

Cordelia moved closer to the water's edge. The landscape provided a stunning backdrop, contrasting her navy wool coat, burgundy scarf, and rosy cheeks. "You really don't believe in Nessie?"

"Historically, the legends date back to Saint Columba in 565 AD and—."

"You're avoiding the answer, Lord Brownell." Her smile teased. "Do you think she exists?"

Royce sat on the log, and repositioned to accomodate for Cordelia curling up in his lap.

"Well?" She fidgeted with the back of his scarf.

"I think some things resist explanation."

"That's very diplomatic of you, but it's not an answer."

"It's the safest option."

"Wow, I've never known you to back down from a debate."

He brushed a strand of hair from her face. "Perhaps I've learned when to let you win."

"More like you know when to admit defeat." She straightened her back and giggled, giving him a quick kiss. Her lips warmed his mouth. "Royce, close your eyes."

"What? Why?"

"Just, close your eyes," she said, closing her own. "Tell me what you hear." A soft smile emerged across her rosy lips as she peeked an eye open. "Trust me, close your eyes." Her eyelids fluttered shut.

Their game—something random that had become a tradition for them since Paris. He'd never shared it with anyone else. Somehow it felt sacred between them. He closed his eyes.

"What do you hear?" she whispered.

"Water. It's moving underneath the thin ice."

"And?"

"Wind. It's whistling in the pine needles. And your breath—shallow, and then deep...but it's calm. Very different than what I heard yesterday in the stables."

Her hand fumbled to cover his mouth. "Shhh. I'm serious."

Royce kissed her hand and mumbled, "Alright."

"Now, what do you smell?"

"Soap mixed with jasmine on your skin. Fresh pine. Wet earth." He drew a deep breath in, "But I smell you more than anything."

"Really? I smell wet earth the most. It reminds me of Venice, but colder."

He opened an eye and watched her chest rise and fall as she smelled the air.

"I can feel you watching me."

He snapped his eyes shut. "No, I'm not."

"Royce," her whisper blew across his cheek. "Tell me what you're feeling."

"The cold air contrasting the warm wool against my neck." He paused and pulled her closer. "Your body against mine. It feels comforting and safe." His hand brushed down her side, moving under her ribs. "I feel grateful—grateful to be here, in this spot with you." His eyelids lifted and met hers inches away.

"I love you," she said.

"I love you too." The words sounded inadequate for what he wanted to express, for what he would finally share. He laced their fingers together. "There's something I need to tell you."

"That sounds ominous."

"It's not. I've made changes to my will and added you as a beneficiary."

Her expression dropped. "Your will?" She repeated the question with a firmer tone.

"Yes, my will. I met with my solicitor—."

"When did you meet with him? Why?" Her voice tensed and cracked.

"Before we left London. But I've been working on for months...since Venice."

"You've been planning this since Venice? Why? What's wrong?"

"Nothing's wrong. I wanted to add you to my will, that's all."

"We shouldn't be talking about this right now."

"Yes, we should. I want to make sure—."

"Don't." She unwrapped herself from him, plopping her hands in her lap. "Royce, we don't need to talk about wills. Not here. And sure as hell, not on Christmas Eve."

"Cordelia."

She gestured, stopping him from continuing. "I know you think I'm overreacting, but I want to share something with you." Her boot made a scraping sound as it dragged across the dirt. "When I was in culinary school my dad called to tell me he'd been diagnosed with cancer."

"You told me. He wanted you to stay in school and focus on your career."

"Right. He promised me he'd be fine, and that his treatments would cure him. Then a month later he called to discuss his will. He swore he was okay. He promised that it was only precautionary, nothing more. Just like what you're saying." She slipped a hand inside her coat sleeve as if she wanted to protect herself from the world.

"Darling, I'm not sick. It's only a gesture of commitment to you."

"Not the way I see it." There was a pain in her voice, a fearful tone. "To me, wills are a death sentence."

"I'm sorry I didn't know."

"No, it's not something couples usually discuss, 'Hey, how do you feel about wills? Freaked out over them?'"

Royce rested his face on her shoulder, hiding a smile that pushed its way onto his face. *Never dull with her.*

"I can't think about losing you, not now. And if we talk about your will then I know I'll obsess over it. Actually, too late, I'm going to anyway. But talking about it, will cause a panic attack, so do you mind if we don't discuss this right now?"

"Of course." He wanted to tell her that it wasn't about the money or preparing for doom, it was his way of showing her the lengths he'd go to protect her—to show love for her. "I didn't mean to upset you."

"I know." She rested her face against his, generating a comforting warmth. A soft wind blew strands of her hair across both of their faces. "You know I have my own money. I don't need yours."

"It's not about the money, Cordelia. I only wanted—."

She jumped up and pointed to the loch. "Royce, look."

Something large and dark broke the surface of the water.

"What's that?" He hurried to the edge. "That's too large to be a log."

Cordelia stood beside him and leaned over the water. "Oh my god, it's moving. It's creating waves."

Soft ripples lapped close to their feet.

"I knew it. It's Nessie." Her wool gloves made a muffled clapping sound.

"We don't know that for sure."

"Yes, we do. Look."

Two eyes peered above the surface as a long, dark body swam gracefully past a thin sheet of ice. Its back emerged and then the creature disappeared.

They stood frozen. Silent. He waited and listened. *It can't be real.* In a small way, Royce hoped it would appear again—prove it existence.

But it didn't.

"So much for skepticism." Cordelia whispered, wrapping her arm around his and resting her head on his shoulder.

"It is Christmas Eve." Nature had just challenged his academic sensibility. And she'd never let him forget it.

3 :oo PM
"We just saw Nessie." Cordelia fixated on the spot where the water rippled toward the shore. "I can't believe it."

"It was something, but we don't know for sure what it was." Royce massaged his forehead. "We can't say definitively—."

"That was Nessie. And you know it."

"Alright, possibly."

She scanned his expression, a conflicted look of wonder and rationale. "You can't tell me *that* was a log. That had a head, eyes, and an f-ing long body."

"I'm not saying it is a log." His hand glided through his hair —a tell-tale whenever something challenged his worldview. "I honestly don't know what to call it."

"Nessie, call it Nessie." Cordelia patted him on the shoulder. "You can't deny it, Royce. She exists." She surveyed the watery horizon, looking for any sign of the creature. "You saw her. Just admit, you were wrong."

Royce cut his eyes at her and smirked. "You'd love that, wouldn't you?"

"Maybe." She batted her eyes, feeling satisfied that Nessie herself had proven her existence to him. "You know you want to admit that what we just saw was something magical."

His arms softly wrapped around her. "You're going to tell everyone about this, aren't you?"

"For sure. That was a once in a lifetime experience. There's no way I'm keeping quiet on that."

His lips curled into a grin. "I love your imagination, you know that?"

"I'm not imagining anything. Just say the words, 'Cordelia, I admit you were right about Nessie.'"

"Shhh," Royce's mouth rested on hers.

"Admit—." A kiss silenced the conversation—playful, seductive, distracting. Her body warmed. *He gets me every time.* It reminded her of Venice after the masquerade when his touch, one simple kiss, expressed a mountain of feelings.

A tree cracked from the rustling wind. Royce paused and looked toward the trail Marcus and Emma had taken. "We should head back. It'll be dark soon." He led her away from the loch, turning onto their original trail.

"Are you anxious to leave because you're afraid Nessie will make another appearance?"

"What gave you that idea?"

"First of all, you're answering a question with a question. Clue number one." He grunted in response, turning his phone flashlight on. "Second, the kiss, the denial, the distracting kiss... need I say more?"

"Alright. I admit we saw what appears to be a large creature, whether it's Nessie or not, I can't say." As he turned around the light created long shadows on the path. She felt his fingers wrapping around her hand. "Does that satisfy you?"

"Sort of." Dusk settled around them, painting the sky in shades of golden grey. "At least I'm one step closer to convincing you that magic does exist."

Royce dramatically sighed, laughed, and tugged her cap. "Come on, let's go."

The trail wound through thin patches of trees, creating tunnels of darkness as they climbed the hill back to the car. The phone light grew brighter as night crept up, causing Cordelia to walk closer on Royce's heels. As they rounded a boulder Cordelia tripped on smaller rocks.

"Are you okay?"

"Yeah, I'm fine." She said dusting her hands off. *Oh shit, that was close.* Her heart pounded as she imagined tumbling downhill and injuring the baby.

"Let me look."

"There's nothing to see. It's just a scrape."

He flashed the light onto her. "Okay." Royce took her hand and guided her to the front. "Would you like to lead?"

She shrugged, "Sure," took the phone, and followed the trail around two switchbacks. "Royce. About your will, I think I should tell you more." They stopped in the middle of the trail, letting the light encircle their feet. The soft glow illuminated their faces. "When my dad called about the will, he said he was leaving me money, to set me up after culinary school. And to take a graduation trip to Europe. He wanted me to experience the food and culture."

Royce's thumb traced circles on the back of her glove.

"I had big ideas of how I'd honor him, but...I met Daniel." She held her breath, feeling into the loss she still felt for her dad. "I am who I am because of him—culinary school, a life in New York, and you." She looked down at their joint hands. "His money helped me build this life. It's like he knew Paris was part of my destiny and I want to thank him."

"You already are, just by being you."

"I miss him."

"I know." He pulled her close. The soft leather of his glove cupped her face. "He knew. I'm sure that's why he left you the watch."

The band gripped her wrist and she imagined his hand on her arm. A cold sting hit her eyes and she buried her face in Royce's chest. "When you said you'd added me as a beneficiary to your will, all I could think about was death and absence. It reminded me that someone can quickly disappear from your life."

"That's not why I did it." He tilted her face up. Their eyes met. "I'm not preparing for death, Cordelia. I'm preparing for our life. Together. I want you to feel secure, to know that whatever happens, whenever it happens, you're not abandoned."

The words settled over her like a soothing blanket.

"I don't know what to say." She cleared her throat. "I still don't like talking about wills, it terrifies me actually, and it's not a Christmas conversation, but I'll listen when we get back to London. Agreed?"

"Agreed." His mouth curved into a dimpled smile. "While we're being honest, I have to admit I was wrong about Nessie."

"Seriously? Wait, say that again and let me record you." Cordelia's laugh bounced off the trees.

"I admit we saw some kind of lake monster. Historically, the Picts and Celts, primarily from Ireland, believed in mythological creatures—."

"Are you lecturing me, Dr. Brownell? In a dark forest where fairies live?"

"I never said anything about fairies."

"No, but I'm sure they're here."

Royce rolled his eyes. "Not you too."

"Now you want to be haughty and flash your academic

skepticism?" His rich laughter sparked the giggles in her. "You realize your doubt makes you an easy target for the fairies."

Marcus and Emma yelled from the top of the hill, causing Royce to startle.

"You're jumpy." Cordelia pulled his cap over his eyes and kissed him. "Don't doubt the fairies. Or magic."

"Alright, alright." He uncovered his eyes. "I believe in your fairies." Royce waved and shouted back at Marcus, letting him know they were nearby.

She handed him the phone and interlaced her fingers with his. "Wait till they hear about Nessie."

"I'm doomed."

They rounded a set of boulders and followed the trail into a clearing. At the crest, Marcus and Emma hovered together, waving their lit phones as Christmas music played. The last glimmer of sunlight created a golden cast on the mountains.

"Hey guys, you won't believe what we saw." Cordelia looked back at the loch and brushed her hand across her belly. It was Christmas eve and life felt magical. "Tell them Royce. What did we see?" Her laughter blanketed the hillside as he chased her back to the car.

Chapter Nineteen

4:30 PM
The estate kitchen smelled like sweet butter and competition.

Cordelia and Marnie tied their borrowed aprons Mrs. MacLeod had selected for them. The faded red stripes wrapped around Cordelia's hips, hiding her bloated belly.

The kitchen had been transformed with matching ingredients laid out on both ends of the oversized butcher block island. Marnie had won the toss and claimed the section closest to the ovens, leaving Cordelia closest to the judging table. Normally the lounge space served as an ideal spot for tea by the fire—a perfect place to watch deer wander across the lawn. But that morning, Luke had altered the area, positioning five chairs around a table and arranging spectator seating beside the windows.

"You're going down." Marnie said, smoothing her apron front. She hummed the theme to *Rocky*.

"Dream on, Nicholsen."

The Earl, Countess, Luke, Mr. Smyth, and Cassandra took their seats at the table. Maisie scooted in between the Earl and

Countess, declaring herself as judge number six. Behind them Marcus, Emma, Ada Rose, and Richard sat waiting for Royce to start the competition.

"Are you ladies ready?" Royce moved a rolling pin between his palms. "Each of you has to create one batch of original Christmas cookies that will be judged blind—."

"Blind? I thought we could watch?" Maisie threw her tiny hands in the air.

"I'm afraid we're being sent to the TV room," the Countess said.

"What? We just got here."

"I agree, it seems very unfair." The Earl frowned. "We promise to remain impartial."

"The rules are, blind judging. Does anyone want to give up their seat?" Royce pointed the rolling pin at the table of judges.

"I don't think I want to be a judge then." Maisie rested her elbows on the table and plopped her head into her hand. "Mommy, can I stay and watch?"

"Of course, baby." Marnie said.

Maisie offered handshakes to the other judges, wished them luck, and took a seat in Richard's lap.

"Anyone else?" Royce paused, "Once the baking is done, our judges will return and cast their votes based on taste, presentation, and creativity. The chef with the highest total score will win."

"What do they win?" Marcus asked.

"Bragging rights." Marnie shot Cordelia a smug grin.

"More than bragging rights," Cordelia knocked on the counter. "Winner gets one no-questions-asked favor that they can use any time in the next year." She stretched in front of Royce and offered Marnie her hand as the group responded in surprise.

"Those are high stakes, Cordy. Are you ready to pay up?" Marnie shook her hand.

"Are you?"

"Okay, ladies, well, if you agree, then as soon as the judges leave, you can begin." Royce waved the rolling pin in the air, motioning for the judges to leave. As soon as the kitchen door swung behind them, he drumrolled on the counter and counted down. "Three, two, one, go." Royce dodged out of the way and sat at the table.

Cordelia measured flour, sugar, and spices for her spiced blood orange shortbread cookies before setting the bowl aside. Next she zested and cut the orange peel into thin slices. *Those three Scots are gonna love these.* Citrus and cardamom aromas filled the air around her work area.

Marnie scooped three cups of brown sugar into a pot, poured heavy cream on top, and added a shot of espresso.

She's making her caramel sauce. Ugh. Smart. Cordelia moved quicker, blanching her peel several times before simmering in a syrup. The sugary smell caused a wave of nausea to wash over her stomach. *Not now.* She pushed up her sweatshirt sleeves, wishing she'd gone with a T-shirt instead. Although the crackling pine in the fireplace soothed her senses, in combination with the hot ovens, Cordelia felt as if she'd stepped into a furnace—a gentle reminder of a little secret she carried.

"How's it going over there, chickie?" Marnie rapidly chopped candied ginger into fine pieces.

"Just another day in the kitchen. And you?" Cordelia cut her eyes at Marnie.

She paused and glanced back, "Hey, no peeking."

"Scared I'll steal an idea?" Cordelia finished mixing her dough and plopped it onto the wood counter.

"More like you're scared I'll beat you."

The spectators whispered among themselves, laughing and cheering them on. Royce rapped his fingers on the table, "Forty-five minutes left. Are you ladies going to finish in time?"

Cordelia pushed the rolling pin over the dough, "Yes, Professor." She caught a glimpse of his grin and dimples. He blew her a kiss.

"Hey, no flirting with the judges." Marnie threw a dusting of flour at Cordelia.

The rolling pin eased across the dough, causing it to stretch and thin. "He's not a judge...doesn't count." She dusted her hands and searched a basket for a square cutter. "He's the host."

"Just as bad." Marnie stirred the sweet mixture on the stove. Hints of ginger infused into her molasses caramel, giving the kitchen a holiday fragrance.

"Did anyone tell you two that you're both ridiculously competitive?" Emma bounced Ada Rose on her knee, who wrestled out of her hands and into Marcus'.

Cordelia and Marnie replied, "All the time."

"This is better than TV." Richard and Maisie played a card game on the rug near the fireplace.

In less than thirty minutes overlapping scents of baked cookies filled the kitchen. Aromas that intensified Cordelia's nausea. "Can someone open a window, please?"

"You okay?" Marnie placed her ginger-molasses cookies onto cooling racks. "Cordy?"

"Yeah, I'm fine." She pushed her sleeves higher. "Time?"

"Fifteen minutes." Royce waved Mrs. MacLeod over, pulling a chair out beside him.

Cordelia's cheeks flushed, and she debated sacrificing time versus gaining relief, but a rush of cold air washed over her after Marcus cracked a window. "Thank you." Her voice cracked.

"Cordy?" Marnie wiped her hands on a towel.

"I'm fine. Focus." She caught a glimpse of Royce—his stare,

his narrowed eyes. *Shit. Relax, Cordelia, relax.* After gulping a glass of water, she tempered a bowl of dark chocolate, checking the temperature three times. *Perfect.* All she needed to do was dip, decorate, and plate.

"Five minutes. Let's get these plated." Royce clapped. The sound rang in Cordelia's head like a gong.

"Seriously? You're taking this role too seriously." Cordelia's voice elevated over the oven fans and Marnie's mixer.

"It's a serious role." He clapped. "Now come on, get those cookies plated."

She ran over to the table and shoved a cookie in his mouth. "Royce, I love you, but please don't."

He nodded and chewed. "Those are delicious. Why haven't—."

"Wait, that's priviledged treatment." Marcus held out his hand, "My darling Cordelia, since you're sharing."

"No. No bribing the spectators." Marnie shouted from the other side of the kitchen. "Cordy, you know better than that."

Cordelia rushed back to her station. "Yes, mom." She dipped a cookie and watched a delicate stream of chocolate fall back into the bowl, leaving a dark coating on the biscuit. *Perfect.* She quickly dipped more.

"Three minutes, ladies. Three minutes." Royce paced in front of the oversized island.

Shit...need more time. Cordelia placed candied orange peel and tiny flakes of edible gold onto the chocolate as it cooled into a smooth, glassy finish. *I've got this.* Light reflected off the gold, adding a touch of Christmas flair to the cream-colored platter that had a aged pattern on the edge.

Marnie arranged her rustic but beautiful ginger-molasses cookies onto a vintage tartan plate, stacking them into three mini towers. They looked homey yet sophisticated with tiny studs of crystallized ginger and a faint dusting of crushed sugar pearls.

Damn, she's good. Cordelia wiped her hands clean and nibbled on a broken ginger cookie Marnie had left on the counter. The flavors soothed her queasy stomach. "Good job." Cordelia felt a bead of sweat trickle down her spine.

"You too." She brushed her hands across the edge, removing a stray crumb.

"Time." Royce said.

"Absolutely fantastic," Mrs. MacLeod approached the island and inhaled. "They smell as good as they look."

"Marcus, will you bring in the judges, please?" Royce set the platters onto the table. "If you two will join me over here."

"You're really taking this way too seriously," Cordelia said, flashing a smile at him.

"But it's adorable, right?" He whispered, moving close to her cheek. "Turns you on just a bit?"

She nodded, looked to see if anyone heard, and brushed her lips against his ear. "Yes."

The judges took their seats and awed at the beautiful platters of cookies. Mrs. MacLeod served each one a cup of honey-colored tea and set dessert plates in front of them.

"Right, bakers if you'll stand over there so we don't influence them," he gestured toward the far wall, near the back hallway, where they couldn't make eye contact with anyone. "Now, judges, this is plate A," he pointed at Cordelia's platter. "And this is plate B."

"They're both lovely," the Countess said, "almost too pretty to eat. One looks professionally designed while the other offers a homemade warmth."

"I agree, plate B makes you want to eat several in one sitting." The Earl leaned closer and smelled Marnie's cookies.

Damn. Does that mean he likes hers better? Unable to stand still, Cordelia glided her slippered foot across the floor, making patterns in the recently vacuumed rug.

"Shall we taste?" The Earl said, looking at the others.

"I can't wait." Luke grabbed two cookies from Cordelia's platter and placed one on Cassandra's plate and the other in front of himself. There was a brief look between them, a partial smile, and her eyes fluttered. *Not now, focus Cassandra.*

The judges ate in silence, taking small bites, making notes on the paper Royce had provided, and whispering among themselves. After each bite, Mr. Smyth would sip his tea, presumably cleansing his palate and then scribble something onto his paper.

"They're both exceptional," Mrs. McLeod said, dusting the crumbs from her fingertips. "Plate A is sophisticated, very unexpected flavors. I'd be interested in having this recipe, both of them actually."

"I agree, they both demonstrated artistry, yet they're very different. I thought I'd be able to guess the chef, but I'm honestly not sure." Cassandra cut her eyes at Cordelia and raised a eyebrow as she nibbled on the shortbread cookie.

"Don't even try to get hints." Marnie playfully covered Cordelia's face.

"What? I'm not doing anything." She swatted her hands away. "Scared?"

"Nope."

"Plate B has incredible depth of flavor." Mr. Smyth smacked his lips together, "I think this chef added bourbon. Is anyone else tasting bourbon?"

"That's what it is. They added bourbon." Luke grabbed another ginger-molasses cookie and took a bite. He made notes and whispered something in Cassandra's ear. She nodded and wrote on her paper.

"It does add complexity, but then so are the shortbread biscuits." The Countess broke one in half. "This chef added a perfect hint of cardamom, and I think there's pepper or some spice in the chocolate that elevates it from a classic biscuit."

Yes. Thank you, Countess. Cordelia fanned her sweatshirt. *Now, please vote so I can cool off.*

"Have you all made a decision?" Royce cut his eyes from the judges to Cordelia and Marnie. "Ladies, if you'll join us."

"Should we hand you our vote, or read them aloud?" The Earl dunked a shortbread cookie into his tea.

"I'll take them, Pop." Royce reviewed the scraps of paper, "Well, we have a tie. Two votes for plate A, and two votes for plate B."

"Wait, that's not possible." Marnie crossed her arms. "There's no way to have a tie with five judges."

Mr. Smyth cleared his throat. "I abstained. I'm sorry, but I couldn't make one a loser. You both did an incredible job."

"But that defeats the purpose of having five judges. Can you pick one?" Cordelia tucked her hands into the apron pockets. "We promise we won't be mad."

"Aye, well," Mr. McLeish appeared from the boot room doorway, pulling trinkets from his jacket pocket. "I thought this might happen." He placed two wooden figures on the table— three inch tall, hand-carved owls. "I carved these from the felled oak, down by the loch." He looked at Royce, "I came prepared, in case someone couldn't make up their mind." He faced Cordelia and Marnie. "You're both good cooks, and no one should be a loser at Christmas, so here ya are, one for each of you."

Cordelia examined the owl in her palm, noting the detailed craftsmanship. "Thank you, Mr. McLeish. These are beautiful."

"Thank you." Marnie's blue eyes sparkled, letting Maisie touch it. "Be gentle, it's very special."

"Well, you know, the owl is the symbol of Waileigh Lodge

and they've been making their home here for hundreds of years. And some folks say, there's magic in these owls."

"Ooh, magic, hear that, Royce." Cordelia elbowed him and winked.

"Right. Can we eat the cookies now? I'm starving." Marcus reached between his parents and grabbed a few, handing one to Emma and a ginger-molasses to Ada Rose.

Royce bit into a shortbread, leaving cookie crumbs on his lip. Cordelia brushed it away, and leaned into him. "Ready to change for the village?"

"Yes. I'm so hot...in this sweatshirt." She clutched the owl, letting her stomach press against his body.

"These are amazing. I think you should make them every holiday season."

"Are we starting a tradition?"

He rested his arms on her shoulders, "I think we are." Royce held up another biscuit, "Here's to new family traditions."

"I like the sound of that." Cordelia kissed his cheek, feeling Maisie tug on her sleeve.

"Auntie Cordy, can I see yours?" Maisie peeled it from Cordelia's hand and compared it to Marnie's. "They're the same. How did he make the same?" She walked off with them, showing Richard the two owls.

The family surrounded the table and finished off both platters. Cordelia nibbled on a ginger-molasses cookie and scanned each face, wondering who all suspected the pregnancy. Two already knew her secret and with a few hours left before telling Royce, she couldn't risk anyone else finding out. She washed the cookie down with a cup of lukewarm tea, and rested her head against Royce. *New traditions. I like that.*

Chapter Twenty

7:30 PM

Royce and Cordelia stood at the edge of a quaint market square, admiring the nearby village's Victorian decorations. Renowned for its Christmas Eve festivities, it hosted the last market of the holiday season, and Mrs. Smyth said it was her favorite in all of Scotland.

Strung above the square were oversized burgundy bows and gold beads wrapped in delicate lights with dangling Christmas crackers. Everyone who passed underneath them strained to touch them. Rows of wooden stalls, decorated in garland and holly, offered everything from mulled cider to hand-knitted scarves to meat pies. The fragrant air smelled of buttery pastry, beef and gravy, and sugar candy. At the center stood an enormous Christmas tree, adorned with hundreds of handmade ornaments, designed by the villagers for the past fifty years. But the eye catcher was the gold star on top. It caught light from every angle and blanketed the square in golden rays.

"It's beautiful." Cordelia adjusted the crimson-colored scarf around her neck—his scarf she'd borrowed, insisting it matched her sweater better than the one she brought. "Now all we need are roasted chestnuts and a town crier."

"There's your chestnuts." He pointed to the opposite side of the square where a younger man roasted the nuts over an open fire pit. "Shall we look for the town crier?" He playfully offered his arm, giving her a head nod.

"How very Dickens of you."

"Anything for M'Lady." Royce's attempt to change his accent sounded unnatural and harsh, causing Cordelia's face to cringe.

"Please don't ever do that again." She laughed and rested her head on his shoulder as they strolled across the square, passing a waterless fountain.

The stone structure was filled with large red and gold baubles with signs requesting 'not to touch', tempting a handful of children to run past and tap. On the other side of the fountain, Emma, Marcus, and Ada Rose smiled for photos with Santa at the North Pole hut. Not far from them, the Earl and Countess drank cider from collector mugs and talked with another older couple in fur coats.

"Oyez, Oyez, Oyez..." The woman, wearing a Victorian dress, banged a spoon against a wooden plate.

"Look, it's a woman crier." Cordelia's voice pitched higher with enthusiasm.

"Can you imagine having had that job?" Cassandra and Luke appeared alongside them.

"Too much gossip for me." She faced them. "Where are you heading?"

"Luke suggested a cider maker—."

"Don't call him a maker, he might not serve you." Luke's hand grazed down her back.

"Right. Well, the cider brewer is at this end of the market. Care to join us?"

"Yeah, come on. You can't enjoy a Christmas market without a good cider in your hands." He rubbed his hands together. "You won't be disappointed, trust me."

"Cider or chestnuts?" Royce said, noticing Cordelia's eyes sparkled from the tree lights illuminating her face.

She shrugged. "Who can pass up a good cider?"

"Cider it is. Lead the way." Royce gestured, noticing Luke's hand pressed against her lower back as he guided her through the crowd. He whispered to Cordelia as they trailed behind, "Please tell me you're seeing this? She's never this warm with dates."

"I know." Cordelia stopped and whipped around. "She's not being pretentious at all. I almost want to ask her if she's alright."

The caught up with Cassandra and Luke, who quickly dropped hands when they arrived. Royce smiled at her, hoping he could read her expression. She looked down and blushed, refusing to meet his eyes. He whispered in Cordelia's ear, "Try talking to her tonight."

She nodded, keeping her eyes ahead.

Royce lingered and smelled hints of jasmine on her neck. Her chest rose and fell as his breath landed underneath her hair. "Actually, forget that. I have something else in mind."

Cordelia smiled. Her eyes cut sideways and she moistened her lips.

They joined the queue, shuffled forward, and listened to Cassandra describe their day ice skating. Her animated laugh sounded genuine, happy.

"Four ciders," Luke said when they reached the front.

"I've changed my mind, just three," Cordelia said.

"Are you sure? It's fantastic."

"Yeah, I forgot I'm doing a charity thing for work. So, I better not." She fidgeted with her right earlobe.

"Darling, I'm sorry. I forgot you were abstaining for the holidays." Royce wrapped his arm around her waist. "If you want I'll give mine away and keep you company."

"No, of course not. I just...I'm not really in the mood to drink tonight anway." Cordelia adjusted her cap and scarf.

She's taking this charity challenge seriously. He studied her face, noticing how her eyes dodged his. *It doesn't make sense.* His fingers caressed her side. *Well, maybe tomorrow night she'll break the rules.* He resisted smiling, but eagerness broke through.

They collected their steaming mugs and wandered toward the center where carolers had taken to a stage and begun singing hymns. Behind them, Royce heard Cassandra ask Luke about growing up in Glasgow. There was a softness to her voice, a tone that she hadn't used in years. Not since Teddy.

"Should we give them more space?" Cordelia murmured, her warm breath tickled his ear.

"Probably." He glanced back, noticing they loosely held hands. "In an odd way, I'm happy for her. Uncertain for him, but happy for her."

"Why, because she's finally coming out of her recession?" Cordelia's girlish laugh snorted.

"Oh, please, that's a thought I don't want to imagine."

"What, Cassandra having...sex?"

"Shhh, I don't think we should say that word when hymns are being sung." He placed his finger over her lips.

"You're being prudish."

"No, I'm being British." He brushed a kiss on her cheek, spun her around and wrapped his arms around her as they listened to the choral music.

The carolers shifted from singing "Silent Night" in English to Gaelic. The melodic, almost angelic voices sent chills down Royce's arms.

"I love this song." She rested her head on his chest. "Do you ever think about living somewhere like this?"

"In a Victorian village?"

"Sort of. Somewhere other than London?"

The question caught him off guard, not because he'd never considered it, but because she'd never suggested it. "Sometimes. However, your job is in the city."

"I know. I just wonder what it would be like to live somewhere small like this, somewhere homey...with a family."

A family? He pressed his lips to her ear. "You mean, children. That kind of family?"

She remained quiet until the end of the song. "Yeah, that kind. But I don't mean today. Just someday."

"Right. I guess I could see us living outside London one day. That's in the future, right?"

She faced him, her expression filled with hope and hesitation. "Oh, yeah, way down the road." Her eyes glistened and she dabbed one dry. "I think the energy of the night has me emotional."

"Ready for a bite to eat?" His finger traced her chin.

"Now that you mention it, I'm starving. How about some crepes?" She turned to walk away.

"Cordelia." He held her hand and pulled her close. "About that someday family. I want that with you."

"Me too."

"And that's why I added you to my document that shall not be named."

"I understand." Her eyes rested on his, enchanting him with a glowing smile.

"I...there's something I—." How could it be the perfect moment when he didn't have the ring? He exhaled. "I had—." Marcus patted him on the back, interrupting his spontaneous proposal. *Wow, I almost said it. Thank you, brother.*

Within minutes, they were surrounded by family members. Everyone talked over each other as Cordelia patted her stomach, indicating she was hungry. He nodded, told his parents they'd be back in a moment, and guided Cordelia to a crepe stand.

Royce glanced at his watch. *Family.* He squeezed her hand and a warm sensation filled his chest. *Twenty-four hours and that someday begins.*

10:15 PM

The wood in the family den fireplace crackled and popped as the logs shifted. Sparks flew upward but dissipated before reaching the hearth. Bright orange flames dispersed light into the room, casting shadows across the floor and the Christmas tree. The aroma of pine lingered above the smell of burning oak.

Cordelia nested underneath Royce's arm and a woven red blanket as they watched a black and white holiday movie. Water pipes creaked in the wall, giving off a ghostly sound. "Sounds like Lady Margaret isn't happy." The pipe groaned in response.

"Perhaps she's lonely." Royce paused the TV and listened to whispered voices that passed in the hallway.

"Because, maybe she doesn't have anyone to spend Christmas with. Maybe all the other ghosts go on holiday for the winter." Cordelia sat up. "What if ghosts really did feel lonely?"

"First lake creatures, now ghosts. Are we going to hunt dragons next?" He sipped a whisky, wiping the condensation with a green cloth napkin.

"Please tell me you weren't this skeptical as a child?"

"No, I—."

Cordelia shushed him, "What's that sound?" A faint, pleading cry neared the terrace door. "What is that? A bird?"

"I'm not sure." He walked softly toward the door. "It's not a bird." Royce froze, straining to hear.

The cry begged for attention and lured Cordelia over. "It sounds like a cat."

"Stay here. I'll check." Royce threw on his sweatshirt. Static electricity caused strands to stick up. "The cats never stray this far from the stables." He smoothed his hair back down.

"Well, whatever it is, I'm coming with you." Cordelia wrapped the blanket around her shoulders and waited for him to unlatch the door. The crying grew louder, insistent, and desperate. When the door popped open, a small kitten paced and looked up at them. "Oh my god, you poor thing." She ignored the cold blast of air, immediately scooping and cradling it against her chest. "Where did you come from?"

"Let's bring it inside." He closed the door, latching it shut. "Why don't you sit with it by the fire, and I'll get some towels."

The kitten was soaked from the snowfall. It shivered and purred as she petted its cold, dark fur. "It's alright, little guy. You're safe now. We've got you." Sitting on the floor in front of the hearth, Cordelia rocked it in her lap.

Royce returned from the kitchen with an armful of yellow towels, the ones Mrs. Smyth used to polish silver. He sat beside her and laid out the towels, making sure the warm stone wasn't too hot. Together, they dried the kitten. At first, the little girl protested, but soon submitted and purred.

The fire's heat warmed Cordelia's face and sent a drop of sweat running down her back.

Soon, the kitten's dry fur morphed into a plush, dark grey coat.

Royce examined her, checking for injuries or signs of illness. "She seems healthy."

"Do you think she made it all the way from the stables?" Cordelia wrapped her in a dry towel and held her close.

"That's my guess. But we've only had one litter this autumn and that was 8 weeks ago."

"She looks too small." Cordelia handed the kitten off to Royce, who rubbed the side of her face.

"Unless she's the runt."

Cordelia slid closer to him, listening as it purred and fell asleep against his chest. The crackling fire hissed. Distant voices faded to silence. A quiet calm settled around them. "What if we kept her?"

"You mean, take her back in London?"

"I know what you're going to say. We live in the city. We work long hours. We travel. But, she did appear on Christmas Eve. Maybe it's a sign to get a pet."

"Didn't you say you'd never owned a pet because it was too much responsibility?" Royce set the sleeping kitten onto the stone between them.

"I don't remember saying that."

His dimples appeared as he chuckled, "Right."

"We can manage. It's two of us and one small kitten."

"You've already decided, haven't you?" He brushed a strand of hair that rested on her cheek. "I guess it'll be..."

"Good practice for the future." She searched his eyes. "You never know when—." Her breath caught in her chest. "Royce, I really want—."

"Okay, we'll figure it out." The kitten stretched and repositioned herself. "Besides, I work from home and Kay's around most days."

"Seriously? You're okay with it?"

He tilted his head, like he always did when he questioned her response. "Yes, if it makes you happy."

"This is the perfect addition..." She cleared her throat. *Oh my god, I can't believe I almost gave it away. Twice.* Cordelia held his gaze, leaned forward, and kissed Royce, hoping it would distract him from her slip-up.

Her heart fluttered. "What are we going to name her?"

Royce looked at the kitten as she slept in a tight curl. "Fortuna."

"Fortuna?"

"Why not? She's lucky we heard her."

"Ah, but the question is, was it luck or did Lady Margaret lead her to us?" Cordelia crawled into Royce's lap.

"Like the ghost of Christmas present."

"Yes. So, what will the ghost of Christmas future bring?" She nibbled on his ear.

"I guess we'll have to wait and see next year."

"Yes, we will."

His lips moved unhurried across her cheek, and when he found her mouth, the kiss was deep—layered with unspoken words. Whisky lingered on his tongue, sweet and smoky. Emotions conveyed through his touch.

Upstairs, someone washed water through the pipes, causing them to rattle.

"Pop really needs to get the plumbing updated." Royce said, resting his forehead against Cordelia's cheek.

"Or he's leaving it for you to deal with."

"That's probably true." His face winced as Fortuna kneaded on his arm. "Alright, my legs are going numb with you two on me."

"Are you saying I'm fat?"

"No. I'm simply suggesting we get back to our movie."

Cordelia stood, stretching her legs and back. The Christmas tree lights twinkled and had become the main source of light as the fire dissipated into glowing orange embers. Royce handed her Fortuna and added a small log to the fire, releasing a smoky fragrance into the air.

Another rush of water through the pipes morphed into groans that came from behind a historic portrait of a man and his horse.

Looks like we have Christmas past, present, and future all together. He just hasn't figured it out yet.

Chapter Twenty-One

1:45 PM

The kitchen dishwasher hummed. The antique mantel clock ticked. The kettle on the stove whistled. Cordelia observed each sound, comforted by their harmonious rhythm. *A quiet kitchen.* Just her and her thoughts. She flipped off the stove and poured the hot water into her mug. *Mmm, peppermint.* With her eyes closed, she paused, enjoying how the steam moistened her cheeks.

While the tea steeped, she searched the island for leftover treats, hoping to find Marnie's ginger-molasses cookies in a biscuit tin. When she found the container, she discovered sugar remnants on the counter, a hint someone else had already indulged in a late night snack. An empty plate with brown crumbs was her second clue.

Cordelia popped the lid. *Oh, they smell so good.* The sweet molasses tempted her to indulge in two cookies, but she refrained, taking only one.

With her tea in hand, she leaned against the counter and savored the soft, chewy cookie. *God...I need her recipe.* She heard voices approaching from the hallway and quickly chewed the last two bites, washing it down with hot tea. *Oww, shit.* Cordelia dusted the crumbs from her face, and positioned herself on a stool, flattening the creases on her green Christmas PJs.

Marnie and Cassandra appeared in the doorway.

Relief eased the stiffness in Cordelia's back. *At least I don't have to explain to Royce why I'm eating cookies at midnight.* She gently slurped her tea and waved.

"What are you doing in the dark?" Marnie's pink fluffy slippers shuffled across the stone floor. They paired nicely with her red and white check PJs and matching robe that hung open.

"I didn't want to wake anyone." Cordelia glanced at the two light sources, noticing the warm glow of the stove light and the sitting room lamp left black holes around the kitchen.

"Darling, in this house, the only thing you'll wake is the dead, and even they're too far from the kitchen to notice." Cassandra swiped a rosy balm across her lips. "But it does give it a cozy vibe...if that's what you're after." She wore a pale pink cardigan loosely buttoned with inky-colored jeans. Diamond stud earrings accented her broad smile.

"That's not what you were wearing at the market. Where are you going?" Cordelia shifted on the stool, pulling one out for Marnie, who busied herself making a cup of tea.

Cassandra glanced at her sweater. "Right. It's the first thing I grabbed." She busied herself on her phone, swiping through social photos. "You know me, I'm always changing outfits." Her phone vibrated and the hint of a grin flickered on her face.

"Cassandra, what are you up to?" Cordelia grabbed a second cookie and broke it in half, offering it to her. She reached for it, but rejected the offer.

"Must we play this curiosity game?" She adjusted her bra, pushing her small breasts upward. "What is it you want to know?"

182

Marnie grabbed the broken cookie from Cordelia's hand and settled onto the stool. "Yes, Cordy, what you're asking?" She smirked and indulged in the cookie.

"Wow, never thought I'd see you two gang up on me." Cordelia twisted her hair into a loose updo. "Cassandra, darling, where are you going in that beautiful sweater at midnight?" She mimicked Cassandra with a snarky tone.

"You know, fresh air is a wonderful thing right before bed." Cassandra moved for the boot room door. "And I agree, this sweater is stunning on me."

"I hope you're not walking alone." Cordelia's nails tapped on her mug. "Luke would be awful disappointed."

Cassandra turned in the doorway, "Luke? What are you suggesting?"

"Who's playing word games?"

"All right." Cassandra scurried back to the island. Her house shoes clicked against the stone. She leaned against the counter, "Yes, I'm going on a walk with Luke. He's bringing his telescope—." Her animated voice had an air of expectancy.

"I'm sure he is." Marnie laughed. "I bet it's a big one, too."

"Seriously, Marnie." Cordelia tapped her knee.

A smile spread across Cassandra's face and she blushed. "Well, I wouldn't mind if he did."

"Oh my god, you two. I can't think about Luke's...telescope." Her face warmed. "God, Marnie, now when I look at Luke, I'm going to picture his giant—."

Marnie's infectious laugh spread and soon they were laughing more than talking, wondering if it was a powerful telescope.

Cassandra wiped smeared mascara from under her eyes. "Well, if you'll excuse me, I'm leaving to enjoy some local culture." She giggled and hurried for the boot room.

"Is that what we're calling it? Maybe I should find some of

this local culture myself." Marnie sipped her tea, choking as she laughed. "I'm fine." Her voice cracked.

"Enjoy stargazing, Cassandra." Cordelia set the kettle onto a burner, igniting the flame underneath.

"That's my plan." She smirked and blew a kiss. Her petite hips swayed out the door.

Cordelia plopped her elbows onto the island counter. "I've never seen her so flirty. It's kinda bizarre."

"She's happy." Marnie stretched for the shortbread cookie tin, grabbed two, and placed them on a plate.

"I know. But I hope she doesn't get hurt."

The outside door of the boot room latched shut as Cassandra and Luke's muffled voices faded into silence. Cordelia watched the burner flames flicker underneath the tea kettle, listening to the water hiss and bubble.

Marnie crunched on cookies. "These are really good. I might have to steal the idea."

"I said the same about yours." Her head tilted sideways. "You know, you haven't changed. You look exactly like you did in New York."

"So do you."

"Clearly you haven't noticed the bags under my eyes."

Marnie pointed at her face. "Check out these. And look, there's these little lines forming. I didn't have these in New York."

Rolling bubbles bounced in the tea kettle. Cordelia pulled it off the stove just as it began to whistle. "Me either." She poured hot water into her mug and joined Marnie, who offered her a cookie. "I shouldn't." She accepted it. "I can't believe I can eat again without getting sick."

"Yeah, that'll pass and then you'll want to eat for two."

Cordelia rested her head on Marnie's shoulder. "I remember. You were eating ice cream every night."

"Oh my god, I know. Chocolate fudge brownie with those little chocolate chips and chewy brownie chunks. It was heaven." She dusted crumbs from her fingers. "We found that place..." She drifted, gazing into her tea.

"Right. You and Darius." A warm sensation travel down Cordelia's throat as she sipped her tea. Hints of peppermint lingered on her tongue. "Do you miss him?" She held her breath, waiting for her reaction.

Marnie sighed, causing the tea steam to float away. "I do." She clicked her tongue. The same habit she had from school—the same noise she'd make during tests. "The older Maisie gets, the less I can escape him."

"That's why you need to be in London."

"Sometimes it's better to move forward than look back." Her upper lip curled, apparently resisting a smile, but her stoic tone suggested Darius was still a closed topic.

"Okay. Then what about Richard?"

Marnie choked on her tea. "What about him?" A bump in the hallway startled them. "I swear there better not be ghosts here."

"I'm sure there are, it's an old house." Cordelia wiped a drop of tea off the counter. "Are you moving forward with Richard?"

"There it is, folks, Cordelia's bluntness." She hugged her. "Kidding."

"Not." Cordelia returned the hug. "I'll keep asking—."

"About Richard." She crossed her legs. "He's nice." Marnie's leg bobbed up and down. "He's great with Maisie. Gorgeous eyes and..."

"And?"

"I don't know, it's different. Darius and I were young. We were friends, and we just fit. We could be laughing one second and deep in hot sex the next."

185

"I know, New York walls are thin, remember?" Cordelia gulped the last of her tea.

Marnie rolled her eyes. "And Edmund, he was all heat." She flung her head backward. "God, just thinking about him still gets me—the man is a genius at cakes and sex."

Cordelia grunted. An unsettled feeling rose from her stomach. *Great, what I've done.* She took a few deep breaths and listened as Marnie described her working relationship with Edmund—creative, respectful, and wildly fun.

"Then there's Richard. He makes me believe there's something stable for me, for Maisie. He's like the guy who comes along when you least expect it, and shows you what could be, even if it's not right now."

"Thing is, he's ready to be that right now guy."

"That's what scares me. What if he's ready, Maisie's ready, but I'm not." Marnie picked at her PJs. "What if, like you said, I need to look back?"

A warm rush of happiness flooded Cordelia's chest. "I'm not telling you what to do. I was only suggesting you give Darius a chance. After all, you burned him, right when his career was taking off."

"Exactly. So, what if I turn away a stable guy because I'm busy chasing the past...a past that resents me?"

Cordelia stood and stretched. "I've told you a million times, Darius asks about you. That's not a guy who's resentful. That's a guy who misses you."

"Only because he doesn't know the truth."

"Don't get mad at me, and this is the last time I'll say this, you're as stubborn as a goat hanging on a ledge."

Marnie laughed, almost falling off her stool.

"Says the woman who's been dodging important conversations about her own future. Cordy, you've got a little secret right there," she patted Cordelia's belly, "and you're stubbornly hanging on for the perfect moment."

"I'm telling him tomorrow, not five years from now." Her eyes narrowed and she felt heat hitting her cheeks.

"Right, because magic happens on Christmas."

"No, but it does add a special flair to things."

"Magic." Marnie stood and mirrored Cordelia's stretches. "Listen, I know you've read way more Jane Austen tales than me, and believe love is out there for everyone."

"And it is." She twisted from side to side, releasing the tension in her stomach.

"I'm skeptical. For now, Richard's a nice guy, who's also a distraction from the reality that I have to restructure our lives again. That's enough for me to deal with, and you certainly don't have time, especially in seven to eight months. You need to focus on telling papa Brownell he's—."

"Got it." Cordelia scanned the room. "I swear I feel like someone's watching us."

"Oh god, do you think they have one of those paintings with the moving eyes?"

They studied the paintings and after a few seconds glanced at each other, shrugged, and giggled.

"Now I'm getting paranoid...I need sleep." Cordelia grabbed their mugs and placed them in the sink. "Guess Cassandra's staying out tonight." She double checked the burners, making sure everything was off. "I swear, there must be something in the water here."

"Maybe it enhances their telescopic abilities." She roared. "Get it? Telescopes?"

Cordelia pushed the stools under the island, shaking her head. "You're determined to make me think about Luke's...telescope." She put her arm around Marnie's shoulders. "Let's go to bed...and please, no more."

"I love it when you blush."

They headed for the hallway, with Marnie falling in line behind Cordelia. Their slippers shuffled across the corridor rug, and there was a noticable temperature drop from the kitchen, at least five degrees cooler. A groan came from above followed by water rushing through a pipe.

Cordelia whispered as they arrived at the foot of the stairs, "I'm glad you're here. I've missed you."

"Me too."

December 25th

The Scottish Highlands

Chapter Twenty-Two

5:oo AM

Royce loved Christmas morning. The world seemed to be wrapped in a special silence—a calm that brought dreams into reality.

Always the first to wake, he strolled into the kitchen, following an amber glow that reflected off the stove's copper hood. His slippers padded across the cold stone floor, a chill that matched the room's temperature. And hints of ginger and pine lingered in the air, like a warm blanket embracing the vast room.

Today's the day. A flash of excitement rose into his chest as he filled the kettle with water. The splashing sound reminded him of a few nights earlier, when a cloud of steam filled the bathroom and water tumbled off their bodies. Being with her freed him.

A sound shuffled in the far corner of the kitchen.

"Hello?" He turned off the water, placed the kettle onto the stove, and ignited the flame.

The sound stirred again. A deliberate rustle followed by faint moans.

"Mrs. MacLeod?" He whispered, walking toward the darkened boot room. "Who's here?" He flipped on the light and noticed two pairs of wet shoes. *Must be Marcus and Emma's.* Royce massaged his forehead, wondering where they would've gone so early. He turned off the light and returned to the kitchen.

A hard knock came from the pantry.

"Okay, who the bloody hell is in here?" Everything quieted. "Marcus?" Nothing. Even the kettle bubbled softly.

I wonder if Mr. Clark decided to join us for Christmas? The old butler had trained Mr. Smyth and stayed on, serving the family until his last day. Royce chuckled and filled two strainers with black tea. Water steamed as it poured across the dried leaves, releasing a creamy honey fragrance. A reminder of Sunday mornings with Cordelia, when neither felt pressured to rush off.

Whispers drifted from the pantry. A shush. A snicker.

I know that voice. Royce popped open a tin of cookies and arranged three chocolate-dipped shortbread and three ginger-molasses cookies onto a plate. He scanned the counter, searching for Mrs. MacLeod's sugar cookies. *Damn they're in the pantry.* He took two steps toward the pantry, stopped, and debated whether to disturb whoever and whatever was happening in there.

He took a chance.

The light switch just inside the door clicked when he pressed the button. "Just grabbing some biscuits." Royce darted his eyes toward the back of the pantry and discovered Cassandra and Luke looking at him like startled deer.

Cassandra stood pressed against the shelf of preserves with messy hair and flushed cheeks. Luke leaned in front of her. He smiled, a boyish grin. Their shirts dangled from potato bins.

"Royce." Cassandra's voice squealed as she smoothed her

192

hair with shaking hands. "We were just... Luke was showing me where the, the jam is stored."

"Right, jam." Luke nodded. "She wanted some Christmas toast with jam."

"Yes, she loves that jam." Royce winked at Cassandra and grabbed the sugar cookie container. "Mrs. MacLeod will be here soon, you might want to finish that...toast before—."

"Got it, darling." Cassandra waved him away.

Royce flipped off the light. "Oh, Luke..."

"Yes, sir?"

"I hear she likes her toast steaming—."

"Royce!" Cassandra's voice reverberated past him.

Luke's laugh followed.

Royce closed the door and returned to the island. Muffled laughter drifted out of the pantry and soon morphed into moans. Anxious to give them space, he placed the tea mugs and biscuits onto a tray and rushed out of the kitchen. He walked down the dimly lit hallway and mumbled his proposal speech to himself. As he reached the stairs he whispered, "Cordelia, will you marry me?"

"I was coming to look for you." Cordelia paused on the landing. Strands of hair draped her face as they tumbled out of her messy updo.

Bloody fucking hell. He grinned and froze.

"Who are you talking to?"

"No one. Myself." He adjusted the tray, making sure the mugs remained stable.

"What are you up to?"

"Nothing. It's a Christmas surprise."

"Oh, okay. Well, I didn't see anything." She dashed up three stairs, stopped, and said, "Merry Christmas, babe."

"Merry Christmas, love." He blew her a kiss and watched Cordelia hurry away. *Tonight it'll all make sense.*

8 :15 AM
Cordelia wrapped a warm, burgundy towel around herself, feeling a trail of water run down her back. The plush fabric provided a soothing barrier from the cool air that invaded the shower.

There was a heart drawn on the glass door with the words "I love you."

Royce stood in the bathroom, taking a last look in the foggy mirror. "I'm heading downstairs. Do you want Mrs. Smyth to bring you anything?"

She shook her head and stepped onto the bath rug. "No, I'm good. I'll be down soon." Cordelia leaned forward and puckered her lips.

He gave her a quick kiss and stepped into the doorway. "It's too hot in here." He turned to leave.

"Babe, save me a scone?" A tender sensation in her breasts caused her to flinch. "I'm starving."

His finger tapped on the door frame. "Is everything all right?"

"Yeah, yeah, just cold."

"Right. I'll add a log to the fire. Do you want a cranberry or apple spice scone?"

"Ooh...both."

"Both? Are you sure? You never eat two."

"Ummm," her mind raced. *Shit, what do I say?* Cordelia buried her face in the towel and squeezed water from her hair. "Well, it's Christmas, so why not."

"Very well, two scones waiting for you." He stepped closer, gave her another quick kiss, and said, "It's going to be a fabulous day. I promise."

A warm tingle rose from her belly and settled in her chest. "Yes, it is."

They held a gaze before Royce left the bathroom.

Moments later, she heard sounds of a wood sparking as it crackled in the fireplace. Cordelia swiped the mirror, exposing her reflection. She cupped her breasts and slid her hands onto her stomach, making a heart with her fingers. What used to be flat and toned had become slightly soft and poochy. *I'm not nauseous.* She stared at her belly. *I could eat a horse...I'm freaking hungry today.* A smile burst on her face. "I can actually eat breakfast. A real breakfast."

Cordelia massaged product into her hair, combed, and dried it, rushing as her stomach growled. Undecided on an updo, she hurried into the bedroom and dressed in a green cardigan with pearl buttons, black leggings, and the Murano glass necklace. She slipped on the gold bracelet Royce had given her, and reflected on the engraving *We met in Paris...* Her fingers traced the lettering and his words lingered in her memory, 'Our story, our beginning'.

She exhaled. Closed her eyes and envisioned their first meeting on Rue Hautefeuille. His smile. His voice. His kindness.

Her stomach growled—a rumbling noise that demanded attention. "Damn."

Cordelia raced back into the bathroom. Her toothbrush, moisturizer, and foundation stood next to one another, lined up and facing her like little toy soldiers. Hurried, she grabbed her toothbrush while reaching to borrow Royce's toothpaste. Just as she looked back, her foundation bottle toppled, spilling beige liquid across the white stone.

"No, no, no." With a handful of tissues, Cordelia wiped and dabbed up the mess. "Dammit." A quarter of the bottle remained. As she cleaned the spill, sweat beaded on her forehead. Suddenly, the bathroom had gone from steamy to oppressively hot. She needed air.

The bathroom window was next to the clawfoot bathtub. It had an old fashioned lock that looked as if it hadn't been opened in years. Cordelia stepped inside the tub, struggling to open the latch. "You've got to be kidding me." She tried again, grunting in hopes that it would help unlock the window. It didn't budge. More sweat beaded on her forehead.

After wiping her hands on more tissue, she removed her sweater, and attempted to open the window again. A wave of heat rolled through her body. Her stomach growled louder, demanding attention. *Alright, already.* She tugged harder. "Just open...please."

The latch screeched—metal against metal.

"Yes!"

Air rushed in. A welcomed relief of cold.

After the sweat dissipated, she climbed out of the tub and finished cleaning the makeup disaster. But soon, the heat fled out the window and a chill ran down her spine. She reached for her sweater, slipped it on, and realized there had been a smear of foundation on her hand. "Dammit, it's Christmas. It's not supposed to be like this."

Cordelia washed her hands, stripped off the sweater, and scurried into the bedroom where she selected a berry cashmere pullover. *Don't mess this one up.*

Ten minutes later, she'd brushed her teeth and applied makeup—without additional disasters. She dabbed on a nude-tone lipstick and did a final check in the bedroom full-length mirror. *Pregnant and stylish, who knew I could pull it off.* Her thick hair cascaded in waves, skimming the top of her breasts. She adjusted and tucked them into her bra, hoping it wouldn't be obvious that they'd grown a size practically overnight. *Well, maybe they'll just think it's the new sweater.*

The fireplace logs cracked and settled, sending sparks up the chimney. Outside the bathroom window, the wind howled, causing one pane to slam shut. "Oh, shit." Cordelia scooted across the carpet and shocked herself when she touched the window.

Out on the lawn, Maisie twirled in circles, catching snowflakes on her tongue. When she saw Cordelia, she stopped, waved, and ran back toward the house. The wind rustled through distant trees. There was a happiness in the air.

Today's the day Royce'll know. She stretched to see the loch barely in view and then closed the window. In the hallway, Emma's faint voice mumbled with the sound of baby talk, followed by a giggle.

We're ready.

Cordelia returned to the bedroom, grabbed her father's watch off the nightstand, and fastened it around her wrist. She double checked her handbag for Royce's baby gift, eager to finally reveal her secret. *I'm ready.*

"But first, I'm going to eat two scones, some eggs, sausages, and enjoy the hell out of my coffee."

8:30 AM
Alone in the library, Royce stared at the pages of a book on Scottish kings and read the same line multiple times. His thoughts drifted to the ring hidden in his drawer. Distant voices invaded the quiet—someone singing a Christmas carol in the kitchen. *Doesn't sound like Mrs. MacLeod.* He shrugged and settled into a woven club chair with large roll arms. He propped his feet onto the footstool and sent Cordelia a text.

In the library, waiting for you.

Seconds later she replied.

XOXO

As Royce re-read the page again, the animated, musical voices grew louder. *Who is that?*

The door clicked open and Richard, Maisie, and Marnie strolled in, unaware he was there. Marnie sang a bubbly song, tickling Maisie as they walked.

"No way," Richard said. "Clearly spaghetti is the superior pasta." As they entered from the alcove, he paused, "Sorry, mate. Are we disturbing you?"

"No, no. Just waiting on Cordelia." Royce set the book aside.

"Uncle Royce." Maisie launched into his lap. "Did you see, Santa came and left some toys." She plopped her head on his shoulder.

"I did. And it looks he left some chocolate in the stockings too." Royce smoothed the back of her red and green reindeer sweater.

"He did?" She looked back at Marnie who'd stopped singing. "You didn't tell me."

"Well you can't know everything." Marnie sat on the sofa beside Richard, leaving a narrow foot between them. "Maybe he wanted you to discover it."

Maisie frowned, looking at Royce. "Then how did you know?"

"Busted." Richard laughed.

"I admit, I looked." Royce playfully dropped his chin in shame. "Am I in trouble?"

Maisie tapped her chin, cutting her eyes away, contemplating the situation. "I guess not. But no more peeking." She shook her finger at him.

Royce held his hand up, "I promise."

"When's Cordelia coming down?" Marnie asked.

"Soon. She's still getting ready." Royce pushed his feet off the stool and adjusted Maisie in his lap.

"Is she okay? Something wrong?" There was an anxious tone in her voice.

"No. Should there be?"

"Oh, no, not at all. I just thought maybe there was...because she wasn't down yet." Marnie shifted closer to Richard. "I don't know why I asked that. Ignore me." She smoothed her hair, tucking it behind her ears, and exchanged a quick glance with Richard.

"Mummy, I'm hungry." Maisie sighed and groaned. "Can we eat now? My tummy's getting angry."

"Soon, baby. Mrs. Smyth said breakfast is in fifteen minutes." Marnie said.

"You could probably sweet-talk Mrs. MacLeod into giving you a piece of toast or bacon." Royce helped Maisie out of his lap.

"But I don't eat bacon." Maisie folded her arms across her chest. "I'm veg...veg-u-darian."

"Really? Vegetarian?" Royce's eyebrows rose. "Since when?"

"Since last night."

"And what made you decide, last night, to become a vegetarian?" Royce sat forward.

She pursed her lips together and stared at the ceiling. "Uncle Richard, why am I veg-u-darian?"

"Do you remember, you learned bacon comes from pigs?" Richard and Marnie shared a look—a smile.

They're enmeshing quickly. Royce glanced back at Maisie. "You learned this last night?"

"Uhhh, they're sweet." She flopped onto the sofa next to Richard. "And I don't want to eat somebody's friend."

"Well, toast it is then." He rested his hands on his knees. "With butter?"

"Yes! And jam." Her eyes lit up.

"A little jam." Marnie rested her hand on top of Richard's arm. "But don't get any on your sweater, please." She pulled her hand away when Maisie faced her.

"I promise." She jumped up and stood directly in front of Royce. Her small hands fidgeted with his fingers. "Do you think Mrs. MacLeod has blackberry jam? I love blackberries."

"I'm not sure, but there's a very well-stocked pantry with an entire shelf of jams." Royce held her hand between his, noticing the difference in their palm sizes.

"I've got to see this." She hurried toward the kitchen, struggling to open the weighted wood door that led down the back hallway. When Richard offered to help her, she insisted on doing it herself. A minute later, Maisie maneuvered it open and disappeared down the hall.

In his peripheral vision Royce caught Richard's fingers graze across Marnie's cheek. "Is there something in the Scottish air?"

Richard fumbled to respond. "Scottish air?"

"Yes, there seems to be a pattern here. Is it the air? The water?" Royce leaned back in his chair and checked his phone. *Where's Cordelia? She needs to see this.*

Richard adjusted his trousers, smoothing and picking at them. "We're all adults, mate, what are you suggesting?"

"Nothing. Other than it seems Scotland has brought out the romantic in everyone." He smiled and cut his eyes at Marnie. "He's a good guy, you made a nice choice."

Marnie blushed a deep shade of red and cleared her throat.

"Well, I...we just met. No one's suggesting we're walking down the aisle."

Richard cleared his throat. "Right. Speaking of happy couples, Marnie said Cassandra slipped out with Luke last night."

"She did more than that." Royce chuckled. "I found them in the pantry this morning. And they weren't looking for jam."

Richard roared with laughter. "Does he have any idea what he's gotten himself into?"

"At the moment, I'm not sure he cares."

"You guys—I shouldn't have told you." Marnie stood. "She seems happy. Isn't that what matters?"

Royce and Richard agreed, acknowledging they wanted nothing but the best for Cassandra and Luke.

"Trust me, Marnie, she deserves to be happy, but Cassandra will be a handful."

Marnie walked toward the door. "I'm going to check on Maisie." As she closed it behind herself, she said, "Don't tease her too much. It's Christmas, remember?"

Royce and Richard nodded and waited for her footsteps to fade before speaking.

Richard slid to the edge of the sofa. "Everything set for tonight?"

"It is. I'll pop into the cellar after lunch and pull a bottle of champagne for Mrs. Smyth. I might need your help in distracting Cordelia."

"Sure, sure. I've got your back."

"The biggest challenge is getting her there before she suspects anything." He paused, running a hand through his hair.

"You've covered it up this long, what's one more lie?"

"Right. Lies and secrets...I don't recommend it." He laughed. "That's why it has to be perfect."

"At least you already know what her answer." Richard patted Royce on the knee.

"Of course. After she gets over the shock that I kept something from her again."

"Cordelia's getting a holiday proposal in the Highlands underneath the stars, pretty sure she'll forgive you."

"I'm sure." Royce ran his hands over his legs. The dark jeans created resistance against his palms. His knee bobbed up and down. "Anyway, it'll be memorable."

Richard agreed and offered more encouragement, reminding Royce it wasn't about the details, but the relationship.

Agreeing and changing the subject, Royce asked about Marnie, hoping she wouldn't return before getting a clear answer.

Just as Richard was about to respond, the door opened and Cordelia entered. Her eyes sparkled when she smiled. Her voice sounded lively and eager for food. Her presence made his heart skip.

Tonight. Royce's eyes dropped to her hand. *It'll all change tonight.*

Chapter Twenty-Three

9:10 AM

The family gathered for gifts.

The drawing room's massive stone fireplace hissed with oak logs, filling the room with the scent of aged wood—an aroma that complemented the twelve-foot Christmas tree's pine fragrance. Red and green velvet stockings lined the front, each packed with surprises. Name cards sat in front of each stocking hanger, although it was obvious by the toys which were for Maisie and Ada Rose.

Glass ornaments on the tree reflected the firelight, sending rainbows of soft light around the room.

Cordelia settled onto the chestnut sofa, tucking her handbag beside her. She'd carried it to breakfast, guarding it, the fresh pregnancy test, and the engraved spoon with her life. She'd managed to keep the contents from spilling when Maisie raced around the breakfast table wishing everyone a Merry Christmas. And when Ada Rose toddled over to her, the Countess rescued the bag, keeping the contents safe. She'd made it to week nine and no one else needed to know, not yet.

Royce I have something to tell you. She rehearsed the line, practicing different tones and pitches.

"Well, then," the Countess said, taking two stockings from the mantel. "Shall we begin with the children?" She handed them to Emma and Marnie. "These are heavy. Santa and the elves have been busy."

Ada Rose grabbed for a stuffed animal that stuck out from the top. Marcus scooped her into his lap. "Nice try, monkey. We have to wait for Gran."

The Countess took her seat and smiled. "Go ahead, darling, what did Santa bring you?"

Ada Rose emptied her stocking in one pull, scrunching her face with determination. She squealed and babbled, showing Emma and Marcus her new toys, socks, and a pink silk hair bow. Emma videoed the unwrapping while Marcus helped Ada Rose explore the contents of her stocking.

Next, the Earl delivered a giant box to her, wrapped in blue and white penguin paper. On top was a giant silver bow that looked professionally made, unlike the ones Cordelia bought off the shelf.

Marcus and Ada Rose tore at the paper—her expression anxiously animated. Inside was a black wooden rocking horse with real horse hair for its mane and a leather seat. Marcus removed it from the box, placed Ada Rose on it, and gently tapped its nose. The horse tilted forward and back. Ada Rose's lip quivered. She reached out for him and burst into tears.

"Oh, baby, it's all right." Marcus lifted her off the horse and cuddled her in his arms. She reached for Emma, insisting she wanted 'Mumma'.

While everyone laughed, Cordelia felt warm tears moisten her eyes. She looked at the fire, hoping the flickering flames would stop the emotional reaction.

Marnie leaned close and whispered, "You okay?"

Cordelia nodded. "Yeah, I'm good. Did anyone see?"

"No. Coast is clear."

She forced a laugh. "Oh, that's so cute. What is it Maisie?" Cordelia dabbed the makeup under her left eye and felt Royce's body press against her right shoulder.

"It's paint! How did Santa know I liked to paint?" Maisie squealed.

"Santa knows everything." The Earl waved her over. "Can I see? What colors did he bring you?"

Cassandra stood behind the Earl and Countess, perched on the arm of a wing back chair, dividing her attention between gifts and the window. She brushed a red lipstick across her lips, pressed them together, and fluffed her hair.

"Cordelia, darling," the Countess said, her voice cutting through a symphony of ripping paper. "I believe this one's for you."

Royce retrieved the large cream shopping bag stuffed with sparkled tissue and tied with a green velvet ribbon. "This is from me."

"From you?" Cordelia accepted the package, feeling the weight and shape before upwrapping. "This wasn't in the car."

"You can't know everything."

"Clearly you plotted against me." She kissed him. "Thank you."

"Well, you don't know what it is, yet."

"No, but it's from you. I know I'll love it."

"Oh my god, you two are so sappy, it's sickening." Marnie elbowed Cordelia.

She removed a buttery Italian leather tote bag—cognac with polished gold hardware and a designer logo. "It's gorgeous." She ran her fingers over the leather. "I guess this means you're tired of my old one."

"The frayed one with a broken zipper? Aren't you?" He

smiled and his dimples appeared. "I was worried it would disintegrate before you bought a new one."

"It's not that bad."

Marnie barked with laughter. "I hear the handles had electrical tape on them."

"She didn't hear it from me." Royce said.

"I told her." Cassandra yelled from the window. "Face it, Cordelia, we all despised that bag."

"So, it was a conspiracy. I get it." She smelled the bag, enjoying the earthy scent of fresh leather. Cordelia kissed Royce. "Thank you. It's absolutely gorgeous, and too nice for someone who spills everything on just about every surface possible."

"Maybe your luck's changing." He said, running his hand down her back.

The Countess handed Royce a gift, the monogrammed tennis racquet bag from Cordelia. His initals were embossed in gold on the navy leather. His face lit up when he opened the box. "Looks like I'm not the only one who snuck their gift up here."

"I like having a few surprises too, you know." A warmth moved from her chest to belly. *I can't wait much longer.* She looked at her watch. *Nine forty-five. This needs to hurry up.*

The morning continued in a warm blur of rustling paper and delighted exclamations. The Earl received a leather-bound second edition of William Blake's poetry from Marcus and Emma. His *keen eye* appreciated the binding as much as the rarity.

Just as everyone thought all gifts had been opened, the Earl handed the Countess a small, narrow box.

"Thomas." She cracked the lid and peeked inside.

"Merry Christmas and happy anniversary, my love." He rested his hand on her knee.

She held up a gold necklace. A blue Faberge egg with a single diamond dangled from it. "It's lovely."

"Open it." The Countess popped the egg in half, revealing an enamel water lily set with another diamond. "I...Thomas, thank you." Her eyes met his and they held a long, silent gaze, as if they communicated telepathically.

A hush fell over the room.

Cordelia cut her eyes at Royce. *The timing couldn't get any better than this.* Their hands reached for each other. His touch tingled as he brushed her fingers.

"Well, it's been an exciting morning." The Countess watched Ada Rose climb into an empty box. "I believe Mrs. Smyth has morning refreshments set up in the family room. And you all know where the Scotch and wine are located."

One-by-one the drawing room emptied, leaving Cordelia and Royce with Marcus and Ada Rose. Excitement fluttered in her chest. "Hey, babe, can we pop into the library for a minute? There's something—."

Ada Rose shrilled, the sound cut like a chainsaw buzzing through wood. Sitting on the floor next to two cardboard boxes, tears flowed onto her pink cheeks. Marcus raced to her.

Emma rushed in."What's wrong?"

"Nothing, she's only offended." Marcus rocked Ada Rose. "Apparently our daughter has no patience for imperfections."

Emma looked down at the partial collapsed boxes.

"Her engineering pride took a hit." Marcus smirked. "Do you want mummy?" The edges of his tone softened.

Ada Rose looked around the room and reached for Cordelia.

"Me?" She zipped her bag closed. "You want me?"

The little girl nodded, stretched toward Cordelia, and babbled.

"Well, darling, it looks like you're on niece duty." Royce rested his arm around her waist.

Her moment gone.

Ada Rose clung to Cordelia's neck as they walked into the dining room. Mrs. Smyth served tea and coffee, while encouraging them to enjoy warm scones, bridies, and Ecclefechan butter tarts.

"Mrs. MacLeod has outdone herself this year." The Earl placed one of each on his plate.

The Countess rested her hand on the small of his back. "Dear, this is meant to be a snack, not a meal."

"Darling, it's Christmas. We can't let all of her effort go to waste." He took a bite of the butter tart, expressing satisfaction at the flavors.

Cordelia situated Ada Rose into her high chair, broke a scone into manageable pieces, and tasted a butter tart. *Wow, I've got to get her recipe.* A note of caramel rested on her tongue. For the first time in weeks, sugar tasted edible and didn't send her racing for the bathroom. She nibbled on the tart and shared her last bite with Ada Rose.

Across the room, Royce, Marcus, and Richard talked— conspirators over something. Huddled together, they appeared deep in serious conversation. Emma joined them, sipping her tea and occasionally nodding as she agreed with whatever Marcus suggested. Royce's eyes darted around the room. *What are you up to?* Ada Rose called for Emma, pulling her away from their schemes.

Marnie stepped in front of Cordelia, blocking Royce from her view. "Did you tell him?"

"I was trying, but we got interrupted. And I can't keep this to myself much longer."

"You waited...two, three weeks, what's a few more hours?"

"That's not the point. I'd planned to tell him this morning, between gifts and lunch." Cordelia gulped her tea that had cooled into a tepid, slightly floral liquid. "I wanted it to feel Christmassy, not an afterthought."

Marnie's subdued laughter caught Maisie's attention. "Welcome to reality where things don't always go as planned."

"Ha-ha, Miss Wisdom." She scanned the room for Royce, noticing he'd disappeared. "Wait. Where'd he go? I'll be back." Cordelia handed her cup to Marnie and hurried off. *My bag.* She stopped in the doorway, remembering she'd left in the drawing room. *Dammit. He's probably there anyway.*

Cordelia found Royce in the hallway near the library, leaning against the wall and on the phone. He listened, unaware she'd walked up behind him.

"Yes. Three o'clock should be fine...The generator—." He whipped around like an animal caught in a trap. "Right." His smile appeared anxious. He nodded, told the person he needed to go, and thanked them for helping out.

"Everything alright?" Cordelia's eyes followed his phone as he slipped it into his back pocket.

"Yes, yes...of course." He kissed the corner of her mouth. "Are you having a good time?"

She found the question odd—something he'd never asked before. "Yes. And you?"

"Definitely. It's hectic, but that's how the holidays typically go." His hands rested on her hips.

"Sure." She studied his expression, his frozen smile. "I wanted to talk to you—."

"There you are, Pop wants to give a toast before round two of gifts." Marcus gestured and knocked on the wood paneling.

"Round two? There's two rounds of gifts?" Cordelia's voice pitched higher. "I don't remember that many gifts last Christmas."

Royce ran his fingers across her lower back. "You never know with Mum and Pop. Sometimes they like to keep things dramatic."

"Wasn't the necklace dramatic enough?"

He chuckled. "Probably. This time it might be sheets and towels or holidays at the beach. We never know."

"Oh...okay."

His hand pressed against her hip, guiding her back into the family room. "Was there something you wanted to say?"

"It can wait."

"Are you sure?" His hand cupped her face. A hint of vanilla lingered on his skin.

"Completely." Cordelia smiled, faking a casual voice, despite the disappointment that knotted in her stomach. "I just wanted to say I'm happy to be here."

They kissed and ignored Marcus calling for them in the background.

Second attempt vanished.

Two hours later, the afternoon emerged like a tennis match, volleying between rapid and slow moments. Time seemed to keep opportunities just out of her reach. Anxiousness loomed and she wondered why she'd insisted on Christmas Day. *I should've told him already...like in London, or out by the loch. No more blowing chances.* She imagined grabbing his hand and blurting the news out—right there in the family room as everyone enjoyed afternoon tea.

Next to her, Royce's fingers rapped on his knee. In less than five minutes he checked his watch and at one point he almost spilt his tea.

What's up with him?

During the second round of gifts, that turned out to be as Royce suggested, Cordelia noticed he and his father exchanged coded messages. At one point, the Earl had tapped his watch, and motioned for them to meet by the main door. They spoke, nodded, and returned to their seats.

"Is there something wrong?" Cordelia said.

"No, no. Pop's giving the staff tomorrow off and he wanted to know our plans." He fumbled over his words. Rare for Royce. His knee bobbed up and down.

"Are you sure that's it? You seem really stressed." She offered a gentle rub on his back.

"That's it." There was a hesitation in his voice, as if he stopped himself from saying more. "I'll be right back. Popping into the loo." He flashed a dimpled smile.

"Well, I..." She watched him walk away. *What the hell is going on with him?*

Royce left through the back door, heading into the kitchen, boot room, and cellar.

Cordelia excused herself and followed, stopping long enough to grab her handbag. She raced to catch up and caught sight of him entering the wine cellar, not the bathroom. *Even better.* When she opened the stairwell door, a damp, earthy aroma made her think twice about going into the cellar. *Now's my chance.* She inhaled, catching a whiff of rosemary and thyme, *That smells so good*, and then stepped inside, closing the door behind her. As she descended the stone stairs, the lighting diffused into a dim glow.

Royce stood in the middle of wooden racks filled with wine bottles. At the far end, five old-fashioned barrels were stacked in a pyramid, infusing the space with a hint of oak.

"Interesting bathroom choice." Cordelia leaned against a pillar at the foot of the stairs.

He startled, whipping around. "Cordelia, darling."

The cold stone seeped through her sweater, sending a chill down her spine.

"Right, well...Pop asked me to select the champagne for

toasts." His voice cracked. He cleared his throat and smoothed the front of his sweater.

"Okay. Now be honest, what's really going on? You've been distracted and jumpy for hours."

"No I haven't." He death-gripped a bottle of Dom Pérignon.

"Promise? You're not hiding something from me?"

"No, no." He took three steps closer. "Babe, I promise nothing is wrong." He set the bottle onto a table and moved closer, pulling her into his arms. "Have you visited Fortuna today? The staff have fallen in love with her."

"I know, when I told them she was going home with us, Mrs. MacLeod looked at me like I was stealing her child."

"Sounds like our baby's a hit."

Cordelia swallowed hard, almost choking as she laughed to hide her nerves. "Our baby?" She gripped her bag.

"Mmhmm." His hands moved across her body. "One of many." His warm lips softened against her skin.

"Many? Do you have an exact number in mind?"

"Hadn't given it much thought. Have you?" His breath brushed past her ear.

An electric charge coursed through her body. "Ummm, not really but I'd never define it as many." Cordelia leaned back, "I wanted to talk to you about something."

"Right, upstairs in the hallway. Is something troubling you?"

"No. Everything's great. I...I just wanted to tell you—."

"Is someone down here?" Mr. Smyth's voice echoed. Footsteps tapped against the stone.

Interrupted, again. Cordelia watched him descend the last two steps.

Third chance stolen.

Chapter Twenty-Four

2:oo PM

Christmas dinner at the lodge had three requirements: informal attire, formal place settings, and an abundance of laughter.

The long mahogany table shined as silver flatware flanked white porcelain plates, while greenery and fresh flowers surrounded small candelabras. Firewood crackled in the marble fireplace, warming the room against the outside chill. Christmas jazz played softly in the background, and the room smelled of herbs and spices. Outside the row of windows, a blanket of white covered the ground.

Royce pulled Cordelia's chair out, noticing she tucked her handbag under the table. "You're very attached to that today."

"Not any different than you were to your phone." She positioned it between her feet.

"Ouch." He sat beside her, shifting his chair to the table. "How about a walk after dinner, just the two of us—no phone, no bag."

"I'd love that." Her hand rested on his, intertwining their fingers together.

Marnie took the seat beside Cordelia. "Sit there, baby." She pulled the chair out for Maisie. "And don't worry, Miss Cassandra can still hear you from over there."

"Of course, darling," Cassandra unfolded her napkin. "Now we can see each other." She placed it across her lap and engaged Cordelia in conversation.

Royce watched them. The differences in the way they touched their hair—how their hands animated when they talked. Cordelia had been tense after gifts, hugging her bag as if she carried precious jewels in it. *Unusual. She's not on her cycle.* She laughed at something Cassandra said, and her fingers massaged an empty wine glass. *She seems normal. Maybe she really is fine.* Cordelia tucked hair behind her ear, letting a strand fall on her face. He felt an urge to touch her cheek. To kiss her. To feel her breath on his skin.

"May I have everyone's attention, please?" His father stood at the head of the table, raising his wine glass to everyone. "Before we begin, I'd like to thank everyone for being here, and to propose a toast." There was an old world pretense in his voice, a tone Royce had come to appreciate in the last year.

The room quieted. Mr. and Mrs. Smyth paused their activities and stood beside a sideboard that had platters of food waiting to be served.

"Thirty years ago, Alia and I decided we would spend Christmas here with the boys, who at the time were more interested in destroying wrapping paper than appreciating family traditions."

Marcus rolled his eyes and smirked at Royce.

"We wanted to create something meaningful. Alia and I wanted you boys to have valuable memories of this home. At the time, we wondered if we were doing anything correctly, but clearly you two have proven that we did." His eyes drifted from

Royce to Marcus to Emma and Cordelia. Each gaze expressed a warm vulnerability.

He continued, "This year I look around this table and see family. Not just my immediate family, but the family we've chosen and the family that our sons have chosen. Marnie and Maisie, you've brought fresh laughter to these old walls. And Richard, you my son, are proof that true friendship is rare and its own form of family."

Richard's moist eyes smiled. Royce remembered their first day at university when they bumped into each other on the dorm stairs and sent papers to flying.

"Cassandra, my dear, I have known you since the day you were born. You are spirited and infectious. You open hearts, after you've infuriated the hell out of them."

She laughed, brushing a tear from her eye.

"But you are a gift and the apple of your father's eye." His eyes rested on Marcus and Emma. "Thank you for the gift of Ada Rose, and teaching us how younger generations think, because without you two, I'm afraid Alia and I would never understand pop music."

Royce felt a lump in his throat as his father's gaze landed on him. His knee bobbed up and down, halted by Cordelia's gentle touch.

"To you, Royce, words do not express how you have challenged and transformed me." A pool sat at the rim of his eyes ready to fall, but he blinked and wiped it away. "I'm proud of you. And look at this beautiful woman beside you. Cordelia, thank you for providing us with many extra pounds of weight we struggle to lose all year long."

Everyone laughed, even Mr. Smyth let out a chuckle.

"Family isn't just blood," he softened his voice. "You all are proof, it's choice and commitment, even when it's difficult. So here's to the family that our sons have built, that we've built together, and to the future that awaits us all."

"Yes, we are grateful each of you are here for Christmas." The Countess' brown eyes sparkled—so graceful, so kind.

Royce's heart swelled. "To the future...and family." He raised his glass to Cordelia.

Her water glass clinked with his champagne flute as the candlelight cast an angelic glow on her skin. "That was beautiful."

"He has his moments."

"I'll say. I even saw Mrs. Smyth crying."

Maisie tugged on their sweaters, insisting on tapping their glasses.

Dinner unfolded with tandoori turkey, gravy, peas, potatoes, and a spicy, aromatic rice. Ada Rose valiantly attempted to eat her peas, but soon realized they made better projectiles at Poppa. Conversations flowed as different ones held the center of attention. Richard debated current tax policies with the Earl, proving family can be on the opposite side of political houses and still find common ground.

Cordelia and Marnie laughed their way through the retelling of a culinary school mishap that involved meringue, a torch, and an apron.

When the laughter faded Mrs. MacLeod brought out the dessert—a flavorful British-Indian chocolate butter cake trifle. It had layers of rose water-brandy cream sauce, candied fruit, and to top it off a cardamom whipped cream.

As they finished off with tea, Royce's mum caught his eye. She tilted her head and raised an eyebrow. Her gestures conveyed pages more than simple words ever suggested.

Understood. The sound of his exhale expressed relief, satisfaction.

"Everything alright?" Cordelia said, touching his leg.

"Just full from the meal."

"Oh, I know. That dessert was decadent."

Royce caressed the top of her hand, a delicate touch that tingled under his fingers. "Ready for that walk soon." He noticed the time. 3:15 PM.

"Definitely." She leaned down for her handbag.

"No bags, no phones, remember?"

"Well, I'm not leaving it under the table." She stood, clutching her bag. "I'll set it in the den. But first I need to step into the restroom."

"Sure. We should probably leave now though, before dusk."

"Okay. Well, I'm ready." Cordelia thanked the Earl and Countess, who encouraged them to hurry and catch the setting sunlight.

She turned the doorknob, paused, and said, "I really need to talk to you about something first."

"Let's talk on the walk." Other than the firewood popping, the room held its breath. "Away from listening ears."

Cordelia studied his face for what felt like a full minute. "Right. Sure."

They headed for the boot room, stopping for Cordelia to use the loo. As agreed, they left their items in the family den, tucked onto a bookshelf. An electric charge raced through his body. *This is it. In less than an hour, we'll be engaged.* He felt for the ring that had been in his pocket throughout dinner. *I hope she's genuinely surprised.*

3:30 PM

Royce's breath hit the crisp late-afternoon air, creating puffs of vapor that dissipated into crystalline fog. He adjusted his wool cap and leather gloves. He paced.

Fresh snow dusted the trail, but Royce knew the path, the slow route to the dome. *Left, right, around the bend, and up along the loch.* The sun shimmered through clouds and hovered above the mountains, giving the sky a plum-grey cast. He checked the inside pocket of his coat. *Ring, speech, pounding heart...definitely.*

Cordelia emerged from the house bundled in layers. Her pink knitted cap and matching gloves enhanced her rosy cheeks, which highlighted her deep green eyes. She zipped up her waterproof jacket and smiled—a vision that still made his heart skip. "Okay, I'm ready." She patted her coat and clapped her hands together.

So am I. The word "ready" never sounded so deep. In seconds it became a word that represented the future, their life, poised to merge the best and worst of them together.

"I thought we might walk toward the loch and work off some of that Christmas dinner." His pulse raced as he pointed toward the far western section of the forest.

"That works." She took his hand and followed his lead. Their boots crunched against the icy patches of snow and created a melodic sound filled with grit, taps, and splats.

The path curved left, where ancient trees rose like a cathedral of interlaced branches that formed intricate patterns. Inside the forest, the bare, moist earth offered a mossy scent that complemented the smell of pine. The soft dirt muffled their footsteps, and nature came alive as winter birds called out in the distance and a nearby water source gurgled over stones.

Ten minutes later, they came to an intersection in the trail. Three paths branched away from each other. Royce stood with his back to the right trail, knowing it would take them directly to the dome. He hoped to distract Cordelia from it.

"Which way?" She rubbed her hands together and bounced on her toes.

"Are you cold?"

"A little, but I'm okay."

Royce crossed his arms and studied the other two paths. "I'm not sure. My guess is that we head that direction, based on the light. But I can't say for certain."

"Seriously?" Her eyebrows lifted. "You spent every childhood summer here, but you don't know which path?" Her tone teased.

"It's been a long time—it's been a while since I ventured out this direction." He tucked his hands into his coat pockets, knowing he could navigate the woods blindfolded. He remembered every cluster of trees and boulders in the forest, even if the undergrowth had changed.

"All right, well..." She looked at each path, "what about this one." She pointed to the trail behind him.

"No. It'll take us back to the house."

"Are you sure? This is the one we were just on."

"Right, but they both lead that direction."

Cordelia shrugged. "Then what about this one?" She gestured to her left.

"If I remember correctly, we need to take that trail." Royce pointed to the far path behind Cordelia.

"Sounds good to me, as long as we don't end up lost in the dark, with no phones." She pressed her chest against his, "Remember, we have no way of contacting anyone if we get lost."

Royce wrapped his arms around her, keeping his left chest pocket from pressing against her. "I know. You're not going to let me forget it, are you?"

"No. I don't want to freeze to death out here."

He laughed, kissed her, and said, "We won't. I promise." He took her hand and they ventured off on the trail opposite from the dome.

Another ten minutes passed and the path veered right and wrapped around a dense patch of trees. Rays of soft golden light streaked through, making the dust particles shimmer like Christmas lights. Around them, the forest seemed to breathe and creak under the soft wind. Their shadows stretched across the path. Sunset had begun.

Royce paused and checked his watch. *Time to end this wandering.* All they needed to do was continue around the bend, but he wanted to play with her a bit longer. "Hmmm, I wonder..."

"We're lost aren't we?"

"No, not at all."

Cordelia pulled off a glove and checked her watch. "I think we should retrace our steps." Her fingers were pinkish and cold.

"Come here." Royce sandwiched her hands between his and blew on them. "You're freezing."

"Well, not yet, but if we're stuck out here then, yeah, I will be."

Maybe this wasn't the best plan. He blew on her fingertips. "I'm sorry, love, I should've kept us on the shorter trail."

"It's fine. But can we just go back the way we came? I...I need to talk to you and at this point I'd rather do it inside, by a fireplace, even if everyone's listening."

"I have a better idea. Come with me." Royce turned to continue around the bend.

"This way? Isn't that taking us away from the house?"

"Actually, yes and no."

"What do you mean, yes and no? Are you saying, you know where we are?" She halted, yanking his arm backwards.

"Ummm," he turned to face her. "Yes, I know where we are, and yes, the trail leads back to the house. But no, it doesn't go there directly."

"Okay. So, this has been a wild goose chase?" She dropped his hand, rubbing her palms together.

"Not exactly. More like an adventure to—."

"To where? Hell? A Frozen hell?"

He chuckled.

"It's not funny, Royce." She giggled despite her frustrated tone.

"I know it's not. Just trust me."

"I have been and look what it's gotten me, frozen fingers. Not to mention the fact that I can't feel my ass."

Royce burst into laughter. "I'm sorry, I never intended—just come with me. I promise this will all make sense shortly." He kissed her cheek, pausing to see if she responded. He moved closer to her lips and kissed again.

"How long is shortly?"

"Two minutes." His lips rested on hers. "One minute. I swear."

She studied his eyes. "Fine. I hope whatever you're up to is worth it."

"It is." Royce reached for her hand. "Come on, let's get you out of the cold."

"That's the first thing you've said that makes sense." Her fingers tightened around his, signaling she trusted him.

Through the trees, a golden glow became visible. Warm. Inviting. Magical.

"Hey, I see light. Are we near the house?" Her tone shifted from frustration to curiosity.

Royce's heart skipped. *This is it*. Months of planning culminated into this one moment. "Not yet."

"But what is that? How come we haven't ever been down here before?"

Royce remained silent. Their footsteps padded across the soft dirt trail, occasionally crunching on a fallen leaf. He resisted using the flashlight in his pocket, forcing their eyes to adjust to the descending darkness. A moment later, they emerged at the edge of the clearing that looked like a romantic winter setting. *Just as I imagined.* The path opened up, lit with soft lights that guided their eyes directly to the dome.

Strung throughout the trees were hundreds of fairy lights with an unlit firepit and bench positioned in front.

The Hypedome glowed against the darkening sky, its glass walls reflecting the last rays of sunset. Warm light spilled from within it, creating geometric patterns of amber. Smooth jazz music played inside with the soulful sound of a saxophone echoing across the clearing.

"Oh, my god." Cordelia stopped. "What...it's beautiful." When she glanced at him the light hit her face, revealing eyes of wonder. "What is this?"

"Our destination."

Chapter Twenty-Five

4:oo PM

The dome looked like a fairy palace hidden in a magical forest with pools of golden light. One step inside the clearing and Cordelia felt as if she'd walked into a romantic world of possibilities. Sparkling lights reflected off the glass structure, giving the illusion that hundreds of fireflies floated overhead. High above, the first stars appeared as clouds parted on cue.

Prismatic patterns dotted the forest floor, illuminated by candles inside the dome. "Is this real?" Cordelia stepped inside the circular space as Royce lit the custom firepit.

"Merry Christmas, darling." The wood sparked and snapped, coming to life in a fountain of flames.

"How did you—." She did a full circle, taking everything in. "Was this always here?"

Royce stood beside her and looked up at the stars. The fire hissed and cast light onto his face. "No." A look of anticipation emerged in his eyes.

"You did this for us?"

"For you." He removed his cap, running his fingers through

his dark waves. "Remember the restaurant in Bath? The one with these igloos?"

"Oh my god, yes." She remembered the candlelit table, the open sky, and faux fur blankets. She remembered the way he looked at her across the table that night, like she was the only person in the world—the only thought on his mind. "Wow. Well, you topped that one."

Royce took her hand. "Come inside."

She followed, unzipping her jacket and kicking off her boots as soon as she stepped inside. Every detail defined the word romance. At least twenty battery-powered candles flickered throughout the space and strung lights hung above, as if he'd captured the stars.

To her left, several dozen red roses, wrapped in brown paper lay on a table beside a wine bucket with champagne. *The champagne from earlier.* And next to it were two cut crystal glasses. To her right, two leather chairs and a small table had been arranged with a charcuterie board. *Every detail...* On the far section of the dome, sheer drapes hung and surrounded a mountain of soft blankets and plush cushions. She counted twenty-five pillows of varying sizes. And tucked in the corner, a small heater pumped warm air inside. Outside, a quiet generator hummed.

Cordelia's chest swelled with emotions. Her eyes moistened. "You did all of this for me?" The thoughtfulness, the mood. It felt as if they'd gone full circle from the Paris bistro where they shared their first glass of wine together to spending Christmas in the Highlands with magical surprises.

"Yes." He took her coat, hanging both of theirs on the back of a chair. "Cordelia..." With a remote, Royce dimmed the hanging lights. "There's something I want to say." He looked at her as if she were a precious diamond, an irreplaceable jewel.

Her breath caught. "I need to tell you something, too."

Royce stepped closer and held her hands. His thumbs traced soft circles onto her palms. "First let me say, meeting you on Rue Hautefeuille not only changed my life, it changed how I viewed love. I thought it was about loyalty, but with you, it's a haven."

Paris. That embarrassing moment when she cried thanks to a cloud of flying dirt in the eyes. "And you offered me your handkerchief." She squeezed his hands.

"What else am I going to do when I see a woman in distress." He laughed, deep but endearing.

"Always the charmer." She felt tears form pools of water, desperate to break free from her lashes.

"It led me to you, and loving you is the most passionate thing I've done." His moist eyes reddened. "Do you remember the night we played ping pong in Paris?"

"Yes. I won."

He burst into laughter, "You did. You were merciless." Royce's hands glided up her arms and down her back, pulling her closer. "I was trying to impress you, but it was clear you didn't care about impressions." The candles added an extra sparkle as he studied her face. "You laughed—you made me laugh and I realized I'd never met anyone so genuine. You were pure joy."

"Oh, I did dominate the game, didn't I?"

He nodded. "You're competitive, and I value that, but only if I'm on your team...not your competitor."

Cordelia flopped her head forward and thought she could hear Royce's heartbeat. "Sorry. It gets the best of me."

"Promise you'll never change."

She nodded, locking eyes with him and felt like her insides were a ball of energy about to go nuclear.

"Ms. Dyer, you showed me that if I wanted to love you, I had to be vulnerable."

"I think we've both learned that lesson." Venice drifted into her thoughts, how her stubbornness and fear almost cost them everything.

He cleared his throat. "I fell in love with you in Paris, and I've never stopped."

A tear slipped down her cheek as she listened. *Is this...Is he?* Cordelia touched his face, feeling him lean into her palm. She held her breath.

"From your messy morning hair in that wild topknot to your late night baking sessions, which are harder to sleep through than a bath."

She laughed through her tears. "Please don't make me ugly cry." If she'd ever questioned his feelings, the doubt had disappeared.

"You could never be ugly."

"That's a lot of pressure." She laughed.

"Cordelia, I want to spend my life with you." Each word rolled from his lips and each held a depth she'd never heard before—from anyone. "I want to spend my life being yours, unguardedly, yours."

Oh my god, her heart hammered against her ribs. *This is real...and I have smeared mascara.*

Royce released her hand and lowered to one knee.

Her breath escaped.

"Cordelia Dyer," his wide eyes full of love and hope stared up at her, "will you marry me?"

He reached into his trouser pocket and revealed a small velvet box. When he opened it, the ring caught the light and cast brilliant blue rays onto his face.

She gasped and nodded. In the box was an art deco sapphire flanked by diamonds with more cascading down the sides of the platinum band. She gripped her glass necklace. "Oh my god, Royce."

"Is that a yes?"

"Of course. Yes, yes, I will." She wiped her tears with the back of her hand. "I love you." Cordelia laughed as she thought about the timing—how two secrets collided in one night. "I love you, Royce Brownell." Her words tumbled out barely above a whisper.

He jumped up and slid the ring on her finger. His hand shook. "This was my grandmother's. My grandfather had it designed for her. And now it's yours. It's a reflection of them and us." His smile could've lit up the forest as he kissed her hand. "It represents how much I love you."

"I, I...can't believe this is real, that you proposed." She stared at the heirloom, a gift that represented Royce's foundation as much as it did their future. "It's incredible."

He pulled her close. "You're stuck with me now, Ms. Dyer." His fingers mapped her face with a light touch. "Or should I say, Mrs. Dyer-Brownell?"

The linger of his lips on hers reminded Cordelia of the masquerade ball, when they held each other in delicate reverence—when his touch felt urgent and fragile like the first note of a waltz. *This...this happened.* She felt every nuance of the kiss, sliding her hands across his chest. His heart pounded as hard as hers. A tear tumbled onto her face. "Royce..."

Pools of elation dripped from his eyes. He wiped them dry. "Not changing your mind are you?"

"No. I think I like this version of Lord Brownell too much."

"Did you suspect? Even a little?"

"I swear I was clueless." She looked at the ring. "When did you—how did you have time to plan this?"

"I've been planning it since Venice." He scanned the dome. "I always loved you. But after Venice, I knew I never wanted to experience life without you." There was an unguarded, raw tone as his eyes dropped back onto her.

"You're my Paris, my Loch Ness monster, my home—Cordelia Anne Dyer, you're everything I never knew to ask for."

"Speaking of home," Her fingers traced his lips. "There's something I need to tell you."

4:35 PM
Outside the dome, the strung fairy lights reflected in Cordelia's eyes, making them shine like the stars high above the forest. The cold air pressed against the glass walls, forming lacy patterns of frost. The generator hummed, a rhythmic sound that synced with her heartbeat.

A single tear trickled down her cheek. "There's something I need to tell you." The warmth of her body pressed against him, her breath brushing past his face. Her hand rested on his chest. "Something I've been trying to tell you all day."

"What is it?"

Her parted lips, moist and pink, paused. She smiled, "I'm pregnant."

"You're..."

"I'm pregnant—about nine weeks."

"How?" The word tumbled out as his mind calculated the timing. *Illogical question*. Based on his estimates it would've happened during their weekend trip to Brighton.

"Well, it's called sex, when we take—." She smirked.

"Cheeky. Yes, I understand the mechanics." His heart thumped against the palm of her hand. "What about your diaphragm?"

"I guess your little guys were determined."

A burst of laughter shot out. "When? How long have you known?"

"About ten days. I took the test three times and they've all been positive. Plus, the—."

"The no alcohol, being sick…and all the crying."

"I haven't cried that much." Her tight lipped expression indicated stubborness.

"You cried during the bonfire, opening gifts, and when Ada Rose threw peas at Pop. You've been crying."

Her eyes dashed side-to-side. "Oh my god, I have bawled a lot." Her shoulders drooped and shrugged. "Well, then I guess you better get used to it." A sparkle of happiness washed over her eyes. "We both do."

"I'll keep plenty of handkerchiefs lying around for you."

Her lips communicated eagerness and uncertainty when she kissed him and rested her head on his shoulder. "Are you happy? Like honestly happy?"

Royce cupped her face, insisting their eyes meet. "Cordelia, to say I'm chuffed is an understatement."

"Chuffed."

"Over the moon chuffed." His hand moved across her body and stopped on her flat stomach. "We're going to be parents."

"I know. That's our little raspberry." She held a wadded navy cloth. "I'd planned a big reveal—I wanted it to be memorable—but I only brought this."

His hand shifted under the weighted velvet.

"I also have the first pregnancy test, and the one I took this morning, in my bag."

"That's why you've been clinging to it. I thought you were becoming bloody paranoid."

She bounced on her toes. "Open it."

He pulled back the corners, running his fingers over the tiny engraved spoon. *You're going to be a dad.* He read the words three times. "You put today's date?"

"Right, so you never forget the day I told you."

"Do you honestly believe I'll ever forget this day?" His throat tightened, an overwhelming emotion swelled in his chest.

"Well, no. I mean, it turned out to be pretty monumental." The sound of her giggle seemed layered with varied emotions.

Royce stared at the spoon. A small object that represented their future—their life together, both extraordinary and mundane captured and expressed in a spoon and ring. When he looked up at her, his eyes moistened. "It's perfect. It's all perfect."

"And I have a journal that I'd planned to give you."

"Let me guess, it's in your bag?"

Her arms wrapped around his neck. "Of course. I bought it the day I found out, and every day I've written notes to you. I wanted you to have something to look back at and add to."

"Thank you." The warmth of his fingers cooled against the spoon.

They kissed and tenderness faded into passion—deep desire that transcended words. In some ways, it felt like lust, but craving her touch represented only a portion of his feelings. Being with her felt like finding something he'd lost before he ever had it, something vital and irreplaceable. She was the tide, and he was finally home.

"I love you." Royce murmured in her ear. He set the spoon aside, letting his eyes follow his fingers as he traced the edges of her arms and hips. "More than those three words encompass."

"Then show me," she whispered.

He carried her to the nest of blankets, pretended to almost drop her, and then lowered her beside the pillows. The fairy lights haloed her in golden light. *She's pregnant.* Royce squatted and held her gaze. A few hours earlier they'd been just Royce and Cordelia, together but separate. In a matter of hours, they'd committed to the future and a family. His breath caught in his chest.

She reached up, touched his lips, and never broke eye contact. Her eyes were pools of wonder. "Big changes ahead." A smile tugged at her mouth.

"Very." Royce crawled on top of her. "But the best."

A slow sensation of her tongue teasing his lips drew him closer.

Minutes later, the winter wind whispered against the dome's glass walls, causing the fairy lights to flicker and briefly interrupt their simmering passion.

Chapter Twenty-Six

5:oo PM

Their kiss had barely intensified when the fairy lights outside the dome flickered again, causing Royce to glance at the door.

"You don't think anyone's out there, do you?" Cordelia stretched to peer through the glass wall.

"No, family knows to give us our privacy. I'm sure it's only the wind." He threw back the blanket. "I'll dim the lights, if that makes you more comfortable." Royce jumped up.

"It can wait." His arm slid from her grip.

"It won't take long."

Within seconds he transformed the ambiance from a dreamy romantic setting to sensual and intimate. Between the subtle orange glow from the firepit outside and the flameless candles that encircled their makeshift bed Cordelia felt as if she rested in the middle of a rare flower that illuminated a fairy forest.

Royce crawled on top, and cautiously settled his weight on her. "I'm not hurting you, am I?"

"No." His skin had the lingering taste of vanilla and pepper from his cologne.

"Are you cold?" Royce's fingers found the hem of her sweater and grazed against her bare skin as he pushed the fabric upward.

"Not at all." The cool air settled onto her stomach, and contrasted the heat radiating from Royce's body.

The warmth of his touch brushed over her tender breasts and down the side of her ribs. Her lips drifted from his mouth to his neck, driving energy to her hips. She pulled her sweater off and tossed it aside, losing it among the nest of blankets. In one motion, Royce removed his sweater, revealing the body her hands had traced hundreds of times, but Cordelia never grew tired of rediscovering him. The candlelight cast shadows across his lean stomach. She pulled him closer and mapped his chest and the ridges of his abdomen.

The same touch, but new meaning. *Pregnant. Engaged. Safe.* Her hand moved lower, desiring what remained hidden.

Royce's mouth found hers again. His control frayed and slipped into urgency—the taste of him shifted from tenderness to raw need. "You're beautiful," he said breathing against her skin, his voice rough with longing. He tossed her bra aside and cupped her breast, gently holding and licking her. "You'll always be beautiful to me."

A dam of energy released as his tongue moved across her breast. She moaned and mumbled, "Come here." Cordelia wrapped her legs around his hips, forcing their mouths to reconnect. Her hands roamed his broad back, noticing the dips and valleys and feeling the way his muscles shifted beneath her touch. "I love you, Royce. More than I ever thought possible."

He paused, looked at her, and tucked his hand under her hips. "I love you." The depth of his kiss consumed her. "More than you know."

Piece by piece their clothes disappeared, tossed into the pillows that formed a cocoon around them. The generator cycled on and pumped warm air into the dome, creating a breeze on her feet. She shivered.

"Let me get you a blanket." His body flinched as he reached for a green cashmere throw.

"Don't worry about it." She pulled him back, feeling desire against her thigh. "I don't need pampering, I need you..."

A smile rose in the corner of his mouth. "Tell me, what do you need?"

They held a gaze. *Nothing.* Their heartbeats slowly synced, and a tear escaped her eye—joy, love, overwhelmingly home.

Royce thumbed it away, smoothing the hair around her face. His mouth glided from her lips to her breast and lingered on her stomach, before trailing between her thighs. "Tell me." His breath washed over her, and the blankets crinkled underneath them.

"Nothing. I already have what I need." A ball of emotions lodged in her chest and released, pleading for more.

He entered. Slow. Deliberate. Sensuous. The sensation stole her breath.

Cordelia coiled her legs around his body as pleasure bloomed and spread outward in waves. Her nails grazed his back. "Oh, God." The breathy words tumbled out.

He stilled, giving her a moment to adjust. His forehead rested on hers. "Everything okay? I'm not—."

"It's more than okay." Her hips rolled and lifted, drawing a deep groan from his core. "Like that." The sensation expanded and pleasure coiled tighter in her belly.

Royce shifted and Cordelia settled herself on top of him. The air sent shockwaves through her skin. Each kiss he placed on her body revealed an animalistic urge—each touch, each nibble laid bare his feelings.

From the moment he entered her, Royce felt a fracture in his reserved nature. Internally, something shifted beyond sexual desire. *Combustion. Consumption.* She straddled him—chestnut waves tumbling over her shoulders, skin flushed and glowing, golden light illuminating her skin. Cordelia smiled, moaned and moved over him with agonizing slowness.

His hands traced her hips and gripped tightly as she moved with teasing precision. He watched her take control, making every move satisfying. Pleasure played across her face and her ragged breathing whispered his name. The air smelled of her scent—her longing, her desire.

Cordelia braced herself against his chest. Her hair fell into his face and traces of coconut lingered on his nose. "Royce...I..." Faint candlelight caught in her eyes, making them shine like dark stars as she seemed to look beneath his gaze. "I love you." Even as she moaned their eyes never broke contact. *She knows me. And I know her.* Simply admiration had evolved into cherishing one another. Love had altered their lives.

Her back arched and she moved faster. Her rhythm became urgent—control slipped away.

He needed to feel every inch of her skin against his. He needed to touch her in reverence. His body wanted to possess her. His hands gripped her hips, letting his thumbs skim the bend of her thighs.

She grabbed his hand, placing it just above where their bodies joined. She kept her hand on top as his thumb traced patterns on her wet skin. Cordelia seemed to lose herself in the blissful world of her pleasure, arching her body toward him.

His palm tingled when touching her belly, still flat and tight. A surge erupted. He sat up, pulling her with him. He wanted to eliminate the space between them. Royce guided her legs around his waist and took her breast into his mouth. Pleasure. Wonder. Devotion. A coiling energy swelled in his chest as they moved in sync. "Cordelia, look at me." His hands framed her face.

Looking back at him, trust, love, complete vulnerability.

Their salty breath mingled as he guided her movements. Overriding, frantic waves. Small sounds escaped her lips. Her nails dug into his shoulders. Her body tightened around his and trembled.

"Royce." She whispered, pleaded his name like a prayer of release.

He held back, resisting the cascade of energy that wanted to rush forward. "I love you." His voice cracked. "Both of you."

A shadow moved outside the dome—a passing deer silhouetted against the winter night.

He held her, breathless and startled by the movement. A floral aroma clung to the sweat that moistened her face.

The deer disappeared into the darkness as quickly as it had appeared, and Cordelia's eyes met Royce's. His heart thumped against her chest as his body craved more. For a heartbeat, they simply looked at each other, letting their breaths wash over each other.

Warm air swirled around them as the heater hummed, while patches of fog formed on the glass walls. Outside, the forest remained silent—attentive to their pleasures.

Royce's hips moved, a slow, sensual reminder of the desire that coiled inside her. His touch sent sensations down her spine as his mouth brushed past her neck, making its way to her lips.

Cordelia rocked backwards, feeling a growing urge for more.

Don't stop. His groans drove her passion and the rhythmic dance sparked more sounds of pleasure.

His mouth crashed into hers and everything else fell away— the deer, the dome, the cold, winter night pressing against the glass. There was nothing but the two of them moving together, building toward something that felt like flying and falling simultaneously.

He guided her movements, controlling the pace and gripping her hips. A sensation sparked inside her like electricity, and she gasped against his mouth.

"That's it," he murmured against her lips.

Beads of sweat formed and their moist bodies pleaded for release. In one motion, he rested her on the blankets. The pressure built, winding tighter in her core, spreading through her limbs like fire. She drove her hips upward, meeting him in a euphoric wave that approached the edge. Her body prepared to leap as the space around them appeared to shatter into golden light. She gasped, "More," and released a deep, muffled cry.

Their hands clasped together and Royce groaned, tightening against her. He followed her over the edge.

La Petite Mort...little death.

He stayed pressed to her body as she trembled, feeling his heavy breath and pounding heart. The charged air brought her back into the dome, where a sweet earthy fragrance blended with the salt of their sweat.

"That was—." She laughed, feeling her breath against his skin. "I can't find the words."

"They don't exist." He pressed a kiss to her damp forehead.

Slowly he shifted off and tucked her against his side. She rested on his chest, listening as his heart raced and made an echoing thump sound. It matched her own frantic rhythm.

"If you have champagne, I'll take the ice bucket." Cordelia said.

"Why?"

"To cool off. I'm so hot—."

Royce rolled onto his side and brushed a strand of hair from her cheek. "That could be intriguing." He ran his finger between her breasts. "A piece here." His fingers walked to her stomach. "Another one here." They skimmed between her thighs. "And one here."

"You first."

He kissed her, mumbled, and flopped back onto the blanket. "Just give me a few minutes to recoup my energy."

Cordelia laughed and propped onto her elbows. "Chicken." She pulled a plush knitted blanket across her legs as the sweat dissipated, leaving a chill on her skin. "I can't believe we're engaged." She rested her head on his chest and stared into the dark night.

The dome walls had partially fogged, leaving trails of condensation dripping to the floor. Outside a few faint stars emerged through the trees.

"I can't believe we're having a baby."

Her fingers drew lazy circles on his abdomen. "I know. Are you okay with the timing?"

"Very." His heart rate and breathing had returned to normal, but the rhythmic sound still thumped in Cordelia's ear. "Did you think I'd be disappointed?"

"No. But I know it's not traditional..."

"So." Royce rolled onto his side, guiding her eyes toward his. "I don't care about societal conventions. You and our baby is all that matters." His warm mouth rested on her lips. "Let people gossip."

"I love you, Royce Brownell." Cordelia flung her leg over his hip, feeling secure in his arms. "I'm your fiancée...and you're my —." She paused, letting a smile curve on her lips. "You're my baby daddy, my bady." She giggled. "Ooh, bady. No wait, Daba."

"Please never call me that again."

"Too late. That's your new nickname. Daba."

He tickled her, insisting he'll torture her every time that name is uttered.

"Daba. You're my *daaa-baaa*."

They dissolved into laughter—happiness, exhaustion, and slight deliriousness overtook them and they curled under the blanket together, listening as the wind began whispering against the glass.

This is what home feels like. Cordelia could be anywhere in the world with Royce and that feeling would go with them. It wasn't London, Venice, or Scotland, home resided in the life they'd built together. *Butterflies.* A sensation fluttered throughout her body.

"Ready to head back to the house?" Royce asked yawning. "Or would you rather sleep here, like this?" His voice sounded satisfied, content. "We can wait until morning to make sure the bears don't surprise us on the trail."

She froze. "Bears? There aren't bears here, are there?"

"Possibly."

Cordelia pressed into him, studying his expression. "Seriously? We're out here with bears?"

Royce burst into laughter. "No. You're safe. They went extinct about a thousand to fifteen hundred years ago."

"I'm engaged to a walking encyclopedia." She plopped her head onto his shoulder.

"Reconsidering things?"

"Never." She kissed him and explored the emotions mirrored in his eyes—contentment, safety, happiness. "You really are my lighthouse."

Royce wrapped the blanket around them, drawing her close. "And you're mine."

A few flameless candles flickered off, leaving half that cast long shadows across the floor. Cordelia stared into the black night and listened as Royce's breathing slowed and deepened. *Everything's impossibly, perfectly right.*

December 26th

The Scottish Highlands
& London

Chapter Twenty-Seven

5:45 AM

The library was always the quietest room in the house. A silence that came from centuries of accumulated knowledge that rested peacefully on shelves. Royce poured himself a cup of dark Scottish tea from a porcelain pot his mother kept in the cabinet for special occasions. The rich, earthy scent rose as the steam floated past.

"Couldn't sleep either?" The Earl stood in the doorway, dressed for the day in tan, wool plaid trousers and a thick black jumper. He wore his freshly washed hair slicked back.

"I slept some." Royce settled into an oversized club chair and sipped his tea.

"May I?" The Earl gestured, waiting like a vampire to be invited in.

"Of course. Do you still drink a cup each morning?" Royce slid an upside down cup on a saucer toward his father.

"Yes, although, against your mother's wishes, I'll sometimes have two."

Royce chuckled, "Living wildly, Pop."

"At my age, that's about as wild as life gets." The Earl sat in the chair across from Royce, poured his tea, and reclined against the back of the chair. "Did everything go according to plan?"

"It did. Better, actually. She's pregnant." A smile curled on his face as he met his father's eyes.

"Pregnant? How?"

He choked on his tea. "I really don't think you want the details, Pop, but if you insist—."

"No, no. Don't be cheeky. I meant, how long?"

"Nine weeks." He crossed his legs, smoothing his trousers.

"Wonderful." The Earl took a slow sip of tea, and they sat in silence for a moment.

There was a comfort within the awkward pause, and the tension Royce used to internalize whenever his father contemplated had evolved into appreciation. The air lightened. *Thank you, Cordelia.* She'd helped him discover new ways of interacting with his father—ways to find common ground rather than resisting.

Subtle sounds from the kitchen drifted down the hall.

When his father spoke again, his voice carried a rare warmth. "I want to tell you something. About Cordelia."

"Yes?"

"She's going to make a remarkable Countess." He rotated the cup on the saucer, adjusting it to the right angle. "Your mother and I couldn't be more pleased with your decision. She's intelligent, graceful, and knows her own mind—all the qualities you need in a wife. And more importantly, she believes in you. She doesn't question her feelings for you, and you'll need her beside you in the future."

Royce's emotions welled up, lodging in his throat. "Thank you, Pop." He cleared his voice. "That means a great deal. More than you know."

"I mean every word." His stared into his tea. "As you know, when your mum and I were dating, my father had significant doubts about whether she could meet the standards of being a Countess. Alia never tried to justify herself to him. She never asked him for a chance. Your mum was who she is—confident, gracious, attentive, and determined. He eventually came to respect her."

"I remember. They had a special bond."

"Did they ever. There were times Alia was the only person who could reason with him." He chuckled and smiled, glancing up at Royce. "Cordelia reminds me of your mother at times. And that kind of self-assurance is rare, which is exactly what this family needs."

"I'm glad to hear you say that." He rubbed his fingers across the soft edges of the leather chair. "She's remarkable." His eyes moistened. *She's my gem.* Clanging metal in the kitchen broke the silent, reflective moment.

The Earl shifted in his chair, placing his tea cup onto the side table. "I've been reading your books. Both of them, actually."

"Really?"

"I have. Finished the second one just last week." His father nodded and smiled, a look of pride washed over his face. "They're excellent, Royce. Truly excellent. Your research is meticulous, and your story is engaging. You've managed to make the history feel immediate and alive. Well done, son."

The compliment hit like a gust of wind. For two years, his father had been skeptical of his decision to leave academia. He'd argued and insisted that Royce wasted his potential, believing he'd abandoned a highly educated and prideful legacy. A fundamental shift unfolded. Of all times to feel a loss of words. He cleared his throat, sipped his tea, and said, "Thank you. I..."

"I owe you an apology. I was wrong to demand you return to the university. And it was wrong of me to suggest you wasted your education or potential as an author. Clearly, you've found something you're passionate about, something you excel at, and you had the courage to pursue it, despite considerable opposition—mainly from me."

"Pop."

"Let me finish, while we have the privacy." The Earl's tone was gentle but firm. "What you've done, leaving a secure tenured position to pursue your dream takes genuine strength. And I'm proud of you. Genuinely proud."

Royce's heart pounded against his ribs. His face flushed. "You've never said anything like that before."

"I should have said it sooner." His father nodded and picked at his trouser's wool fiber. 'The truth is, I never had your courage. You take after your mother in that area. I spent my entire life doing exactly what was expected of me—taking the seat in the Lords, managing the estate, fulfilling title duties, practicing law. The only time I truly defied expectation was when I insisted on marrying your mother. She gave me the courage to defy my father, and it was the best decision I ever made."

"You're mistaken," Royce said softly. "I have courage because of you." He sipped his lukewarm tea, placing it on the side table.

"I doubt that, but perhaps. You have truly displayed great strength, and I'm proud of you. You've built an entirely different life for yourself—as you say, on your own terms and talent. You challenged your inherited obligation. To my demise, I might add." He chuckled. "That takes gumption and it's admirable."

Something eased in Royce's chest, a tension he'd denied. He cut his eyes away, resisting an emotional reaction. "Thank you, Pop." In his peripheral vision, he saw his father brush away a tear. Royce approached him, squeezed his hand, and noticed his father still wore the same herbaceous cologne. "That's the third-best Christmas present, thank you."

248

"Third?" The Earl reached in his pocket and blew his nose. "Well, I'm glad this is in your top five."

Royce settled back into his chair. "Most days, you'd be first."

"Yes, well...heaven forbid I tried to compete with a fiancée and child."

They laughed and relaxed into a companionable silence. Mumbled voices approached, but faded before they reached the library door.

"So," the Earl said, his tone elevated and slight conspiratorial. "Have you and Cordelia discussed the wedding yet? Venue, timeline, guests?"

"We've barely been engaged twelve hours." Royce tapped the chair arm, amused at his father's enthusiasm.

"Yes, but these things take considerable planning. You'll want to wed at Hayton Chapel, naturally, or if Cordelia prefers, St. George's Chapel at Windsor is an option. Although, Marcus and Emma—."

"Pop."

"And the guest list will need careful curation. We must invite Lord and Lady Ashland, especially after we overlooked them at your brother's wedding. He's never forgiven me for going against him on the agricultural bill."

"Pop." Royce tapped his fingers on the chair.

"Then there's the question of formality. You'll want white tie, obviously. Cordelia and your mum will need to coordinate with the florist—."

"Pop." His tone was sharper than intended but at six in the morning, his father's enthusiasm overwhelmed his senses. "Slow down."

"Son, these events require proper planning." The Earl's eye twinkled with excitement while his tone remained dignified.

"Let us have twenty-four hours before we start planning *an event*." He sat forward. "And when we do, the final decision is

Cordelia. I know you want to be involved, but I'm not going to hijack her wedding."

"Of course, of course. I'm simply discussing details."

"You're suggesting a white tie event with at least four hundred guests." Royce affectionately shook his head no.

"The chapel doesn't hold four hundred."

"That's not the point. I'm happy you're enthusiastic, but this is Cordelia's day, not yours or the Ashlands, and she might have very different ideas about what she wants."

The Earl frowned. "I suppose you're right. Though surely she'd agree to a formal reception at the house."

"You're talking several hundred guests."

"Give or take a few." He smirked.

"Pop. No more planning. Not until we've had a chance to discuss it ourselves."

"Fair enough." His father gestured and surrendered. "Although for the record, St. George's Chapel is quite lovely."

"You're relentless."

"Well, you should know your mother's already making lists. She's more excited than I am."

"I'm sure she is." Royce leaned back in his chair, watching his father sip the cooled tea. How life had changed since meeting Cordelia. His father had become warm and engaging. "Honestly, Pop, I appreciate your excitement, and I promise, when we start planning, you and Mum will be involved. But let us have today, let us celebrate with everyone before it becomes about table linens and music."

"Of course, of course. You deserve today."

"And tomorrow." Royce stood, stretching his legs.

"Yes, yes. But don't take too long."

"Pop."

"Right. Not planning, only celebrating." The Earl stood, patting Royce on the arm.

More noise drifted in from the kitchen.

"Right. Well, I'm going to get a fresh pot of tea and take it to Cordelia...Before you start organizing a christening."

"That will be next on the agenda." His deep laugh rolled out like a gentle wave on the beach.

"See you in a bit, Pop." Royce shook his head and walked toward the hallway. *How do I top this? Engaged, baby, and a proud Pop?* He glanced back at his father who'd settled back into a chair and begun reading from a book. *It's not possible.*

7:oo AM

Royce recorded his thoughts in a journal while Fortuna purred and slept in his lap. Situated beside a drafty window, the floral wingback chair seemed caught between two worlds—the damp darkness of pre-dawn and the warm comfort of a fresh crackling fire.

His black and gold fountain pen raced across the page, leaving a few smears of blue ink on the page.

Cordelia stretched in bed, tightened the comforter around her shoulders and curled on her side. Her hair spilled across the pillow in waves and a small smile rose on her lips. "Morning."

"Good morning. How did you sleep?" Royce capped his pen and placed it in the journal fold.

"Like a baby." She stretched again, glimpsing at her new ring.

"There's a cup of tea on the nightstand for you."

She propped herself up, "Thank you," took a sip, and flopped back onto the pillow. "What time's our flight home?"

"Five-thirty, but I want to leave here immediately after lunch."

"That's fine. Wake me in thirty?" She slid back under the blankets. "Or maybe, you'd like to join me?"

Royce's laugh woke Fortuna. She arched her back and repositioned in his lap. "I think she has other plans for me."

Cordelia patted the bed's open space, encouraging him to join him. "There's plenty of room." Her eyes held a flirty yet sleepy gaze.

"In a moment." He refocused on his journal, steadily moving the pen across the paper as he organized his thoughts.

<u>Housing</u>, he wrote at the top, followed by a column of practical thoughts:

*Current flat - two-bedroom, Mayfair

- Pros: familiar, close to BL for C, established
- Cons: no space for baby - unless I give up office (not ideal), no garden, not ideal for family

<u>Considerations</u>:

- Chef's kitchen (C's standards)
- Nursery with natural light
- Nanny's room (discuss with C)
- Garden or outdoor space
- Reasonable commute to BL London

P<u>ossible New Neighborhoods</u>:

- Kensington
- Notting Hill
- St. John's Wood

- Marylebone

<u>Timeline</u>: Spring (before baby's due date??)

H e placed the pen and journal on the side table and carried Fortuna to the bed. As soon as he set her onto the comforter, she found a spot and kneaded.

"Were you already making lists?" Cordelia rested her head in his lap.

His back nestled into the three pillows leaning against the headboard. "Only a few."

"Royce, we have time. It's not like this baby's coming tomorrow."

"Eight months isn't a lot of time when planning a wedding and a new home."

Cordelia rolled over. Her wide eyes scanned his face. "Seriously? Who said anything about moving?"

"I am. We can't stay in our current flat, there's not enough room."

"But it's a baby. They don't take up much space." She sat up and sipped her tea. "I don't think we need to move."

"Well, I disagree. We need to resettle before the baby's born, so he...she doesn't have to move homes."

Cordelia gulped her tea. "Moving as a child isn't the worst thing in the world. They do survive. Look at me."

"Right." He moved closer to her, avoiding Fortuna who lay curled beside his leg. "I'm not saying you didn't turn out well adjusted, but I'd like for our children—."

"Children? Let's start with this one first, please." She laughed with a tense tone.

Royce wrapped his arm around her, pulling her into his

chest. "Noted. I didn't mean to stress you." He guided her leg over his as she rested it against his body. "I won't push the issue, all right?"

"Good. I love our home." She rested on his chest and for a few minutes they relaxed in silence. Not even a ghost stirred. "Who knows we're engaged?"

"My parents, Marcus, Emma, and Richard. And the staff, of course."

"Right, staff."

"Who knows you're pregnant?" His fingers fidgeted with her hair.

"Mmmm, Marnie...and your mum." Cordelia bit her lip and smirked.

"Mum? You told her?"

"No, it's more like she figured it out on her own."

"She's perceptive."

"Try psychic." She petted Fortuna, who stretched and repositioned into a ball. "And I thought I was doing a good job hiding it."

"I told Pop this morning."

"And he was surprised? Your mum hadn't already told him?"

"She's a vault, as you like to say."

Cordelia giggled. "Well, what did he say? Is he excited?" She rolled over in his lap, facing him. "Disappointed?"

"Not at all. He's already making mental guest lists and selecting the venue." Royce shifted. The thought of his father participating in planning caused back tension.

"Oh God, did you stop him?"

"You don't restrain Thomas Brownell."

"Unless you're Alia Brownell." A burst of laughter erupted between them. Cordelia did her best British accents, imitating Royce's parents having a conversation about the wedding plans.

"Alia, you don't understand." She straddled him and deepened her voice, tucking her chin in slightly. "Thomas, it's not your wedding."

Royce rested his hands on her thighs, laughing and catching his breath. "So cheeky." Her lips softened against his mouth as she giggled. "Promise me you'll never change."

"Never."

He widened his legs, dropping her between them. Cordelia repositioned, sitting with her back against his chest. Royce wrapped his arms around her. Remnants of the night before—powdery, salty scents lingered on her skin.

"I love you." Her soft voice emphasized each word. "In case I didn't make that clear last night."

He nestled his face in her hair, breathing in her aroma. "You did But I don't mind hearing it again."

"I love you, Royce Brownell. My Bady."

"God, you're never going to let me escape that, are you?"

"Nope. You're stuck with it." Her laughter filled the room with warmth. And his heart with joy.

Chapter Twenty-Eight

9:30 AM

The dining room buzzed as comfortable chaos erupted over breakfast with voices talking and laughing over one another. The air smelled of coffee, bacon, and Mrs. MacLeod's gingerbread scones. Cordelia paused in the doorway and inhaled a deep breath. *No nausea.* The salty bacon scent made her mouth water.

Royce stood beside her, resting his arm on her waist. Sunlight streamed through the tall windows, revealing patches of condensation and fog. Her engagement ring caught the light and threw rainbows across the table.

"Oh, my god." Cassandra set her fork down, letting it rattle on her plate. "Is that?"

The Earl peeked around his morning paper and grinned. Next to him, the Countess puffed her chest and nodded at Royce. She squeezed the Earl's arm, beaming with excitement.

"Good morning, everyone." Royce took Cordelia's hand and casually escorted her into the room. Her nerves fluttered as the table quieted and all eyes landed on them.

"We've had such a difficult time keeping this to ourselves?"

The Earl stood and greeted Cordelia with a kiss. "Hello, darling."

The Countess followed his lead and hugged her. She whispered, "Does he know?"

"Yes, he does." They locked eyes and hugged again. "And so does the Earl."

"Thomas." The Countess turned, grabbing his attention from Royce. "You knew and didn't tell me?"

"Knew what?" His expression shifted from a frown to a smile. "Oh, that. Yes, dear, not all of my secrets are yours."

She patted his arm, "It's all right, dear. I already knew." She refocused on Cordelia, encouraging her to take the empty seat beside her.

Royce kept his hand on Cordelia's lower back, pulled out her chair, and sat next to her. Under the table he wrapped two fingers around hers.

She felt his heartbeat. *Maybe that's mine.* Cordelia glanced over at Marnie, who was busy helping Maisie back into her chair. They weren't in the room when she and Royce arrived. *Please don't know, please don't know.* Cordelia watched the way Marnie placed the napkin in Maisie's lap and encouraged her to keep her elbows off the table.

When their eyes connected, Marnie gave a slight wave and mouthed, "How are you?"

"Great." Cordelia said, keeping her voice silent and mimicking Marnie.

"Wait, mum, you knew?" Marcus asked, wiping oatmeal from Ada Rose's face. He and Emma sat opposite the Earl and Countess with the high chair in between.

"Of course I did."

The Earl returned to his seat. "Your mother's psychic," he said placing his napkin across his lap. "Or so she claims." He chuckled to himself.

"I thought the circle was small." Marcus looked down the table. "Who here knew?"

Emma and Richard raised their hands.

Cassandra, at the far end of the table, glared at Richard. "You knew and didn't tell me? I thought we were closer than that." She pursed her lips, giving him a pouty, sad-eyed look. Her head whipped the other direction. "Royce Brownell. How could you not tell me? I would've kept it in the...vault, as Cordelia says."

Why is that word suddenly so infectious?

"Cass, we all know that's impossible." Marcus patted her on the shoulder.

"Mummy, what's in the vault?" Maisie whispered.

Definitely a buzz word today.

Marnie's tone had a touch of confusion in it. "Baby, it means keeping a secret."

"Then what's the secret?" Her whisper held the table's attention.

Cordelia held up her hand. "This." She locked eyes with Marnie. "Looks like you have another reason to be in London next year."

Marnie's eyes widened. "What? Oh, my god." She jumped up and raced around the table, wrapping her arms around Cordelia who tried to stand while Marnie clung to her neck. "Oh, my god, for real? Royce...this is amazing. And the timing's perfect with the—."

"Yes," he cleared his throat. "Yes, right, well, only you and Mum know." Royce straightened his flatware to the edge of the table.

"Don't forget me," the Earl said.

"And Pop."

"There's more? How many secrets are you keeping?" Cassandra jumped up and joined Marnie in drowning Cordelia with hugs.

"Wait, wait. Before that, aren't you going to officially announce this, or must we all infer the meaning behind grandmother's ring?" Marcus handed a baby bowl of food to Emma and sipped orange juice from a cut crystal wine goblet.

"Everyone already knows—." Royce said.

"Yes, but do it." Marcus tapped the table's edge. "Say it."

"I agree with Marcus." Richard shifted his chair back from the table and crossed his legs. "Let it out of the vault, mate."

Are they mocking me? That's my word. Cordelia adjusted the collar of her pink cardigan, noticing how the diamonds caught the light. *Damn that sparkles.*

Richard and Marcus continued pushing Royce, despite the obvious, while Cassandra shared the first time she met Grandmother Brownell.

"Come on, mate, we're waiting." Richard clapped, encouraging Marcus up out of his chair.

Royce's cheeks flushed, "All right, all right." He fidgeted with a fork on the table. "If you insist." He stood and stared into Cordelia's eyes. "Last night, by the loch, I asked Cordelia to marry me." His voice softened. "And she said, yes."

The room erupted in cheer. Cordelia felt the blood rush to her face as a wad of emotions lodged in her throat. She squeezed Royce's hand, grounding herself in his touch.

The Earl clapped and whistled as if he were at a tennis match—reserved excitement.

"It suits you perfectly, dear." The Countess dabbed her eye. "Your grandmother would be so pleased."

"Yes, we couldn't be more pleased. Congratulations, you two."

Emma and Marcus congratulated them, while Ada Rose studied everyone's reactions.

A few minutes later, they'd all settled into their seats, giving

Cordelia and Royce a chance to breathe. The room felt hotter than when they arrived thanks to a fresh stack of wood Mr. Smyth had arranged in the fireplace. Like a footnote on a page, the fire crackled and calmed the room.

Cordelia sipped her coffee, letting the rich taste rest on her tongue. *Perfect.* She lingered over the subtle notes of dark fruit.

"Have you thought about a Spring wedding? The gardens at Hayton are lovely that time of year. Or perhaps early Summer, before—." She caught herself, smiled, and took a bite of toast.

"Mum, let's get through breakfast first." Royce sliced his sausage patty and swirled it into a runny egg yolk.

"I'm merely thinking out loud."

"Be prepared, Cordelia, they'll have the venue selected before you even make it back to London," Marcus teased. "And the flowers, too."

"We're simply offering the chapel at Hayton, if you're interested. It can comfortably seat seventy-five guests or if you prefer a larger venue the village church would be beautiful."

"So many decisions." Cordelia gripped the coffee cup to her chest before taking a sip. "I think we'll probably take some time to think about it first."

"I know it can be overwhelming." The Countess rubbed Cordelia's shoulder, leaned closer, and whispered, "How are you feeling?"

Cordelia nodded, "Good. Very good, actually."

"I seem to remember you two having very strong opinions about our wedding, too." Marcus leaned back in his chair, handing Ada Rose a pink, rubber giraffe toy.

"That was different," the Earl said. "You wanted to have it in that barn."

"It was a converted royal stable with historical significance."

"It was a barn." The Earl's firm tone as he repeated the phrase caused a few snickers around the table.

"What time is your flight back to London?" Emma asked, leaning toward Cordelia and Royce. "Ours is at five-thirty."

"Oh, we are too." Cordelia was grateful for the change of subject and a chance to enjoy her eggs that grew colder by the second.

"Well, Mrs. MacLeod is preparing take away snack boxes for everyone." The Countess placed her fork and knife at the four o'clock position on her plate, sparking Mrs. Smyth to immediately remove it from the table.

One by one they finished eating breakfast. dishes clinked as they were placed on a tray, disappearing through the wooden kitchen swing door. Mr. Smyth refilled coffee and tea cups and refreshed the cream pitchers.

Royce cleared his throat. "We have one more piece of news to share." His eyes drifted to Cordelia.

A table full of curious expression stared at them, except for the Countess who folded her hands together in prayer-like fashion and smiled with a Cheshire cat grin.

"We're expecting," pride resonated in his voice. "We're having a baby next summer."

Cordelia scanned each face as the additional news settled in —surprise, gasps, slight giggles, especially from Marnie who was the first to express her joy with a high pitched squeal.

"Cordy, you're going to be a mom." She clapped and hugged Maisie. "Are you excited?"

"A baby? Where?"

"In her tummy." Marnie placed Maisie in her lap. "I'll explain later, okay, baby."

Maisie agreed and celebrated despite her confusion.

"This is wonderful news. Isn't it, Thomas?" The Countess, tapped the Earl's hand. "Another grandchild."

"Which you already knew about." He chuckled at her reaction.

"I didn't...how did you know?"

"Our son." The Earl pointed at Royce. "What's the phrase the kids are using, 'you kept it in the vault'." His belly laugh sparked rolling laughter around the table.

The congratulations and conversation flowed through a round of questions from when they each found out, when they'd move to the suburbs, and the big one—will Cordelia continue to work. She answered that with an emphatic yes, insisting that they could and would balance parenthood with their careers.

"We'll work our way through it," Royce said with a gentle firmness while caressing her hand under the table. "Just like all of you have...one step at a time."

Cordelia relaxed in the comfortable chaos of family excitement as everyone talked about the future and the upcoming year. But there would be one person missing from the picture— her father.

He'd be proud of everything she'd accomplished in her career, but Cordelia knew his greatest pride would be in her new family, in the love she'd found. *I miss you Daddy*. A deep well of emotions rose as she imagined him by her side at her wedding. She cleared her throat, forcing tears to stay hidden, at least until she could be in the safety of their home, in the safety of Royce's comfort.

Royce brushed his hand across her cheek. "Everything okay?"

"Yeah, yeah. I ate too much. It was just so good, but I think I stuffed myself." He was here family, her future and the past had truly faded into memories—ones that sometimes got locked in the vault like a treasured diamond ring. She glanced at her hand, noticing the way each diamond supported the sapphire, just like her new family.

The Countess tapped her arm, "When Royce told us he was proposing, Thomas and I were thrilled. As a mother you pray your children will find happiness, and both of our sons have found something special." Her red manicured fingers wrapped around Cordelia's hand. "Just like Emma, I consider you a daughter."

Her eyes fluttered as she fought back more tears. *Not now.* Cordelia's voice rattled over her emotions, "Thank you, that means so much to me."

"Oh, dear, I didn't mean to make you cry."

"It's okay. I do it all the time now."

"I remember those days." The Countess handed Cordelia a monogrammed handkerchief from her pocket.

She dabbed her eyes, thumbing the navy initials embroidered on the white cotton. Cordelia laughed to herself, remembering Paris and a similar handkerchief with the initials RBG. *This is where it all began.*

A familiar scent of vanilla lingered in the air. Nestled against her ear, Royce whispered, "No regrets?"

"None." Cordelia rested her head against his forehead. "Absolutely none."

Chapter Twenty-Nine

7:50 PM

The elevator dinged and the doors opened. The foyer's black and white tile glistened when the lights illuminated the space. Cordelia dragged her suitcase across the threshold while Royce followed, maneuvering his luggage as the doors closed behind.

Fortuna cried as the soft carrier rattled on top of Royce's hard luggage, but her pleas softened after he set her on the floor.

"Home." A white rose scent permeated the air. "Kay must've been here today. It smells like our candles."

They paused, kicking off their wet boots.

"I asked her to stop by and drop off cat supplies." He unwrapped his scarf, folded it, and set it inside a cabinet drawer. "Knowing her, she also stocked the fridge."

Cordelia hung her navy wool coat and slung the scarf around the collar. "That reminds me, I need to stop by the boutique tomorrow and get another one for the bedroom."

Royce dusted the back of his black jacket. "Is that your excuse for going to work tomorrow?"

"No." Her voice rose higher than she'd intended. "We need another candle, and while I'm—."

"While you're there, you'll make a quick visit to the shop, just to make sure they survived. Am I right?" There was a dry playfulness in his voice, reminding her how well he understood her hidden motivations. Royce hung his wool coat in the color-coordinated section of the closet.

"I can't help it if the boutique is right next door to BL."

Inside the carrier, Fortuna pawed the side and meowed. Her lonesome cry pleaded for attention.

"Right." Royce slipped on his brown leather house shoes, which were tucked inside the closet beside her pink fluffy ones. He slid hers closer to her. "Will this be an all day candle shopping event?"

"I'm buying a candle, that's it. But you're welcome to come with me." She wiggled her toes as her feet settled into the plush slippers.

Royce unzipped the carrier, letting Fortuna emerge at her own pace. His silence implied doubt, but his dimpled smile conveyed something else—cheeky amusement.

Fortuna stepped out, took in the surroundings, and sniffed the air. She explored the flat, slowly at first, but within minutes her grey-blue eyes filled with curiosity. She wandered from room to room, discovering her new home like a tiger strolling the jungle.

Cordelia and Royce stayed a few steps behind, watching as she rubbed against a chair and quickly discovered a scratching post tucked behind the furniture.

"Kay thought of everything." Cordelia said, curling up next to Royce on the sofa after discovering a basket of toys and self-cleaning litter box in the utility room.

He agreed, igniting the electric fireplace with one click.

Cordelia scrolled Jessica's number on her phone, feeling the warm glow on her cheek as the realistic flames danced behind glass.

"We've been home five minutes..." His hand rested on hers. "I thought we agreed, no work tonight."

"I'm just giving her a quick call. It'll take two seconds."

"BL survived four days without you, I think they can manage another twenty-four hours. Besides, you need to minimize stress, not add to it."

She opened her mouth to protest, but caught the hopeful look in his eyes. *He's right, I have to consider the baby.* Cordelia sighed and watched the phone screen go dark. She wanted to challenge his logic but knew her strategy to work had to change.

"Can we have tonight before the world rushes back in?"

"Yes, of course." She set her phone upside down onto the coffee table, and leaned against his chest, stretching her legs across the sofa.

"Which would you prefer, food or suitcases?"

"I guess suitcases. I'm really not in the mood to cook."

"Then don't." He kissed her again, nuzzling his lips against her neck. "We'll order takeaway and then make passionate love all night." His laugh tickled her skin, sending a chill down her spine.

She flinched and giggled, wiggling as his pinned her down. The deep sofa cushions molded around her back.

Soon their suitcases lay open on the bed and clothes filled two baskets, one for the cleaners and one for the wash. Cordelia paused and smelled her Christmas day sweater, flooded with memories from that night. *Yes.* She glanced at Royce, remembering him on one knee proposing to her. *I'll always say yes to you.* His scent lingered on the fibers.

The sapphire and diamonds caught the light as she tossed the sweater into the basket, casting sparkles across the duvet.

She paused, watched him fold the fisherman sweater he'd

worn the day they hiked out to see Nessie, and then toss it into the dry cleaning basket.

"Why are you staring at me?"

"No, I'm admiring. There's a difference, remember?"

He chuckled and folded his arms. "Enlighten me."

"If I recall, a certain someone explained it this way—staring is idle, admiring is active appreciation."

"Is that right? Very wise person."

"I think so." She moved around the bed. "You see, I'm admiring someone who makes me..." Her lips hovered an inch from his mouth.

"Stimulated?"

"And?" Her lips barely touched his.

"Adored?"

Cordelia agreed as she kissed him, tasting a lingering peppermint flavor on his tongue. Her heartbeat throbbed against his chest. When she pulled back, their eyes locked onto each other. His three day old beard scruffed under her fingertips. "I'm admiring someone who's my home, my best friend."

His eyes softened. "Then don't let me ever stop you from staring." He squeezed her butt cheeks and lifted her toes off the floor. "And I promise I won't either."

"Deal."

Royce set her back down and drummed her butt. "Now, before we feed that appetite, what do you say, we finish unpacking and then pop over to the pub for burgers?"

"Oh, I'm down for that." She pushed off his chest and scooted to the other side of the bed. "It's been weeks since I enjoyed food. I'm doing double cheese and extra pickles." Cordelia tossed the last of her clothes into a hamper and zipped up her suitcase. "I'm ready."

"Give me five minutes and then I'm yours."

She looked at her watch. "I'm clocking you."

Royce grabbed an armful of shirts and trousers, tossed them into the wash bin, and tucked his suitcase in the corner next to his favorite reading chair. "Done."

"Wow, less than a minute. Impressive." Fortuna struggled as she tried to jump onto the bed. "Come here, sweetie." Cordelia placed her on a folded throw blanket at the foot. "There you go."

Fortuna kneaded and walked in circles, purring loudly and holding their quiet attention. When they left the room, Royce turned on the lamp closest to the chair and window.

In the living room, Cordelia grabbed her phone and noticed a belated Christmas text from Jeannine Gosselin-Larue. She responded, waiting to share the engagement-baby news until she saw them in person. "Babe, I need to schedule a trip to Paris to see Bastien and Jeannine. Maybe the first week of January? I have a call with him next week to discuss the spring/summer menu, but I wanted to share our news in person. What do you think?"

"Sure. How many days did you have in mind?" He joined her at the foyer closet and reached for a black trench.

"I don't know, two, maybe three with travel. You could come with me if your book deadline allows. We could schedule dinner with them at Pièrre Claud's new place by the river."

"That would work for me." Royce selected a red scarf and wrapped it around his neck. "It would give me a day of research before finalizing my book outline. Charlie's already sent two emails wondering when he'll get first pages."

Undecided on what to wear, Cordelia tried on two coats before settling on a white parka. "That man's relentless. I don't know how you stay calm around him. I'd be stressed out every time I got a message from him."

He laughed and pressed the elevator button. "That's what Cassandra says. She despises him."

"Well, he did screw her over for that role."

The elevator dinged and the doors opened. As they stepped on, the living room lights automatically dimmed. "Oh, and did Richard talk to you about New Year's Eve?"

Royce placed his hand on her lower back, moving his thumb in circles. "Yes, and I told him we had the museum gala that night."

"Oh."

"Is that a 'I don't want to do the gala' oh or is it 'I told him differently'?"

"Both. But before you remind me about our duty and how we're expected to attend, like every year, what if we did both?"

"And go unnoticed? You know Pop's on the board, and there will be—."

"I know, but what if we made an appearance, satisfied your father and social gossipers, who clearly will be talking about this?" She held up her ringed hand. "Then snuck out and went to where we really want to be, with our friends?"

"It's possible, but you know Pop will frown over it."

"Let me handle him." Cordelia touched her belly. "He likes me."

Royce yanked her close. "Does he."

The elevator doors opened as soon as it dinged, and staring at them was Stephen Johnson, the sports journalist who had an ego as wide as the Thames. Cordelia tucked her hand into Royce's pocket and attempted to exit the elevator with more than a hello. Unfortunately, Stephen decided neighborly conversation was necessary.

Five minutes later, Cordelia removed her hand from Royce's pocket, and together, they exited the building.

They walked through Mayfair's quiet streets huddled close as the cold December wind whipped at their faces. The street lamps scattered soft light and cast oddly shaped shadows onto the pavement. They walked a block in silence, listening to distant music spilling out from a club. After greeting Oscar and Leo, a couple they knew from the neighborhood, they continued toward the pub.

Royce wrapped his arm around her waist. "Leo sure was excited over the engagement."

"I know. I think he'd be crushed if we didn't hire him as coordinator. Although I don't know when I'll have time to think about that."

"Soon, I hope." They turned the corner and nearly collided with a woman walking her tiny dog. "You're not going to keep me waiting too long, are you?"

"No. But I can't promise I'll have the time for a lavish affair. Or that I want one."

"I'd marry you in here and now, if I could."

She halted, faced him, and said, "Then do it. Say it here and now. We'll declare ourselves married, and go on with life."

He cupped her face as the wind tugged at her wool cap. "Cordelia Dyer, in heart and soul, I'm yours here and now, but you know I'm bound by duty as the future Earl. I have obligations, and eventually you will too. Besides, my mother would be devastated if she didn't get to throw us that lavish party and show you off to her friends."

"I know, even though she has many times."

"This is different."

"I know." Cordelia placed her hands on top of Royce's. "And I love you for respecting your family's role." She pressed her body into his. "I'm yours here, now, and in a grand display of our wedding."

"Thank you." He kissed her, ignoring the group of university students that brushed past. The smell of grilled meat reminded them why they'd ventured out into the cold night. "Come on, let's get inside."

When they reached the pub, warm light and lively sounds spilled onto the street. Through the windows, Royce spotted Richard and Marnie at a booth, talking and laughing. *What the... dodgy mate.* He pulled Cordelia back and pointed at their friends huddled together.

"Well, I guess we're about to blow up their little game."

"We can go somewhere else."

"Oh no, I want my double cheese, extra pickles burger and this place has the best."

Royce laughed, opened the door, and gestured, "After you, Ms. Dyer." He followed her in and realized they were crossing a multitude of thresholds together, each leading them to the next.

Cordelia snuck up on Richard and Marnie, startling them as she slid into the booth. She lit up the room with her love for people. *She's my home...* He slipped in beside her, feeling her hand rest on his thigh. *We're building our future one mundane, yet extraordinary moment at a time.* Royce wrapped his arm around her waist as she leaned into him. She continued talking with Marnie and never missed a beat.

Here's to those wintery landscapes that spark cozy dreams.

Reviews

One More Thing...

If Cordelia and Royce's story touched your heart, please consider leaving a review on Amazon, Goodreads, or your favorite book platform. Your words help other readers discover their next favorite escape, and they mean the world to me as I write the next book in this series.

Thank you again for choosing to read this book and the entire Hayton Collection series. For me, stories are meant to be savored and shared, like the perfect macaron among friends.

With heartfelt gratitude and warm wishes,

Shannon

A Gift for You

To you, a romance-loving friend—

Thank you!

You're the final piece of their story. By choosing to continue Cordelia and Royce's journey with me, you make it feel complete. So, thank you for spending time in their world, from the snow-covered Highlands to the warmth of Waileigh Lodge, and of course for being with them for the magical proposal under Scotland's winter sky.

Your support means everything to an author, and I'm delighted to offer you this small gift bundle.

Your Gift Awaits

To celebrate Cordelia and Royce, I've created a downloadable bookmark featuring the book cover. Plus, have you ever been curious about how Cordelia ended up in London or her painful backstory in New York? Well, here's a chapter I wrote that never made it into *We Met in Paris*. Enjoy!

Download Your Free Bookmark Here: https://BookHip.com/WAAGWKK

For best results, print on cardstock, and let it transport you back to those cozy winter nights every time you open your next book.

Download Your Bonus Chapter Here: https://BookHip.com/HRRJBTH

Stay Connected

Stay Connected for More Sweet Escapes

Did you love Cordelia and Royce's continuing story? Their journey continues between pages, and I'd love to share what's next:

Join my Reader's Club for exclusive bonus scenes, author's musings, recipes, and be one of the first to know about upcoming releases.

Sign up at: https://shannonsteevesauthor.substack.com/subscribe

Shannon

Also by Shannon Steeves

<u>The Hayton Collection</u>

We Met in Paris

We Danced in Venice

We Wed in Mayfair - *coming May 2026*

Sweet Surrender - *Cordelia's Cookbook*

<u>Union of Immortals</u>

Fire -

A romantic fanatasy series coming February 2026

Acknowledgments

Every book is a journey, and I'm grateful to the incredible people who helped me navigate the journey, from that first spark of an idea to the story you hold in your hands.

First and foremost, to you, the reader. You make sharing these stories exciting and fulfilling.

My deepest gratitude goes out to the incredible writing group I've discovered through Reedsy. You all have provided feedback, support, and encouragement while helping me to develop as a writer. Thank you.

To my editor, Steffi Waters, whose wise editorial eye and unwavering belief in Cordelia and Royce's story helped me bring their voices to life. Thank you for pushing me to dig deeper and for knowing exactly when to add "more interiority." Your patience is legendary.

Special thanks to Katarina (nskvsky) for creating a cover that captures the romance and style perfectly.

Additional thank yous go out to Ariana Brenal, beta readers, and reviewers who assisted me along the way. You all remind me that the writing process may be solitary, but the journey is never lonely.

My husband, Ford. Words do not capture my appreciation and love, but thank you for encouraging me to never give up. To my children and grandchildren—I'm reminded why happily-ever-afters matter.

To every librarian, bookseller, book blogger, and social media influencer, thank you for your support.

To you, my readers, thank you for choosing Cordelia and Royce's story. Thank you for believing in second chances, romantic moments, and the transformative power of love. Your support makes this journey possible.

With gratitude and love,

Shannon

About the Author

Shannon writes across romance genres, from contemporary to fantasy. She loves writing about women who master their worlds, navigating both authentic ambition and fantastical destiny.

In real life, she's still working to conquer the elusive, perfect croissant, and she plans her vacations with the same intensity she plots her novels. A lifelong student of European folklore, English history, and French culture, she brings passion to her love stories, researching everything from Celtic magic to high court etiquette.

Shannon lives in Atlanta with her loving family.

Connect with her at shannonsteeves.com or shannonsteevesauthor.substack.com/subscribe for updates, bonus scenes, Cordelia's recipes, and tales from Royce's latest historical discoveries.

Find her on Instagram *@shannon.steeves.author* or TikTok *@s.steeves.author*